THE LOST KING

The Bewildering Adventures of King Bewilliam Book One

DEVORAH FOX

Other books in *The Bewildering Adventures of King Bewilliam*
series:
The King's Ransom, Book Two
The King's Redress, Book Three
The Redoubt, Book Four

Also by Devorah Fox
Naked Came the Sharks with Jed Donellie
"Turning the Tide" in *Masters of Time, A SciFi/Fantasy Time Travel
Anthology*
"Blackwing" *in Magic Unveiled, An Anthology*
Murder by the Book, A Mystery Mini
One Bad Apple, A Mystery Mini
Detour, A Big Rig Thriller
The Zen Detective
Lady Blackwing
:

DEDICATION

for Mike, who said I should write a book

THANKS

to my friends who agreed and especially to Barb and Anet for
helping get this out the door

.

AUTHOR'S NOTE

This is not a doctoral dissertation on life in the Middle Ages. I have taken liberties with many aspects of medieval life and technology. Others, I simply made up. (Although really, who's to say it didn't happen this way?) For that, I apologize to those who would have preferred to see history portrayed more accurately.

But this is a work of fiction. Therefore, names, characters, places, and incidents are the product of my imagination or used fictitiously. Any resemblance to actual events, places, or persons living or dead is purely coincidental.

CHAPTER ONE

"Moo."

Moo? King Bewilliam frowned. What was a cow doing in the throne room?

"Moo."

King Bewilliam no sooner had set his gaze on the Bell Castle's richly-veined marble floors, the opulent woven tapestries, the straight lines of courtiers resplendent in their gold-braided uniforms than it all vanished.

His heart jolted and he felt a pervasive icy chill.

"Moo."

I'm asleep, the King thought. I'm dreaming. I need to wake up. He opened one eye. He had been dreaming but what vanished was not the cow but the throne room. Instead, the sight that greeted him was another eye: big, brown, and deep.

King Bewilliam opened his other eye and found himself face-to-face with a large Guernsey regarding him with mild curiosity.

"Moo, moo," said the cow although to the king it sounded distinctly like "Who, you?" which, it seemed to him, was an excellent question given the circumstances. Was he not King Bewilliam, ruler of the Chalklands, master of Bell Castle?

So what was he doing here staring down a cow? He shook his head to clear the fog of slumber. One by one, the details of his surroundings impressed themselves on him: the cool, moist dawn air; the dewy grass on which he lay; the dark canopy of the oak tree arching over him. And the cow.

King Bewilliam eased into a sitting position and looked about. In the thin light of daybreak he saw many cows grazing in the pasture that surrounded him. What was he doing sleeping in a cow pasture? his waking mind struggled to know.

Oh yes, it was where he had come to rest after walking all day. He hadn't talked to a single person, having kept his distance, avoiding questions about who he was and what he was doing here. He knew who he was: first-born son of a noble line, raised to rule, trained to lead and now, a grown man, husband to Queen Daya, and father of princes. What he was doing here in this unfamiliar place, his crown nowhere to be found, his fine tunic and leggings tarnished and soiled, his boots scuffed, was a mystery to him.

Well, an inquisitive cow wasn't all that unfortunate an encounter. At least there would be breakfast. He rummaged his mug from the pouch at his belt, then hesitated. He scanned the area for onlookers who might accuse him of poaching. There were none.

"Here, Boss." He stroked the cow's sturdy flank to gentle her, then milked her. As he worked, he observed how strange many might find it that a king would, much less could, milk a cow. Certainly, Bell Castle's milkmaid who had shown him how had thought so. Yet even as a young prince, the workings of things fascinated him. He would pester every maid, knave, squire, knight, and lady to show him the why and how of what they did.

His meager breakfast done, he turned the ermine-lined cloak that had been his bed inside out and knotted the ends together, making it into a shoulder sack. It would have been easier to wear the weighty cloak across both shoulders than to lug it on one but he knew he mustn't be seen wearing it. No one would believe that a vagabond like him rightfully owned such a fine garment. It would be seized and he might be imprisoned as a thief. Nevertheless, he was reluctant to part with it. The cloak had served well as bedding when he found himself sleeping out in the open.

He finger-combed the grass from his red curls and observed that his hair had gotten unseemly long. So had his beard, he discovered as he ran his hand over his face. When he reached a town, he would need to visit a barber. First, however, he would need to raise some money to pay a barber, not to mention buy a decent meal. His stomach growled in agreement. Apparently the birds had beaten him to the berries. He quickly banished from his mind the image of the generously-laid groaning boards to which he was accustomed before it could further exacerbate his hunger.

He sighed, hefted his improvised sack, and set off.

The morning sun had strengthened by the time King Bewilliam spied the first sign of civilization. In the distance, a farmer's oxcart made slow progress across the horizon. King Bewilliam strained to see clearly. It was headed toward town, he surmised, as the wagon was laden. He aimed his feet in the same direction and hurried his pace in hopes of overtaking the cart and begging a ride. He was already tired of walking and the day had barely begun.

"Eh! Friend! Where are you bound?" he called when the driver was in earshot.

The wooden cart slowed but did not stop. The driver turned his head, showing a long face shadowed by a broad-brimmed hat.

"To market, of course, Stranger," the driver replied.

"Is it far?" asked Bewilliam.

"Far enough." The driver sounded weary. "And my long day truly begins only when I get there. I don't have time to waste chatting with strangers."

"Perhaps some entertainment would make your journey pass more enjoyably." King Bewilliam withdrew a harmonica from his pouch and whistled a phrase, light and sweet as the chirping of the red-breasted robins roosting in the trees that lined the wagon way.

The cart slowed yet more.

"A pretty tune, but how do I know this isn't some ruse to rob me?" the driver asked.

King Bewilliam flung his arms away from his body. "I have only this knife for a weapon which I would entrust to you for the length of the journey." He was close enough now to see the driver's eyes narrow in concentration.

"And that sack of yours?"

Were it not for his sack's ermine secret, Bewilliam would have offered to allow the driver to search for weapons. "I'll give you custody of that too," he said and came alongside the wagon.

The wagon stopped. "Hand them over, then," the driver said, "and climb aboard. And play another tune. You do pull some fine notes from that thing."

King Bewilliam did as bidden. He settled himself in the rope sling strung from the cart's side and appraised the cart's load. "Radishes," he said, inhaling the spicy, earthy aroma.

"Aye."

"I like radishes," King Bewilliam said. "These are rather small...no offense."

"None taken. Would that I could grow them bigger."

"Hmm. Have you tried feeding the earth with the refuse of your meal from the night before?"

The farmer frowned. "Would that help?"

King Bewilliam explained that apparently when certain items such as onion peels and melon rinds rotted, they returned beneficial humours to the soil, so the decomposed refuse could be used as fertilizer. "But don't use meat scraps or bones. That just attracts vermin."

The farmer pursed his lips and nodded. "How know you this? Do you farm?"

King Bewilliam shook his head and smiled. "I like radishes."

"Have you one, then," replied the farmer. "Then play me a tune, Friend." He put out his hand. "I am John."

No "Your Majesty," no bow. King Bewilliam had not encountered many people lo these unnumbered days of wandering but when he had, not a single one offered anything more than the most common of courtesies. It was taking some getting used to. No one took him for anything more than what he seemed to be: a vagrant. The only part of his appearance that merited any attention was his footwear. Though shabby, his boots were somewhat grander than the flimsy slipper-type shoes most plebeians wore, suggesting that he had seen better days. That was certainly true.

His own hand halfway toward accepting the greeting, King Bewilliam stammered, "I'm... I'm..." He took a cue from the birds that had inspired his tune. "Robin."

They shook hands. With the slap of the chains, John put the cart in motion. "From whence you come, Robin? A far piece, from the looks of you."

Robin nodded. "A far piece." In miles, an untold number. Much farther than that in terms of what he had left behind and where he now found himself. He dusted the soil from the radish and ate it in one bite. "You might have left the radishes in the ground longer."

"Would that I could have, but I have a need for cash. I have a loan that's come due."

They rode for three songs and one lengthy tale that Robin told of a night in a tavern. It so amused the farmer that he cried with laughter. Then Robin took the reins while Farmer John slept. Jouncing in the cart's rope-sling seat didn't do Robin's bottom any favors. He wished for the gentler ride of Bell Castle's royal carriages with their cushioned seats and a springy suspension that he had invented. His feet were grateful for the rest, however, and riding spared his already shabby boots.

The morning was warm, warmer than he remembered spring mornings being. Maybe it was no longer spring, but summer or fall. Had he been walking that long? It felt like a lifetime. However the tender green of the leaves on the trees and shrubs told him that they were still in the earlier part of the year.

"Eh, Farmer John, I believe we're nearing town."

John raised his head.

"Must be Market Day from the looks of all this traffic," said Robin. The number of farmers and merchants using the wagon way had gradually increased until it had become quite crowded.

"Nay, this is only Tuesday," said Farmer John. "It's often like this."

"Indeed?" Robin handed over the reins.

"This is a popular trade center."

Clearly it was. The carts alongside them were heaped with produce and goods.

"I hope to sell the entire load," John said.

His face was tight and Robin suspected the debt that the farmer owed preyed on his mind. "The loan of which you spoke?"

The farmer nodded. "Yes. I had a drainage problem at the farm. My fields flooded with every rain and my crops were ruined."

"Your lord was not inclined to help?" I would have been, Robin thought. After all, his fortunes rose and fell with those of his tenants.

"I own my land," John said. "It's not much but it is mine, and I am proud to be able to bequeath it to my sons when the time comes. Farming here is a challenge. Our weather is downright devilish. Some days are brutal hot, others bitter cold. Sometimes we have terrible storms with great winds. We have droughts followed by downpours that could drown an ox. This last deluge about swept me away." He shook his head. "I was told, 'Send word to Lord Bernard.' And yes, I had heard that this lord had provided assistance to others, for an obligation. One day I was approached by one of his knights who said that I needed to dig a ditch. Well of course I did, but I didn't have the wherewithal to do it."

Robin nodded. Farmers, he knew, were busy from sunup to sundown and beyond just getting the farming done, much less making capital improvements.

"Before long," said John, "the knight returned with a small loan for me. It was just enough for me to hire a ditch digger."

"And now?"

"My crops have been doing much better. It looked like I was going to be in a position to pay back the loan as agreed but the knight visited me and told me that Lord Bernard demands payment now."

That didn't sound at all right to Robin. What was the worth of an agreement if both parties did not honor the terms? "Perhaps you are dealing with a rogue knight who seeks to fill his own pouch."

Farmer John shook his head. "I don't think so. He seemed to regret having to pressure me, and I think was fearful of what would happen if he didn't return to Lord Bernard with money." John frowned. "You have not heard of Lord Bernard?"

"No, I can't say that I have."

The farmer shrugged. "No matter. I hope to get out from under this obligation and then truly, I have learned my lesson. I will make the best of what I have and not aspire beyond my means."

Alongside the road, a trellis covered with rambler roses marked the settlement ahead. To Robin, the absence of a defensive ditch, wall, or gate spoke of a loosely-organized settlement not even worthy of the term "village."

"That's Rose Bank, the trade center, up ahead," said Farmer John. He handed Robin his sack and knife. "Where go you from here, Friend?" he asked as Robin dismounted the wagon.

"Don't know." It would be helpful if he knew where he was.

All he could remember was walking. Perhaps he had set out for a hike. There was nothing unusual about his leaving the castle. He often toured the countryside, partly to escape the pressure of court and partly to see firsthand how fared his subjects. However, rarely did he go without his retinue and most assuredly did not go on foot.

This last time, apparently, he had set out alone, walked beyond the castle gates, and kept walking. He remembered walking and walking and walking until he could walk no more, sat to rest, and fell asleep. He awoke and realized that he was in a strange land, definitely out of his realm. Could he have been enchanted while he slept? An enchantment would explain his lot. If not a spell, what other reason could there be for his mysterious transformation from honored and respected ruler to homeless vagabond?

He remembered trying to make his way back to his kingdom. Yet the harder he tried, the further he got into unknown territory. He sorely missed the ease and luxury of royal life. He felt adrift in the absence of challenges presented to him daily, and the satisfaction of reaching solutions where benefits outweighed the cost. He tried not to think about his wife and two sons as that brought a longing that was too painful to bear.

If he even could make it back to his realm, what would he find? Did his family and subjects await his return? Would the kingdom have fallen to ruin? Had he been deposed? Did someone else now rule in his place? If that were true, would he even be able to reclaim his throne? Certainly it would take more than simply reappearing, ragged and worn from life on the road. Hell, he might need an army to recapture his throne. At the very least, he would need a king's ransom to redeem it.

A king's ransom. What a joke! At the moment he didn't have a coin to buy a haircut or a crust of bread to eat or a bed in which to sleep. He sighed. Here in this settlement there would be no sleeping in the open, for he would be arrested as a vagrant. Perhaps, though, he could find some employment and raise a few coins.

CHAPTER TWO

The crunch of Robin's boot heels was not quite loud enough to drown out the growling of his stomach. Good as it was, the farmer's radish had served only to whet, not satisfy Robin's appetite. Would that he had had some nice bread and butter to accompany it. And a turkey leg. And a beer to wash it all down.

At the carts and stalls that clustered in the settlement's market square the fruits of farming, ranching, and hunting changed hands briskly in trade for manufactured goods and coins. Robin had neither coin nor anything to sell and no one was likely to be interested in a harmonica tune that wouldn't be heard over the cacophony of the market. He ambled along, looking for an opportunity. Here there was a wagon with a split plank, a stall with a torn canopy, a butcher cursing knives too dull to make a clean cut. Robin cadged tools from nearby stalls and repaired the cart, mended the torn canopy so at least it hung as one piece, and sharpened the butcher's knives.

By the time the sun had crossed its course's midpoint, Robin had bartered his skills for lunch from the butcher and a handful of coins from the other merchants. As he worked, he had observed the merchants to be of good spirit: industrious, fair, even generous, as they responded with grace to paupers seeking alms. Robin suspected that he too could have filled his pouch with coins by begging rather than by the sweat of his brow, but that was not his way. Charity came at too high a price; he would be indebted to the donor until the obligation was discharged. No, the scales had to be in balance. Some good or service had to be rendered in exchange.

His hunger sated, he stepped away from the market and strolled past the timber-framed structures that lined the road through Rose Bank, housing a blacksmith, potter, and weaver. Surely, somewhere here there was a stable, a room — something with walls and roof. Before night fell, he would need a place to sleep.

Tantalizing aromas teased him as he passed the baker's, and his mouth watered at the sight of the ale-wife's flag. He marked the location of the leatherworker. Robin knew his boots would need patching before they would take him much further. At the barber's he paused and fingered the coins in his pouch. Had he enough for both a bed and a trim?

Deciding that he did, he stepped through the door into a thick clutch of stubbly, bushy-haired men. Others wore makeshift bandages and pained expressions that spoke of the need for doctoring. The men shifted their weight from foot to foot, grumbling with impatience as they awaited their turn. At the back of the room, the barber clipped, stropped, swabbed, and sheared without pause. Robin would have described the man as tall had days of bending over his customers not rounded his posture. Gray peppered his short hair and beard, and hair clippings of many shades furred his tunic. Though he said nary an unkind word, the barber's wrinkled brow and drawn face betrayed his stress.

Robin counted the waiting men and sighed. It would be some time before his turn came around. He tried to engage one or two in conversation but they were too ill of sorts for small talk. Finally, Robin drew his harmonica from his sleeve and piped a tune by way of amusing himself.

The man next to Robin hummed along, softly at first, then with vigor. Next to him, a fellow sang the words to the popular tune. A second man joined in, pitching his tone to harmonize. Another man lent his deep bass voice to the chorus and a fourth man made it a quartet. Before long, the front of the shop was home to a lively concert. At the rear, the barber swayed to the rhythm, the click of his shears providing the percussion. Harmonies ebbed and flowed with the traffic of men entering and leaving the shop.

At last it was Robin's turn in the tall, high-backed chair. Though he put away his harmonica, the singing continued. The barber hummed along as he clipped, shampooed, and shaved Robin's russet curls.

The dust of many trails removed, Robin felt fresher, even lighter. He withdrew a coin.

The barber shook his head. "Oh, no, sir, this one's on me. Your playing has entertained my customers. I have made the price of your cut many times over." He waved his hand at the men remaining in the vestibule. "Had you not kept them amused, their impatience would have driven off many and I would have lost business."

The barber laid aside his scissors and took a long drink from a tankard. "Ah, the first break I have had all day!" He grinned. "In fact, would you be inclined to stay and play until closing? I would be most grateful and happy to compensate you for your time and talent."

Extra coins! Robin envisioned another meal already bought and paid for, perhaps even a bath to go with his bed. He took up position in the front of the shop and kept the tunes coming until the last customer had left.

The barber sank into his chair and wiped his brow. Robin took a broom from where it leaned against the wall and swept at the multicolored carpet of shorn hair.

"You don't have to do that," said the barber. "I will get to it."

11

Robin shrugged his broad shoulders and continued sweeping until he had brushed the clippings into a pile. He retired the broom and headed for the door.

With a raised hand, the barber signaled Robin to wait. The man filled his tankard from a small cask in the corner. He held out his other hand. "Your cup, sir?"

Robin handed his mug to the barber who filled it and retook his seat. Robin settled on a bench, braced his back against the wall, and took a long drink. Beer! Parched though he was, Robin drank slowly, savoring the beverage.

The barber nodded his head. "A good day's work, my man." He took another drink. "So, music-maker, how are you called?"

"Robin." He suppressed a chuckle. The name suited his new lot of flitting from perch to perch. He held out his hand.

"David," said the barber. He clasped Robin's hand firmly.

They drank in weary silence. The shop grew ever darker as the day turned to evening.

Robin drained his mug and stood. "I had best move along. Night falls and I need to find me a bed."

"Why not stay here?" asked David. "I have room, a spare blanket, food."

"I couldn't take your food," Robin replied.

"You could if you agreed to help me on the morrow," said David with a grin.

Robin gazed out the open door at the dark street and around the shop. "What's for supper?"

CHAPTER THREE

David's trade, already brisk, grew as word spread of the entertainment offered for no more than the price of a regular visit to the barber. Robin kept the customers amused, the shop neat, and the scissors sharpened. In exchange, David provided a roof, food, and the occasional free trim. Satisfied customers sometimes dropped a coin in Robin's lap.

David kept long hours at the shop, rarely pausing for a break, even working by candlelight on occasion. Robin worked just as hard. David remarked on it.

"I need the money," Robin replied. "I came here with nothing and I mean to change that."

"Money you have now," said David.

"Not enough," said Robin. "Not near enough to do what I want to do." Not near enough to recover a kingdom.

"Well, I won't ask you what that is," said David. "Perhaps someday you will tell me. Meanwhile, I am glad that you're here. Not only have your efforts contributed to the growth of the business, I enjoy your company. We have quite the partnership."

Partners? Well, not exactly. After all, David owned the shop and Robin owned nothing. If anything, Robin was hired help. But, if that was how David felt about it.... Robin held out his hand for David to shake. "Partners."

The days passed quickly and companionably. Like Farmer John and several others in the area of Rose Bank, David owned a plot of land and owed no service to any lord. David's holding was small but it did provide for his family. David's wife Carolyn and their sons tended the land. When times were good and they had a little extra, David's family would visit Rose Bank's market square to trade. If the workday was short, David would spend the night with his family at the farmhouse, leaving Robin in the shop alone with his torturous thoughts and questions.

Robin much preferred when the day was long and wearying. Then he and David might sup together and sometimes visit an alehouse before retiring, David to a private nook at the back of the shop and Robin to his spot on the stamped-earth floor, cushioned by his ermine cloak. On rare days when the shop was closed, Robin would help with the farm chores. The work was hard but he preferred chasing chickens and pigs to chasing his unanswered questions. Besides, his contributions of labor left him feeling less beholden to David and Carolyn for their sustenance.

One evening found Robin sweeping up and David seated in his own barber chair, resting his weary feet and massaging his aching hands after a long day. Evening light swept across the floor as the door swung open.

"We're closed for the day," Robin said to the tall man with the proud bearing. It seemed the man could easily afford to wait until the morrow. His trim white beard and close-cropped hair were not in need of barbering, nor did he appear to require medical attention. Though his broad-brimmed hat, long coat, and sturdy breeches bore the dust of much time on the road, the fabrics of which they were made were fine.

"Nay, Robin," said David. "He is not here for a haircut." To the tall man he said, "Come in, come in. Be seated. I'll be with you in a moment."

The tall man moved to the rear of the shop and seated himself on the bench.

David glanced around the shop. He picked up an uneaten apple left over from the lunch that he had been too busy to finish and handed it to Robin.

"Robin, why not go have you some supper?" David asked.

Robin took the apple. "I believe I will." Though he was curious as to what business the man might have with David that didn't involve the removal of unwanted hair or the leeching of bad blood, he respected David's wishes and stepped outside the shop.

Straining against a hitching post and snorting was a mount that Robin assumed belonged to David's mysterious customer. The horse's livery suggested an explanation for the man's regal appearance. Moonlight glinted off the bridle and stirrups, shone in the fine-grained leather, and made the white horse appear almost ghostly. Metallic threads in the saddle blanket glittered. Robin thought that he could make out a heraldic crest: an eagle, perhaps, although it could have been a bat. Could David's customer be a member of a royal court? And what could he want with David, a humble barber?

Robin longed to be privy to what transpired between the two men. It took all the willpower he had to remain outside the shop where he amused himself by munching the apple and talking to the restless animal that continued to rear and stomp.

"What know you of your master's errand?" he asked. He managed to stroke the horse's soft muzzle. The horse calmed and finally stood quietly. It whinnied, which sounded to Robin less like "neigh" and more like "hay." Robin wondered if the horse was hungry. "Have you not been fed?" he asked. The horse nudged Robin's hand. Robin looked at his half-eaten apple and held it out. Gently, the horse wrapped its big teeth around the fruit.

"Step away! What have you done to my horse?" came an angry voice from behind.

Robin turned to face David's customer. Even in the scant moonlight, Robin could make out a menacing scowl.

"Begging your pardon, I was just —"

"I have never seen him so obedient," said the man. "We thought to train him for battle or jousting, but he is willful and nearly impossible to control. The only fight we're likely to get out of him is the one he's given me this journey. Yet you have him eating out of your hand, quite literally, it would appear."

"I simply said kind words to him," Robin replied.

The horse whinnied and butted Robin's shoulder.

"He must have liked what you said." The man chuckled. "You must be a magician like your friend the barber." The man mounted his horse. "Well, now, perhaps we will have a nice gentle ride home."

The horse neighed as if in response.

"I may come back to find out exactly what you did say to him." With another chuckle, the man shook the reins and steered the horse away into the dark night.

Robin returned to the shop to find David wrapping something in a scrap of purple silk.

"So, of my visitor tonight, you are no doubt curious," said David.

Robin shrugged, he hoped not too convincingly.

"His kingdom would like to incorporate Rose Bank," David said. "Provide us supplies, equipment, and labor to build fortifications, which we don't need, for a price, which they do."

"Indeed," replied Robin. The lord probably also coveted the small farms of David's and his neighbors, and the labor force that went with them. Though of course this was a common practice, Robin had rarely used such a strategy to enlarge his own kingdom. He preferred instead to increase the royal coffers through his proficiency as a dragon slayer. He liked dragon slaying and was so good at it that other kingdoms sought out his aid. The gifts that he received in gratitude nicely fattened his treasury. He vaguely remembered having gone on one such lengthy campaign, but could not have said when that was, except that it seemed a lifetime ago. "And he spoke to you of this because...?"

Now it was David's turn to shrug unconvincingly. "Of those here who might call themselves burghers, I have probably been in Rose Bank the longest."

And was the most influential, Robin decided. The casual intimacy of David's tending to their grooming encouraged many to confide in him. Since he knew so much about so many, his advice was also often solicited.

"I see." Robin cleared his throat. "Are you a magician?"

"What?" David laughed. "Where did you get that idea?"

"Your visitor said you were."

"There's no magic in it." David turned the silk-wrapped bundle over in his hands. "The cards just help me to focus."

"Cards?"

David unwrapped the silk to reveal a stack of heavy paper cards decorated with woodcut prints.

They looked similar to those used for children's games or sometimes for gambling in taverns. Yet they were different, the images more detailed and exotic. Tarot cards they were, for divination. Robin wondered if he should admit that he was familiar with them and their use. From time to time, various soothsayers had employed them to answer Robin's request for an opinion on some course of action that he contemplated. The exercise had disappointed him. He had expected more considered wisdom from his ministers than a reliance on a dubious fortune-telling device. A tarot reading rarely told him anything that he didn't already know. He would have to admit, though, that sometimes a reading helped him to see the situation from another angle or brought to the fore some aspect that he had overlooked. Or, as David had said, to focus.

"Would you like me to do a reading for you?" David asked.

CHAPTER FOUR

R obin hesitated. What if there was something authentic to this tarot? Would David be able to divine Robin's true situation, that he was a king without a kingdom? Something more than idle curiosity made him answer, "Yes."

They straddled opposite ends of the bench where a short candle at the center cast a pool of yellow light. David directed Robin to shuffle the cards just so, then David cut and restacked them in a deliberate manner. Finally he dealt cards one by one onto the bench in an elaborate pattern.

David studied the cards in silence for a few moments, tilting his head to the left, to the right, frowning, pursing his lips, and muttering "hmmm, hmmm."

At last he spoke. "You are a man who had much, my friend, but it is gone. Taken from you, it seems, perhaps because your attention was diverted."

As with other readings, this did not tell Robin anything new. He had had an entire kingdom and then, like magic, it was gone. Maybe it was magic. Maybe he was under a spell of some kind.

"You seek to regain it," said David.

"And will I?"

David held up an index finger and frowned at the interruption. "First you must come to understand how you lost it."

Now it was Robin's turn to frown. Perhaps he should devote some time to consulting with necromancers, to uncover the spell and learn what it would take to break it.

"Look to your past," said David. "Therein lie both the question and the answer."

The past? Perhaps David was saying that necromancers weren't necessary, that if Robin searched his memory he would recall how he had been bewitched and by whom.

"You have many struggles ahead," said David. "Some dark moments of deep despair. You will call on every ounce of strength you have, and press onward. You will not be without allies." David patted Robin's forearm. "Yes, you will struggle mightily."

Robin sighed. He felt weary already. Perhaps he should simply give up. The effort to amass, one coin at a time, the fortune he would need to reclaim his former life was like scaling a mountain whose peak disappeared into the clouds.

"But there's a potential for the outcome to be favorable."

Robin raised his head. A favorable outcome? Could it indeed be that he would regain his throne? That he would once again be the master of his own fate?

"You see all that there?" he asked.

David shrugged.

Robin stood at David's shoulder and perused the cards. One in particular caught Robin's attention and he wondered why David hadn't remarked on it. It pictured a smiling king sitting on a throne and holding a huge gold coin. That the card was upside down filled Robin with dread.

He tapped another card which portrayed a man carrying an armload of staves, his back bent by the weight of them. "Is this a symbol of struggle?"

"A struggle, yes, and strength."

"It's upside down, though. The image is facing away

from me? Does that have significance?"

"That can mean that ultimately there will be a laying down of burdens."

"The favorable outcome of which you spoke?"

"A potentially favorable outcome, if and only if when he lays down his burden he does not pick it up again, or take up another."

Robin studied the other cards on the bench. The scenes of men and women, of staves and swords, goblets and pentacle-stamped coins did seem to have a story to tell if only one understood all the symbols. He regretted now having dismissed summarily the soothsayers of his court without first having learned more about the cards. He tapped another card which pictured a fair-haired sweet-faced maiden wearing a star-studded crown and a rose bedecked gown, seated on a throne. The card's legend read "The Empress." He wondered if it might have some reference to his wife, Queen Daya. "And this? Who is she?" he asked, almost afraid to hear the answer. "Is it her realm in which I now find myself?"

"The Empress? Rose Bank is not a part of that or any realm, much as some would have otherwise." David chuckled.

"Like tonight's visitor?"

David simply smiled. "Besides, even if that were the case, it's unlikely that it's as simple as that. The Empress card doesn't necessarily always refer to a specific person, or even a woman. It bespeaks of certain qualities, such as a passionate approach to life, creativity, fertility, and abundance. Nurturing and generosity."

He cocked his head to one side and studied the cards for a moment before gathering them into a stack and rewrapping them in the silk.

"Hmph," said Robin. "A simple deck of cards, yet you see my past, present, and future. It must be magic."

Again David chuckled. "Not magic. No, I'm just a good reader of men. As I have read you, lo these many days."

Which surprised Robin not at all. David spent his days listening patiently and without comment to his customers' chatter as he attended to their barbering, and in between sweeping and music-making, Robin overheard many tales of daily troubles and trials.

Now it was Robin's turn to chuckle. Indeed, there was much that David could surmise simply from Robin's appearance, demeanor, and behavior, even if David didn't know the specifics of an entire kingdom lost, seemingly in an instant.

"And you did a reading for your visitor?"

David winked. "I told him that an alliance he sought just wasn't in the cards. Well, my friend, now it is truly time to call it a day, or shall we say 'night,'? Even the light is ready to quit."

As if in agreement, the candle sputtered and went out, the dark room lit only by the silvery gray moonlight that filtered around the edges of the front door. David bade Robin goodnight and retired to his private quarters.

Robin spread his bedroll on the floor, but found that he could not sleep. Wrapped in the ermine-trimmed cloak of his past, he lay in the gloom. Before his waking eyes, men jousted with staves while a star-crowned, rose-bedecked maiden smiled. He counted the pentacle-stamped coins of which he had pitifully few, and nowhere nearly enough to reclaim his kingdom.

As he had many mornings now, Robin woke to the strengthening sunlight outlining the door, thinning the pall of night. He quickly folded his cloak, stowed it in a cupboard, and stepped outside to empty a full bladder behind the cover of a hedgerow. When he had first arrived at David's, he noticed that amongst the shrubbery was a puny rosebush with nary a bloom. In the ensuing weeks it appeared to have strengthened. It having, to Robin's knowledge, received no other attention, he attributed the improvement to his early morning dousing. It pleased him that there might be some beneficial humors in his water.

Back inside, he pulled on his tunic and vest and stoked the banked cooking fire to life. With his mug, he ladled up some hot water in which he steeped some bracing herbs. He took his tisane to the bench, sat, and reached for his boots. No sooner had he noticed that one felt unusually heavy than a small furry head appeared over the top. Startled, he dropped the boot.

"R-r-r-ow!" came the angry protest from the gray kitten that tumbled out.

"Well, now, where did you come from? Before my boot, that is?" Robin said.

The kitten sat on its haunches and regarded him with big golden eyes.

It must have been unobtrusively hanging around the shop for some weeks, Robin surmised, judging from its well-fed appearance and the relative lack of rats and mice. "Stay then, little furry one, and keep our place rodent-free," he said. Indeed, cats were useful to have around for that very reason. There were those in Robin's kingdom who thought them evil consorts of witches and strove to eradicate them. Robin had noticed an increase in the rodent population after each of these campaigns, and an attendant decrease when cats made a reappearance.

"Meeyoo," said the kitten, and padded over to rub its jowls against Robin's ankles.

"Well, that's very nice, Chum, but if you're looking to me to provide you with breakfast, I'm afraid you're on your own. I have no milk, you see. But you get started on finding a mouse or two."

The kitten sat, cocked its head to one side, then the other, stretched up a paw and placed it on his ankle. "Meeyoo."

Robin scratched the kitten between its shoulder blades, the one spot cats could not reach themselves, unleashing a flood of purrs. "Now that I've got your gears turning, you'd best be off about your business and me about mine."

The day progressed as many of them did in David's shop, with a steady stream of repeat customers who now expected not just to be shaved and groomed but also to be entertained. Having watched Robin put an edge on David's scissors between cuts, many now also brought knives and other small blades to be sharpened. David gave Robin the use of his sharpening stone and let Robin keep the tips he received. Robin had offered to turn these coins over to David but he refused, saying there were many helpful things that Robin did about the shop for which he was not compensated, and for which David was grateful.

Not the least was the improvement that Robin had made to the clipping scissors. Robin had noted how sore David's wrist and hand were at the end of every day. Not surprising given how much force was needed to use the spring-operated scissors. Robin had wondered if he couldn't improve on the design to make the tool more efficient. He found that spending his sleepless nights pondering the question was more satisfying than lying awake brooding over his misfortune. After much experimentation, he worked out that it made sense to separate the two blades, then join them with a pin upon which each blade could pivot. A finger loop at the end of each blade made for an instrument that David could use all day with less discomfort.

"You're quite handy with that sharpening stone, aren't you, my good man?" said one of David's regular customers, Oliver John by name, a cutler by trade. Oliver John's home was many a day's ride away, but he traveled widely, seeking new customers. He spent much time on the road and when in the vicinity of Rose Bank, would make a point of stopping at David's to attend to his grooming, maintaining that a cared-for appearance was critical to his success with his customers. Robin had hoped to overhear some conversation that might suggest Oliver John's travels had taken him near the Chalklands, but such had never been mentioned.

"I'm glad you think so," said Robin.

"Oh, indeed I do. You put a keen edge on these blades, and you're quick about it, too."

"Thank you."

"Ah, I see David is almost done and ready for me." Oliver John exchanged a coin for his newly-sharpened dagger.

"Most generous of you," said Robin.

"I can afford to be. My cutlery business is truly taking off."

Robin imagined that it would be. With the area's growing prosperity came an increasing interest in the finer things such as personal armor, and the wherewithal to afford it. Would that Robin could afford to buy a sword from Oliver John. Handy as it was, a knife would hardly be up to the task of retaking a kingdom.

"I would be doing even better if production could keep pace with demand," said Oliver. "If, say, I had a swift and able man to attend to sharpening the blades." Oliver fixed Robin with a stare. "A man such as yourself."

"Are you offering me a job?" Robin asked.

"It would be much harder work than playing the harmonica and sweeping floors," said Oliver. "But I'd wager you'd find the pay better. Of course, I have no idea what your arrangement with David is, or what are your obligations. Ah, I see it's my turn." He headed for the barber chair, saying, "If you are interested, let me know and we will talk further."

Throughout the remainder of the day, Robin's thoughts drifted off to ponder Oliver John's offer. When playing the harmonica or sharpening blades, which claimed his full attention, he pushed those thoughts aside. But when sweeping the floor, they returned.

He hadn't considered seeking other employment. He was content with his situation at David's. Here he had shelter and work. True, the work paid little. Most of the coin that he received as tips went for food, for while David would accept no money for the shelter that he provided, he did allow Robin to stand for the price of a meal or a tankard of ale now and then.

It was over one of those tankards that Robin struck up an acquaintance with Dolores, a young woman who often helped the ale-wives for tips from the overworked brewers and their thirsty patrons.

And he had another new friend. Every evening when he retired, the kitten he had discovered in his boot would reappear. It would enjoy the occasional morsel of food that Robin had saved from his own meal, then wait for Robin to settle in for night, at which point it would climb onto his chest and purr until Robin fell asleep. In the morning he would find the kitten curled up in one of his boots.

Yet, while life in Rose Bank was comfortable, even pleasant sometimes, Robin had to admit that the nest egg he sought to build was not growing very fast. At the rate that he was going, he would be a very old man by the time he had enough to buy himself a decent sword, much less reclaim his kingdom.

One evening over a late supper of roasted turkey leg and cider, David said, "You seemed preoccupied today. Is something the matter? Are you ill?"

"Ill? No," Robin replied. "Preoccupied, yes. I apologize if I left something undone."

"You didn't. My remark wasn't meant as a criticism, just an observation."

Robin took a swallow of cider. "I was simply ruminating on that loss of which you spoke when you read the Tarot. I was thinking about that, and how I might regain it."

"Indeed," said David. "This is ever present on your mind."

Robin shrugged. "I should leave off thinking about it, I suppose. It's a lot to recover and the chances that I will ever be able to do so are thinner than the strands of hair on old Mr. Greery's head."

David chuckled. "And yet the desire lingers."

Robin nodded. He took the loaf of bread that they shared and tore off a chunk. He popped it in his mouth, chased it with a bit of turkey, and chewed them together. He liked the blend of flavors and often contemplated wedging the meat into the bread somehow. There seemed no way to cut slices of bread thin enough to make a combination that could be enjoyed in one bite. A well-sharpened blade would slice off wafers of turkey, but not even the sharpest knife would cut thin slices of bread, which would only crumble or crush under the blade's pressure.

"Then if that is your true desire, it should not be denied," said David. "It will only haunt your dreams and gnaw at your soul."

That it did, although of late Robin had been devoting some sleepless nights to the bread-knife problem.

"What's yours?" Robin asked.

David smiled. "I believe I've satisfied mine."

Robin found that easy to believe. David too had shelter, food, and work. As long as men had hair, David would always have work, and therefore food and shelter. He was well-liked by the townspeople, a valuable member of the community. Clearly the rich and powerful sought his counsel, if not for his power to sway the community's will, then for his ability to see hidden meanings in a deck of cards.

And David had a family. Robin enjoyed the time he spent with Carolyn and the boys. They were hard working but light-spirited people. Yet at night as he lay on the floor of David's shop, Robin so missed his family that tears stung his eyes. The eagerness with which David's sons endeavored to master the skills that their father sought to teach them reminded Robin of his sons. They were of an age now when their lessons would shape the men they would become. And Robin was not there to teach them. Who was, he wondered, and what were they learning? He ached to be with them now, to share what a lifetime of experience had taught him.

Robin took a long, thoughtful swallow of cider and pushed thoughts of his family away. He should be grateful for what he did have. It wasn't that long ago that he slept in a cow pasture, not a farthing to his name. He was not unhappy. The days passed agreeably enough, with visitors to the shop happy to chime in with one of his tunes, pleased with their newly sharpened blades. His evenings were agreeable, too. He would swap tall stories with David, or take some pleasure with Dolores who was not only very pretty but also seemed to find Robin immensely charming. That she could also provide her own ale was an added benefit. Though Robin never quite forgot that somewhere, a wife mystified by his disappearance might anxiously await his return, he did not dwell on it. Like his vacated throne, she seemed part of another world, someone else's life.

Still, his nights alone were restless. He often roused from slumber, concerned about the welfare of the kingdom only to realize with heavy heart that it was no longer his. Sometimes only the purring of the kitten on his chest got him back to sleep.

This night, the words of Oliver John kept Robin's eyes open long after the room dimmed with nightfall. Oliver John could not know, of course, but it was true. The few coins that Robin earned in the course of a day were adequate for his basic needs, but no more. Robin stared at the ceiling. There would be no reclaiming his kingdom, not unless he could find a powerful witch to cast a spell greater than the one that had already changed his fortune. Or unless he made his own magic. And that would require men, arms, and all the other accoutrements of a major military campaign.

It was unlikely that Oliver John intended to reward Robin for his labors to such a great extent. However it was sure to be more than he had now.

CHAPTER FIVE

"What are you going to do?" asked Dolores. She snuggled a little closer to Robin.

"I haven't decided," he said, and tried subtly to extricate himself from her clingy embrace. Their coupling was pleasant enough, perhaps a degree more than merely pleasant. Dolores was a beautiful woman and a lusty lover. Robin sometimes wondered if it was the ale that unleashed her passions. At first he had found that amusing, perhaps even attractive. She could hold her liquor so well that she could laugh, sing, and flirt until the beer vat had been drained, and still had energy left over to satisfy Robin. Of late, though, he had become concerned. The tips that she made were generous, yet hardly amounted to a living wage.

She had little money for lodging, so had no permanent residence. The women who kept Rose Bank in ale sometimes let her curl up in a corner. Other times, she bunked with friends or sometimes former lovers, the latter seeming imprudent to Robin.

She had little money for food either, although that didn't appear to be as much of a problem since she hardly ever ate. Robin remarked on it once and Dolores had laughed and said that ale filled her belly.

She certainly drank a lot of it and Robin had begun to wonder if that influenced the decisions that she made, some of which were unwise, even dangerously daring.

When she wasn't tipsy, which wasn't often, Dolores could be bright and intelligent company. She was a talented seamstress, a skill that she did not pursue which Robin thought unfortunate. She had made for him a rucksack in which he stowed the ermine cloak and the few personal possessions that he had acquired. At one point he had asked her to craft a sort of scabbard to accompany the refashioned scissors he had made for David. Robin envisioned a tabbed pouch with slots in the tab such that a belt could be threaded through it. With such a pouch, one could easily keep the scissors handy. Dolores had made a promising start on the project only to abandon it for a night drinking with friends.

He had wondered why her young sons did not contribute to her support. "They're off making their own fortunes," Dolores told him. "As they should be. I can take care of myself," she had said, and she refused to ask them for assistance.

"If you leave Rose Bank, I would go with you," Dolores said. "A traveling companion might make the journey more enjoyable. I am very fond of you and there's not much keeping me here."

The latter was certainly true. It might even be an act of kindness to take her away from an environment where ale came all too easily to hand. Her life as she led it in Rose Bank was likely to end prematurely, even badly.

He could see that having Dolores along might indeed lighten his steps. If he knew where he was bound and what he would find when he got there, he would be tempted to ask her to join him. But what if the road to Oliver John's did lead Robin back to his kingdom? He had no idea what he would find once he arrived there. If he had to wage a battle, how would he look after Dolores? And what of Queen Daya? Robin shook his head. Every line of thought regarding the fate of Queen and their two sons ended in aching despair.

"That is a generous and attractive offer, Dolores," he said, sliding from her embrace. He pulled on his leggings and tunic. "I don't know that I am leaving. I still have much to consider before I make a decision."

Dolores gave him a weak smile. "You will let me know what you decide, won't you?"

"Of course." Robin pulled on his boots, gave Dolores a parting kiss, and headed for David's and another restless night of contemplation now complicated by yet another decision to make. If he accepted Oliver John's offer, should he ask Dolores to come with him?

At daybreak, Robin completed a now familiar routine of hiding his cloak and watering the rosebush. He took his morning beverage outside to enjoy the mild late spring morning. As had become its custom, the kitten followed him. Robin would sit on a stool and the kitten would settle at his feet. Robin would speak his thoughts aloud and the kitten talked back with purrs and growls. The kitten would fix Robin with an attentive gaze of its yellow eyes and let fly a string of utterances. Robin would imagine that it was relating its own adventures, tales of victory in finding a rich nest of mice, or defeat in being outrun by a particularly fleet-footed prey.

This morning Robin found himself more than usually anxious. It seemed as though Oliver John was about due to report to the shop for a trim.

"I think he is going to expect an answer from me today, Cat. What to do?" Robin said.

"Mee-yoo," the kitten replied, somewhat insistently, Robin thought.

"That's no help," said Robin. He drained his cup and headed inside to get the shop ready and open for business.

There was enough to do that Robin had little idle time and few opportunities to ruminate. Indeed, Oliver John did put in an appearance. Though he said nothing to Robin, his penetrating look spoke louder than words.

Oliver John paid David for his services, nodded to Robin, and departed the shop. Almost as if they had a will of their own, Robin's feet followed and swiftly brought him alongside the man.

"If the offer's still open, I would like to take it," Robin heard himself saying. He held out his hand.

Oliver John at first seemed puzzled, but then took Robin's hand and shook it. "I am glad to hear it. Come along, then."

"On the morrow," Robin said. "I have yet to explain it all to David."

Oliver John nodded. "I understand. I know that your services will be missed. Tomorrow, then. You will find my home and my shop outside Riverington. It is several days' ride from here. Ask for directions to the ironworks."

Several days' ride. Since Robin had nothing on which to ride, that meant even more days walking. Robin was already weary just thinking about it. "I will be there."

Robin returned to David's shop quite a bit more slowly than he had left.

At day's end, Robin told David of his decision.

David cast his eyes down. "I can't say that I didn't see this day coming. I know that you have a dream that bedevils you and you see this as a way to make that dream come true." David expressed regret, not just at the loss of an assistant, but also of the company. "I think you will agree that lo these many days we have forged a friendship. So you will know that I am sincere when I say that you are welcome to return any time."

"Thank you. And should you ever find yourself in dire need of my help, just send word."

That night when he retired, Robin assumed that having finally made a decision, he would at last get a decent night's sleep. Yet he lay on the floor watching the light that limned the door wink on and off as clouds drifted across the moon. He sighed. The kitten rose from its prone position on his chest and stood, somehow heavier on all four paws than when it was stretched full-length across him. It fixed him with a stern look, eyes glittering in the low light, as if to complain that Robin's restlessness was disturbing its sleep.

"I'm sorry, Cat," Robin said. "I just hope that I made the right choice. I feel almost as though it was impulsive. I'm not unhappy here, in the shop with David and the customers. My leaving will so inconvenience David, who has been nothing but kind to me. But happiness will not buy back my kingdom. Nothing that I'm doing is moving me toward that. Working for Oliver John could. I would be a fool not to accept his offer."

The kitten yawned, resumed its position stretched out on Robin's chest, and purred.

Robin could not say when he finally fell asleep but he awoke as usual at daybreak. This morning, he hurried his routine so that he could ready the shop as his last act before leaving for Oliver John's.

He gathered his few belongings in his rucksack and glanced around. As it had many times in the past, the kitten placed a paw on his ankle and said, "Mee-yoo."

Robin scratched its ears and neck. "Well, little one, I must be going. You've been doing a great job of controlling the rodent population here. Just keep it up." He shouldered his rucksack and walked toward the door. The kitten trotted behind him. Robin chuckled. "No, no, Cat. No tea and talk this morning. I must be off. You stay here."

"MEE-YOO!"

Robin stood still, goosebumps radiating outward from his spine. As clearly as if it had spoken actual words, he heard the kitten cry, "Me! You! You dumb ox! That's what I've been saying. Me! You! That means 'us!' Together! Forever!"

"Well, umm, OK. But understand, you may not be welcome everywhere I go. There may be times when we'll have to be secretive about it."

Robin could have sworn he saw the kitten nod its head.

"Come on, then, Meeyoo." He stepped out the door, the kitten at his heels. They went a few paces, Robin striding and the kitten skipping along. Robin stopped and chuckled. "Meeyoo, not that you haven't been doing a stellar job of keeping up, but I think from here on in you are going to have to ride rather than walk." He made an opening at the mouth of his pack, scooped up the kitten, and put her in it. As he walked, he could feel the kitten's breath as little warm puffs at the back of his neck until it decided to snuggle into the pack and sleep.

As he walked the road leading out of Rose Bank, through a home's open door he spied Dolores stirring a vat with an ale stake. Realizing that he had one more decision to make slowed his steps.

CHAPTER SIX

"Ah, Meeyoo, what am I going to do about Dolores?" he murmured, but got no reply. That made sense. In all his albeit one-sided conversations with the kitten, he had not once mentioned Dolores or her offer to accompany him on his travels so Meeyoo hadn't had a chance to form an opinion. Robin hadn't devoted any time at all to considering it and now the hour was at hand. He felt somehow that it would be a righteous gesture to take her away from Rose Bank. On the road, there would be little ale. Exercise, fresh air, and good country food might put a blush in her cheeks where now was only the pallor from too much time spent indoors and drinking.

Yet his steps did not turn toward her and instead continued on the road leading away from Rose Bank.

"I'll work really hard for Oliver John, Meeyoo," he said. "I'll save up some extra coins and come back here before starting on my quest for the Chalklands. Buy a nice little house for Dolores so she won't have to beg, borrow, or, well, 'trade' for a place to sleep. I'll make her a good pair of scissors. Maybe that will interest her in sewing." The more he spoke of it, the more the plan seemed to have merit. He nodded his head. "Yes, Meeyoo, that's what I'll do. I'll see that Dolores is taken care of."

Robin's heart sank a little on the journey to Riverington. Though he had passed farmlands, settlements, and substantial cities, he doubted that this was leading him any closer to his kingdom. Certainly there was plenty of lush foliage. Yet the landscape seemed a bit less green, more yellow than that of his realm. Some of the shrubs and ground covers were unfamiliar.

The "several days' ride" turned out to be many days on his feet and too many nights sleeping in fields. Wherever he could, he performed small jobs in exchange for food or lodging. His spirits lifted when he noticed an increase in cleared land spotted by tree stumps. An ironworks would need much lumber to feed the fires that smelted the ore. He must be nearing Oliver John's enterprise.

Some of that lumber had been used in construction as well, as Robin observed brick-and-timber structures.

Ahead he spied a sign much like the one that marked the site of Rose Bank. An elaborate wrought iron post marked the settlement of Riverington. He stepped off the road into the cover of some bushes, shrugged off the rucksack, set it on the ground, and pulled back the flap. Meeyoo turned her face up to peer at him through the opening.

"You had best hunker down, little one," Robin said. "I need to stop in town and we have no idea how folk here feel about felines."

He patted the kitten on the top of its head. The little animal padded around in a small circle atop his folded cloak, laid down, and closed its eyes. Robin laid the flap over the sack's opening, took the pack up once again, and returned to the road.

He strode toward the well in the market square but before he reached it, he spotted an alehouse. He stopped there for something to eat and drink and to ask how he might find the ironworks and Oliver John. Tired as he already was from his journey, once Robin learned that he had another half-day's travel, he did not linger. He quenched his thirst with a tankard of ale and ate half his order of bread and cheese, keeping the rest for his and Meeyoo's supper should they not reach Oliver John's by nightfall.

Hours after leaving Riverington, Robin came upon the intersection of which he'd been told. Another metal signpost indicated the side road to take to reach the ironworks. From here, Robin had been told that he had yet the better part of another hour's walk. He stopped, let Meeyoo out of the rucksack, and seated himself on a stump. The kitten stayed close to the rucksack at first, looking up, down, and in all directions, and sniffing the air. A rustling in the grass caught her attention. Bemused, Robin watched as Meeyoo adopted a fierce attack posture, nose and forelegs low to the ground, hind legs cocked. With a few shakes of her rump, Meeyoo charged off. Robin followed her progress as she half leaped, half ran through the grass. The race was over quickly. Meeyoo's return was slower than her advance. When she reached Robin, she sat and gazed at him with what looked like disappointment.

"It got away from you, huh?" Robin chuckled and broke off a bit of the cheese. Meeyoo swallowed the morsel in one bite, then busied herself with grooming. After a few moments, Robin declared that their break was over. He returned his traveling companion to the rucksack, shouldered the bag, and resumed their journey.

They were no longer alone on the road. Many times he had to step aside to make room for traffic coming and going. Though he knew that Oliver John was prosperous, Robin had not anticipated what he found as the road neared his destination. This was not merely an ironworks, it was The Ironworks. Thatched-roof brick-and-timber buildings lined the road. To his right a mining camp towered not far from flowing water in which stood a dock and a watermill. Habitations dotted the field near a marshy area. The metal roof of a warehouse glinted in the late afternoon sun and Robin could see the ebony gleam of peat bogs. Two halls flanked the two-story octagonal center building of a factory. Despite the late hour, all about thronged men, oxen, horses, donkeys, and wagons.

At some distance from the factory stood a veritable mansion with leaded-glass windows. Robin realized that this must be Oliver John's manor house. Robin had underestimated the man whom he had assumed to be a cutler, the owner of perhaps a town smithy. As owner of the house, the lands, and the factory and as employer of all these people, Oliver John was clearly a lord.

Robin decided to inquire after Oliver John first at the factory. He started across the central yard when over the din of manufacturing he heard someone call his name. He looked right, left, and behind but every man appeared to be busy with his task. Hearing his name again, he looked up and saw Oliver John waving from the factory's upper story's parapet. The man was dressed much as he was when would visit David's barbershop: sturdy clothing suitable for a day of hard travel, or in this case, work, but nevertheless made of the quality material and attention to detail that suggested the wearer was a man of means.

"Wait there!" Oliver shouted and after a few moments, joined Robin where he stood. He clapped Robin's shoulder. "I'm glad to see you," he said. He caught the elbow of a passing man and said, "A couple tankards of cider, if you would please, Stephen, and a few buns as well if any remain."

Stephen bowed and took off at a trot.

Robin realized with a guilty start that while Oliver John was clearly a person of importance, Robin had not once acknowledged that with the requisite obeisance. What Oliver John made of this egregious lack of respect Robin could not imagine. In Rose Bank, where there were no lords, no one had expected to be honored. Although Robin was used to being on the receiving end of bows, he realized that in keeping with his new social status, he was going to have to remember to offer them. He tucked his chin in what he hoped would pass for homage.

While they waited for the man to return, Oliver identified the various buildings: the foundry where huge fires

37

burned in furnaces, the stockpiles of coal and lumber for stoking those fires, the smithies for shaping swords and knives.

Stephen arrived, bowed, and handed out the refreshments. Oliver raised his tankard to Robin. "A toast, to you, my friend, and to the greater prosperity that we both will enjoy."

Robin clanked his tankard against Oliver John's. They drank and handed the tankards back to Stephen who bowed and carried them away. He returned with a horse-drawn cart to carry Robin and Oliver John on a tour of the Ironworks compound. To Robin it seemed larger and more populated than the settlement of Riverington through which he had passed earlier that day. Everything that was needed to support production surrounded them: ore from the bogs, flowing water to drive huge wheels and gears, trees to fell and mill for lumber, coal to feed the fires, stables to house the animals, and small farms to feed and clothe the workers and livestock.

At last they arrived at a tiny hut. Shaped like an inverted V and covered in thatch, the windowless timber hovel had a front and rear wall. "No one's using this at the moment," said Oliver John, "so this can be yours if you choose. It's not very large but the rent is equally small."

The shed appeared to be no deeper than the length of a man lying down, but how much room did he need? Robin thought. Having his own private lodging was already an improvement over sleeping on the floor of David's barbershop. "I'm sure this will suit me fine," he said, quashing an image that sprung up of his large and luxurious king's chamber in Bell Castle.

Oliver John chuckled. "Indeed, it's a bit close but you won't be spending much time in it. I mean to keep you very busy. So, I will give you tonight to get yourself settled. On the morrow, report at first light to the same spot where I found you today." With that, Oliver John mounted the cart and instructed Stephen to take him back to the foundry.

With a somewhat queasy feeling, Robin realized that he was now a serf and wondered if this was indeed an improvement in his status.

Exploring the little hut didn't take much time. Rushes covered the pounded-earth floor. Robin was fairly certain that one of his first domestic chores would be to scour the nearby marshes for fresh material. Outside the hut he found the remains of a cook fire but saw that he would need to fashion a tripod and obtain a pot if he planned to do any cooking. He would also need a candle or lantern to light the windowless interior, which in the fading light was already getting quite dark.

He set his sack on the floor in the corner and lifted the flap. Meeyoo lifted her head and peered out, the pupils of her eyes wide in the growing dark.

"Well, Meeyoo, looks like this is home for the near future."

Meeyoo placed her front paws on the edge of the sack and scanned the surroundings for a long moment before creeping out. As she had in the field, she skulked around in ever-widening circles to make a thorough examination of her new environment. At the open door, she again stopped to peer out first before venturing beyond the structure's shelter.

While Meeyoo conducted her reconnaissance, Robin combed the field for something on which to sit. He found a suitable rock and rolled it to the hut. He positioned it where the wall of the hut would support his back. It was a far cry from his capacious and cushioned throne and he found himself wondering who now sat there. Perhaps his wife, the Queen? If so, she might be managing to hold the realm together, for she had a good head on her shoulders and was a skillful manager. Perhaps one of his sons had had taken his place. They had been taking to their lessons well but they were still only youths. But for the young man's age and thus lack of experience, Robin's eldest might manage to cope in his father's stead, for the boy had a sharp and inventive mind.

Robin shook his head. He had no time for such idle thoughts. He wanted a fire. En route to the Ironworks, he had spent too many nights in the open, half-awake and on guard against predators both animal and human. As the sun headed for the horizon, he scraped out the fire pit that the previous occupant had left and piled a few dry twigs into it. Without even a flint, he knew he had serious work ahead of him and no good prospect for success. Tomorrow, Robin resolved, he would look for a bit of flint and a piece of steel that he would undoubtedly find around the foundry. For now, he would have to try to start a fire with wood alone. As a boy, he had pestered the royal forester to learn whether this could be done, then tried it himself. What he remembered of the experience was that he had spent hours at it, and he had failed. He knew that he would need a piece of softwood to make a fireboard and a hardwood shaft.

Fortune smiled upon him for he found the necessary raw materials. He took his knife and carved a long narrow groove into the plank of soft willow he would use for the plowboard. Next he whittled one end of the hardwood stick to a point. He laid the plowboard on the ground and rubbed the shaft back and forth in the groove to create a tiny pile of wood dust. He propped one end of the plowboard on his thigh so the dust would collect at the bottom, then set about rubbing fast enough to create the heat that would cause the wood dust to smoulder. It was hard work. Several times his heart leapt to see a whiff of smoke and he paused, thinking he had met with success, only to have the smoke vanish and the dust go cold.

He sighed. His back and shoulders ached. He was tired from the long day's travel and meagre nourishment. Though he had worked up a sweat, he realized that with nightfall the air was growing cool. Soon, he realized, the chill would further work against him.

CHAPTER SEVEN

Despairing, he looked about. He had slept out in the open without a fire before. He told himself that he could survive another such night. At least here he had shelter.

He took a deep breath. "We'll give it one more shot, Meeyoo," he said. He redoubled his efforts and was rewarded by a healthy puff of smoke. The pile of wood dust emitted the hint of a glow. Gently he blew a tiny flame to life. When that small fire at last burned strongly enough, he used it to ignite a scrap of tinder with which he touched off the kindling in the fire pit and got a proper fire going. He fashioned himself a torch to light his way back to the marsh in search of potable water and returned with his mug full. His supper would be water and whatever crumbs he might find in his pouch. Meeyoo would undoubtedly eat better tonight than he would.

By leaping onto his chest, Meeyoo woke Robin well before sunrise. The hut was nearly as dark as pitch, with just the thinnest line of moonlight outlining the door.

Robin groaned. "Oh, Meeyoo, you could have let me sleep a little longer. There will be no tea this morning, and no breakfast, not unless you fetch it." He rolled to his side, got to his knees, then stood. His shoulders, arms, and back ached, his legs, knees, and feet hurt. His stomach felt cramped as if it were collapsing in on itself from lack of something to fill it.

He stepped outside the hut, the cat at his heels. She took off bounding and skulking through the grass.

At the left side of the hut, the fire that he had built the night before had gone out. Around him, the dark silhouettes of buildings, bushes, and trees were just barely visible against the predawn sky. A scrawny bush just outside the hut struggled to put out some leaves but for the most part offered scanty coverage. At least at this hour there was no one in the immediate vicinity. Yesterday had been a long dry day and Robin didn't have much in the way of output. Certainly there was no rosebush to water. Robin sighed as he realized that he would not get to enjoy the summer blooming of the rosebush that he had tended at David's. Perhaps he'd be able to cultivate one here.

There was no barbershop to ready this morning nor had he any belongings to put away save his cloak. Robin stood in the dark hut, for the moment at a loss as to what to do. He did not fancy carrying the heavy garment in his pack throughout what was likely to be a long and wearying day but there was no place in the hut to hide the garment. What if brigands came by while he was gone and stole it? Even the chance that a curious passerby would discover it was too great a risk to take. At last he decided the only course of action was to take it with him for the day. Tonight he would dig a pit or something in which he could hide it.

He turned at the sound of an odd mewling. In the doorway of the hut sat Meeyoo, a fat starling clamped in her jaws. She set the bird at his feet. Robin felt his heart squeeze. Meeyoo had returned from a successful hunt to David's barbershop on several occasions. Robin had never quite figured out whether she brought dead animals into the shop because she was returning with prey to what she considered her lair, or to show off her prowess as a hunter. This morning he wondered if she had taken seriously his challenge to find breakfast for him.

42

In the event that was the case, he said, "Thank you, Meeyoo, but I would need to cook that. However my fire's gone cold and I don't have time this morning to start a new one."

Oliver John had told him to report at first light and the dark of night had thinned to gray.

He set out across the field towards the foundry. Around him the Ironworks community came to life. The light of lanterns flickered on and grew brighter within the huts. Doors opened a crack and a dog would emerge to nose around the hut or a figure would come out to nudge a cook fire to life or to "watch the sun rise." Smoke puffs from the mining camp and the foundry told Robin that the workday had already begun. He had an hour's walk back to the foundry and was already late. He hurried his steps.

As he hustled toward the foundry, he was on the lookout for flint, for steel, for something to use as a cooking vessel, and for something edible. He did spy a pepper bush that by its bedraggled appearance seemed to belong to no one. It was of the hot-pepper variety and the animals had left several pieces of wrinkled fruit behind. Robin knew that he would have to remove the seeds and membranes carefully to be able to eat it without wanting for ale to put out the fire. Several of his new neighbors had vegetable gardens that showed signs of early yield. Perhaps he would be able to beg, borrow, or, if he had to, buy some seedlings. He spotted herbs growing wild and made a mental note to pick some on his way home this evening. With any luck he'd be able to have tea tomorrow morning.

While he ruminated on various schemes to ensure a supply of food and quickly, a welcome sight ahead urged him almost to a run. Oliver John stood in front of the foundry holding two mugs.

"Good morning, Robin," the man said, and handed him one of the mugs.

Sincerely grateful for the sustenance, Robin made an awkward bow.

"I thought you might not have had time to procure provisions," said Oliver John. "You will find that at the

Ironworks' store, we have a few items for sale that will save you a trip into Riverington. And you could buy your supper here and leave your pack behind. I believe you will find wearing that on your back all day a real burden."

"Thank you, sir," Robin said, trying not to drink the cider in one greedy gulp. "I'll look into that."

"Today, I want to orient you to our industry here. By the end of the day, you will have your charge. Come with me."

He led Robin into the octagonal center building. Four workhorses harnessed to an armature overhead walked in a circle around a central shaft.

"You may have seen the watermill near the dock?"

Robin nodded.

"That drives the saws for the lumber mill. It takes much coal to make steel, and making coal requires much cut lumber. These horses drive the wheel that turns the gears and arms operating the larger grinding wheels," Oliver John explained as they passed by what appeared to be a watermill-type apparatus that had been rotated ninety degrees.

Robin followed Oliver John up the stairs to the second story that overlooked the entire property, and listened intently as the man explained the art and science of blade-making.

"Our main enterprise is swords," said Oliver John. "First we make a blade blank. We used to procure the blanks already made by specialists from distant lands and have them delivered by wagon or ship. However recently we have begun to create our own blanks. Thus we are mining ore from the nearby bogs and smelting it in our own bloomery."

He pointed toward the mining camp. "We load the ore into a puddling furnace and heat it with forced draughts of air. This reduces the ore to an almost spongy mass that we call bloom."

Robin observed men driving air into the furnace with bellows. "It's hard work but it was harder before we employed the bellows. Before that we had apprentices blowing into the furnace through straws."

He directed Robin's attention to a roughly conical brick building with a dark arched opening at the base and a smoking chimney.

"We remove this material and while it is still glowing hot, pound it with sledges to separate out some of the impurities. Sometimes this alone can produce steel but mostly what we get is wrought iron. Wrought iron can be shaped, but is not well suited for sword making as it is too easily bent. If we add the right amount of carbon and reheat the mixture in yet another furnace, the iron absorbs enough carbon to form a steel that can be shaped but which will also hold an edge.

"You can see the cast iron being transferred to the bloomer furnace where we introduce air and strive to keep the fire at a critical temperature. It takes many hands to man the furnaces, to hammer the bloom, to drive the bellows, and keep the fires hot."

That was something that Robin could easily see. Although the day had just begun, scores of men thronged around the furnaces. Working with huge horse-power-driven saws, blazing hot fires, and molten metals looked like grueling and dangerous work. He felt respect and admiration growing for all those involved in every aspect of sword-making and felt a new appreciation for just what a fine instrument a good sword was.

"For the most part, we create stock blade blanks. We manufacture blanks of several different lengths and profiles. We do have some customers who want a custom-made sword but for the most part, the custom-fashioning is in the hilt and scabbard, not the blade.

"Once we have made a blade blank, it's handed off to heat-treaters, grinders, and polishers and finally assembled. Meanwhile, the scabbard maker is readying the scabbard. A scabbard maker, as you can imagine, must be leathersmith, jeweler, and metalsmith combined. Our scabbard makers are among the finest." Oliver John smiled. "Well, all our designers and craftsmen are. Sword-making is very complex. The contour of the blade, the weight distribution, the shape of the edge, all must work together. We adhere to the principle of the Golden

Section, and aim to attain harmonious proportions at every step of manufacture."

Robin had heard of the Golden Section, although he didn't understand it all that well. It was an almost mystical mathematical concept relating the ratios of a sum of two quantities to the larger quantity. This produced a result that was not only functional but also pleasing to the eye. Robin wished that he was back at his court where his ministers could further explain the concept. He could now see how it would be important in the making of a sword that would not only serve as a trustworthy weapon that would give long service but also be an implement that would bring pride to its owner.

Robin and Oliver John had arrived at a small workshop behind the foundry. "This is where you come in, Robin," said Oliver John. "Here is where we do the grinding and polishing. Getting a good edge on a sword is no trivial matter. Watching you sharpen knives in David's shop has led me to believe that you could be well-suited for the task. With some training from our artisans, you could become a fine swordsmith."

For the moment, Robin had no words. He had been vaguely aware of the steps that went into making a sword, but had never given it much thought. Most of his attention had been applied to perusing a selection of blades his armorer had presented. Those swords had already met the prerequisites Robin had set for features, composition, and quality. The decisions that had been left for Robin to make had more to do with balance, with aesthetics, with whether the instrument felt right in his hands than anything else.

He was impressed with the skill and artistry that sword-making called for at every stage of production. Were he to be given a choice as to which task he would prefer, he would be hard pressed to choose. A swordsman's life could easily be lost over a mistake made at any point in the production.

"I'm eager to get started," he said.

"Very well," said Oliver John. "Let me introduce you to Franklin."

CHAPTER EIGHT

They descended to ground level and Robin followed Oliver John into one of the factory wings. The workshop there boasted the large grinding wheel of which Oliver John had spoken earlier. The chimneyed furnace at the center had already warmed the room. Sledges, hammers and tongs, rasps, and files hung from racks on the furnace's sides. Worktables flanked it and a line of stout tree stumps supported anvils and tubs of water. Lanterns hung from the ceiling. A lever-driven bellows occupied a stand next to the furnace. Tall stools stood next to frames holding grindstones of various sizes, some driven by cranks, others by treadles. The wooden floor was powdered with a light coating of grit and sawdust but otherwise relatively free of debris. Buckets held scraps of wood and metal. Robin made a mental note to retrieve a small scrap of steel before day's end.

"Frank!" Oliver John called over the noise of the fire and the mill just outside.

A slender man in worn, stained, and singed work clothes hunched over work at one of the tables. He turned to regard them through magnifying glass lenses mounted in a frame perched on the bridge of his nose. He dismounted his stool and acknowledged Oliver John with a bow.

"This is Robin, the apprentice of whom I spoke," said Oliver John.

Now uncertain of what was expected, Robin hesitated. Franklin resolved the matter by holding out his hand for Robin to shake.

"Teach him everything you know, Franklin," said Oliver John.

"If I do that, sir, you won't be needing me anymore," Franklin replied with a grin.

Oliver John chuckled. "True. Well, then, teach him everything that he needs to know."

With that, Oliver John took his leave.

The man Franklin said, "A little old for an apprentice, aren't you?"

Robin shrugged. "I was in another line of work but can no longer pursue that, so I am starting over."

Franklin nodded. "I'm told you're handy with a sharpening stone."

"Oliver John — L-l-lord Oliver John — seems to think so. I've sharpened scissors and knives."

"What do you know of swords?" Franklin asked. "It's a bigger instrument, more room for error."

"I know that they can do some serious damage when driven into a man's belly."

Franklin rolled his eyes. "I meant, what do you know of how they're made?"

"I have discovered that I know very little," Robin replied.

Franklin folded his arms and leaned his back against the workbench. "You will learn a lot by doing, but briefly, there are three processes: forming, heat-treating, and finishing. The men who do the forming take the steel, shape it into a billet, and draw it out, tapering it to create an edge and a point. Then they might put it through some cycles of heating and cooling. That takes care of any stresses that might have built up during the shaping which could leave weak spots.

"The heat-treating tempers the steel so it's less brittle and easier to shape, so it will take an edge better."

"And that's the finishing," Robin guessed.

Franklin nodded. "There's a little more to it than just taking a sharpening stone to it."

Robin glanced around the workshop. "I can see that. Many different types of grindstones..."

"Because they each have different degrees of roughness. Grit, we call it." Franklin slid off his stool and with a wave of his hand, beckoned Robin to join him alongside the grindstones. "Feel," he said. "And we don't always use these stones. They move quickly and create heat, too much heat for part of the task. There's still quite a bit of handwork involved.

"You might think that it's that point you're driving into that man's belly that does that damage, and that's true enough. But armor is becoming stronger and more impenetrable every day. It's important that the swordsman be able to cut as well as pierce. That calls for a deadly edge, and it's no mean feat to get an edge right. It has to be sharp, but strong. It has to be thin enough without being brittle. You understand?"

Robin nodded.

"Once we've got the sword to its final shape and polish, we'll be doing any engraving that's been ordered. We might, for example, carve out a fuller, which would make the blade a little lighter and easier to handle but no less effective. Then, we'll craft and assemble the grip, the guard, and the pommel."

Franklin pointed to the sack Robin wore on his back. "You can set that on the floor there and take a seat." He indicated a stool at the worktable. Before Robin he placed a blade, a wood block, a small dish of oil and one of water, a whetstone, and a metal rasp. He pointed to the lantern overhead. "Light this lantern if you need to. You must have plenty of light for this work. Here, rest the blade's point on the block. Now, with the file, I want you to start shaping the edge. Angle the file like so." Franklin turned Robin's wrist so that the file angled against the blade's edge at about thirty degrees. "Now, take even, measured strokes in one direction only. Don't try to create an edge. The edge is there. You just want to reveal it."

Franklin's voice had taken on that dreamy quality that Robin's ministers' did when they talked of Golden Sections and harmonious proportions. He looked up to see if the man was joking, but Franklin wore a serious expression. Then Franklin smiled. "You'll come to see that it really does seem that way.

"Be careful not to take too much off any one side. Keep turning the blade over and working alternate sides until you see a rough edge start to appear. And it will look rough, but don't let that concern you. You will improve its appearance in the next steps."

Franklin watched as Robin worked, occasionally stopping him to reposition his wrist or caution him to lighten his pressure.

"That looks good," he said at last. "Now, put a little oil on the whetstone. You're just polishing now, not grinding, so go slowly. Use that same angle, pass the blade across the stone. Back and forth, not in a circle. Check your work here, see? No, no, just look at it, don't feel it, not yet. Keep working that stone against the entire surface of the blade. Be careful — don't make any one spot too thin. Keep it even. Can you see the edge?"

Robin said that he could, in some spots.

"So," said Franklin, handing Robin a piece of parchment not much bigger than the tip of his finger. Fine grit coated one side of the parchment. "Now you want to wet this and very carefully run it along the edge of the blade. It's easy to cut yourself at this point so you want to pay close attention to what you are doing or you could lose a digit." Franklin held up both his hands and Robin could see old scars on most of the fingers. "Your focus must be complete. At this point your world must be only you and the edge of the blade."

Robin stopped and turned to look at Franklin as his voice had once again turned dreamy. Robin found Franklin's expression to be sincerely serious. Once again, Franklin smiled and said, "You'll come to see that it really does seem that way. You may even get to like it."

Franklin straightened and stood at Robin's shoulder while he worked. Robin could not have said just when it was that he lost awareness of Frank, the workshop, the noises and smells, the heat, and the ache in his empty belly until he heard Frank say, "That looks good. What do you think?"

"I think I'd like to make one for myself," he said. He straightened his back and realized that his back and shoulders ached. He arched his back and kneaded his left shoulder with his right hand.

"Ah, you've discovered that you can easily become a hunchback at this job," said Franklin. "We still have much work ahead of us so now would be a good time to take a break." Franklin pointed to Robin's rucksack. "You brought your supper?"

"Not exactly. I arrived only late yesterday and have not yet laid in any stores. I have nothing at home except mice." And he wouldn't have those for very long, either, with Meeyoo around to police the place.

"No matter. You can probably get what you need at the Ironworks' store. Or you might wish to wait until later. Many of the men here do not have wives and take their meal break later in the afternoon when a maid from town brings around a food wagon."

"I don't have much in the way of coin."

"That shouldn't be a problem. You can establish an account with the Ironworks' store and they will deduct your charges from your wages. The food wagon is usually cash."

It was clear that there would be no such thing as a free lunch. Yet the prospect of getting something to eat and drink far outweighed Robin's reluctance to become indebted before he had had even his first payday. "Well, as long as we're stopped, I might as well go to the Ironworks' store," he said, and shouldered his pack. "Will you be coming along, or...?"

"I will go home and take my midday meal with my wife," Franklin replied.

At the Ironworks' store Robin found fresh loaves of bread; preserves, conserves, and pickles; cured, dried, and smoked meats and fish; condiments, spices, and oils, and ciders, wines, and ales, even some housewares. He felt rather like a long-at-sea sailor who has finally made port. Had he a budget, he would have gone over it. He filled his pack with preserved food, telling himself that even if he started a garden tonight, it would be months before it would bear fruit.

On his return to the workshop, Franklin said, "Lord Oliver John expects to see a significant improvement in output as a result of bringing you on. We should strive to reward his faith in you and have a productive afternoon lest he regret his decision, don't you agree?"

Robin nodded.

"Do you think that you can sharpen and polish some blades on your own without lopping off a finger?"

"I should hope so."

Franklin frowned. "You should more than hope. Be speedy, but not at the expense of caution." He indicated that Robin should retake his seat at the worktable, then dragged over a tall crate of rough swords. "I will be at the grindstones. If you have a question or need help, you will have to yell. Loud. Very loud," he said.

Robin took a deep breath and dug in. At first he wondered how he would be able to concentrate on his task with all the noise inside and outside the workroom. Once he got a rhythm going, he found it a little easier to focus. It came as almost a surprise when he realized that hours had passed and that Franklin stood at his shoulder.

Robin carefully laid the sword that he had been working on flat on the worktable and lifted his hands away.

"The workday is ending," Franklin said. He removed the magnifying glasses from the bridge of his nose, revealing raw spots where the clamp had pressed all day. "You can stay and continue to work, if you want, but you should light more lamps."

Robin slid from the stool and stretched, now aware that almost every part of him ached. His hands felt cramped, the skin dry and cracked with many small stinging cuts. His ears rang, his eyes smarted, and his lungs felt choked with dust. He had sweated so much from the heat in the workshop, he thought he must look like a piece of jerky. He certainly felt like one. "I hope you'll say that this is a respectable accomplishment for one day."

"For a first day," Franklin said, and Robin waited for him to smile to indicate that he was joking, but the expected smile did not come.

Robin felt a vague sense of dread. This was going to be very hard work indeed, much harder than working at David's barbershop, and not nearly as enjoyable. Singing and joking with the customers had been pleasing. True, he had kept busy enough, and had been on his feet a good part of the day but the work wasn't nearly as taxing physically. Maintaining this afternoon's pace all day for days on end was a daunting prospect.

Of course, there was no going back, and no quitting, not now that he had incurred a sizable debt at the Ironworks' store. He would need to work at least until he had paid that off, made enough to sustain himself, and was able to make himself a sword. If he were to retake his kingdom, he would need to outfit an army, starting with himself.

"Well, if you're done then, we need to straighten up," said Franklin. "Tools must be stowed in their place, the fire banked, and the floor swept." Franklin directed Robin to help pick scraps out of the sweepings and sort them into the various buckets.

Sweeping up was something in which he now had plenty of experience. "Why not just sweep it all into one large bin if it's just going to be discarded?" Robin asked.

"Because very little is discarded," Franklin replied. "Wood scraps can be burned and metal scraps can be resmelted. Nothing goes to waste."

Robin felt a twinge of guilt about the piece of steel that he had slipped into his pouch. Surely, neither Franklin nor Oliver John would miss one tiny scrap, or if they did, would begrudge it to him.

"You said that you hadn't anything at home yet," Franklin said. "You are welcome to join me and my wife for supper."

Robin felt his face grew warm at the embarrassingly generous offer. He patted his rucksack. "I bought some supplies earlier at the store."

"Well, stop and have an ale at any rate. I believe my house is on your way."

CHAPTER NINE

Franklin's house proved to be small but tidy. His wife, Babs, greeted her husband at the door with a tankard, and quickly fetched another for Robin. Babs had a personality that was as warm as the red color of her hair. She and Franklin were apparently quite fond of cats as several prowled around the house and throughout the yard.

"You don't mind them, do you?" she asked. "We think they are fascinating creatures, clever and proud. Independent, although they can be affectionate when they want to be."

"Like you, my love," Franklin said, and wrapped his arm about her shoulders.

"No, I don't mind them," Robin said. "I like cats. I have one myself."

Babs clapped her hands. "Well then you must have this." She foraged in a basket by the hearth and returned with a small knotted muslin bag. "A catnip toy for your cat to amuse herself while you're at work."

"I hope she'll stay amused catching mice," Robin said with a laugh. "But I guess she can't work all day, so thank you."

"You and I did work all day, however," Franklin said. "And we have another day just like it on tap for tomorrow. Be on time."

With a wave of his hand, Robin said, "Say no more. I am certainly ready to find my bed." Which, unfortunately, he did not actually have. At least he had a roof over his head, and would have a fire.

The walk back to the hut that evening seemed to take far longer than it had the previous night. Packed with foodstuffs and household goods, his pack, already heavy with his cloak, now felt like a boulder on his back. For the first time in as long as he could remember, his feet did not hurt although every other part of him did.

Tonight, getting a fire going was less of a challenge. With the flint that he had picked up this morning and the steel that he had cadged this afternoon, he was able to strike a spark and ignite some kindling.

Meeyoo sat and watched with interest as Robin rigged a tripod from which he could suspend the small iron pot that he had bought at the Ironworks' store. He filled the pot with water from a stream feeding the river. "I'll have tea, Meeyoo," he said. "For you, though, I have a different herb." He produced the catnip toy that Babs had given him. Meeyoo sniffed at the little pouch, then rubbed her jowls against it, and finally rolled back and forth over it with such enthusiasm Robin doubted the toy would survive the night.

One last challenge remained for him, and that was to solve the problem of his cloak. He simply could not tote that around every day and even leaving it stowed in his pack in the workroom was risky. Anyone could take it into his head to examine the contents, even Franklin. But an idea had come to him while he had been focused on the more perfunctory aspect of blade sharpening, when random thoughts cropped up like bubbles coming to the surface of a mug of ale.

He propped open the door to the hut so the cook fire could cast a little light into its depths. At the corner furthest from the entrance, he scraped aside the rushes to uncover the earth beneath. With the hardwood plank that had served as a fireboard the night before, he dug a small pit.

He took a seat on his rock and in the firelight, with his knife he carefully cut away the ermine fur trimming the cloak. He stowed the fur in a tin box that he had bought at the Ironworks' store. He secreted the tin in the pit, packed dirt over it, and put the rush covering back in place.

All that was left to do now was remove the royal crest from the cloak. He blinked away the tears in his eyes and with the point of his knife, one by one he picked out the threads that formed the red shield of the warrior and the orange chevron of ambition. Gone was the white bull, the sign of bravery. He would miss the inspiration of the falcon, the symbol of one who does not rest until he has met his objective, but he was wryly content to remove the blue barry waves that spoke of a mettle built when besieged by troubles. Troubles he now had in good supply.

Done, he wiped his eyes with the back of his hand and sighed. He told himself that although he would have not the outward symbols of what he knew about himself, the truth would abide in his heart and his bones.

His days were long as Meeyoo would wake him well before dawn with a cry of "Meow! I want out! Now!"

Robin now had a small rosebush to tend to and a garden to cultivate before work. The rosebush he had found growing wild and had transplanted it. The vegetable garden was courtesy of Franklin's wife, Babs, who had spared him a few seedlings.

Robin felt that he had returned the favor when he presented his latest invention to Franklin. Robin had observed that the pincers of the magnifying glasses that Franklin wore all day left the sides of his nose raw. He gave the matter much thought and then spent several very long nights in the workshop. He crafted a frame to hold the eyepiece, two side pieces that would hook over Franklin's ears, and two tiny pins to attach the earpieces to the eyepieces. The earpieces would help support the weight of the eyepieces and Franklin wouldn't have to clamp them on so tightly.

Frank regarded the construction with suspicion. "Where did you get the metal for this?" he asked.

"I..."

"Certainly you didn't take any from stock, or from the rubbish bin? I told you—"

"I know. The material in the rubbish bin is not trash, it gets reused." Still, Robin thought, no one would actually miss the tiny bit he had taken. With less discomfort, Franklin would be more productive. The value of the scrap metal would be earned back in no time. Besides, though he hadn't admitted to taking the scrap metal, he also hadn't said that he didn't. So it wasn't as if he lied. "Try them on!"

Gingerly, Franklin positioned the construction on his face.

"Well?" asked Robin.

The smallest of smiles tugged at the corners of Frank's mouth.

Work was demanding and interminable, as there always seemed to be more to do than time in which to do it. Robin and Frank would work until the sun began its descent, and as summer advanced, that descent began later and later each day. The ceaseless work left him with little energy to spare outside the workroom. On a very rare occasion, he might tip an after-work tankard of ale with the other laborers. He enjoyed learning about their crafts almost as much as he did the relaxation and camaraderie. On even rarer occasions he might take some pleasure with Jane, the maiden who brought the food wagon.

Forays to Riverington were few and far between, but Robin had made enough visits to learn that Mary, Jane's mother, was an ale-wife and her husband, Paul, the de facto leader of a settlement that like Rose Bank appeared to belong to no lord. Robin had been surprised to learn that Oliver John did not own it.

When he had a bit of energy to spare, Robin devoted some after-work hours to sprucing up his dwelling. Since he did

hands. You could grip the blade partway up, you see, which would offer you the option of the horizontal thrust."

"It's good to have every possible advantage in a battle," Haden murmured as he studied the grip.

"Well, then, you might want us to apply a ricasso. That's a blunt section here, just forward of the guard. It enables the swordsman to choke up for close-in fighting." Robin demonstrated. "We can even put a small guard to protect that position.

"Speaking of guards, that option is for your protection. It helps to keep your hand from sliding up your own blade. Of course, we can assemble the sword without any guard at all, or with a simple straight crossbar, and you do see those on, uh, lesser personages. But to my way of thinking, why would you want to wield a weapon that can damage you as much as your opponent?"

"Robin!" Oliver John said with a scowl. "Lord Haden is not here to listen to your opinions."

"Not at all, John, let him speak. He makes sense."

"But he's just the apprentice."

Haden shrugged. "The man clearly knows his swordcraft."

"Go on, Robin," Oliver John said in a near-growl.

Robin scouted about the worktable for a guard that he had been working on to fulfill a commission that Oliver John had been given by a wealthy merchant who had more pride and money than actual enemies. "Now this guard has many important protective features. See how this loop here and this branch here would shield your hand?"

Haden nodded. "And this?" he asked.

"Ah, the strap. Not every swordsman has one, of course, but it's an extremely useful option. You loop it around your hand so you're less likely to lose the sword if you should happen to drop it. We can make the strap out of simple leather but a fine strap is not only practical, it puts everyone on notice that you are someone to be reckoned with."

Haden pressed his lips together. "John, I see that I did myself a disservice when we first discussed this sword. I really should have a pommel like this, and a guard like that, and a strap like this one."

"Well, Haden, you understand that..."

Robin feared that Oliver John was about to point out the extra expense of adding these features and tried to head him off with pleading eyes.

"... that it will take a little longer than we had originally estimated to bring the sword to completion."

Robin breathed a sigh of relief.

"And well worth the investment of a little more time," said William Haden. "More money, too, that goes without saying. But it would appear having a superior weapon will justify the investment. And it will be you who does the work, Robin?"

"If you wish, milord. It would be an honor. I will endeavor to build in an extra measure of confidence, at no extra charge."

William Haden chuckled. "Excellent." He turned to Oliver John and clapped him on the shoulder. "Well, what's next?

"I believe it's time for a glass of that fortified wine of which I spoke earlier." Oliver John flung an arm across the man's shoulders and chuckled.

"Yes, I believe you're right," said Haden and the two men shared a laugh that spoke of other glasses savored in enjoyment. They exited the workroom but a moment later, Oliver John reappeared in the workroom doorway. "We shall speak of this on the morrow," he said with a stern look that left Robin filled with dread.

The next day, when Robin reported to the workroom, Franklin was already at the grindstone. "Lord Oliver John said that he wishes to speak with you, and he did not seem pleased," he said. "What's that all about?"

"I'm sure I don't know," Robin replied.

"Well, you're to find him at the parapet," Franklin said, looking upward.

With heavy feet, Robin climbed the tower stairs.

"Milord," he called.

Oliver John turned and gestured for him to approach.

"About yesterday —" Robin began.

"It was not your place to speak," said Oliver John.

"I realize that, sir. But —"

"You are but an apprentice. A talented one, but an apprentice nonetheless. It was Franklin that Haden should have spoken with."

But Franklin had not been there. Even had he been, Robin doubted that he would have been as effectively persuasive. Franklin was a skilled blacksmith, a proficient and diligent worker, and a good teacher, but he was more craftsman than salesman.

"How come by you with so much knowledge about swords?" Oliver John asked.

Robin could hardly tell him that he had learned these things ages ago, as a young prince from his father and as a king himself from his armorers and craftsmen.

"I talk to the other men," he said, which was not untrue. Over the weeks, he had learned enough about the other crafts at the Ironworks to feel as though he could do any one of them.

"Well, I don't want you for a minute to think that I am ignoring, much less rewarding your impertinence," Oliver John said. "Nevertheless, the fact remains that you talked William Haden into commissioning a much finer sword than what he originally had in mind."

"I only pointed out the advantages —"

"Yes, that you did. And I have no doubt that he will be well pleased with the finished product. As I will be well pleased with the additional coins that he will be spending with me."

His hands clasped behind his back, Oliver John walked away a few paces, turned, and walked back to Robin. "You are a skilled and productive smith. You put in many long hours, rather like a younger man bent on building up his stake. For whatever reason..." He held up an index finger, arresting any explanation that Robin might think of providing. "I don't need to know what it is. I do see that you have yet another talent of which I'd like to avail myself.

"I'd like you to visit with some of our other prospects and commissions. Perhaps they too are not fully aware of all the benefits to be gained from some of the optional features that we can incorporate. Should, as a result of your visit, a customer decide to commission us to craft him a sword or 'increase the value' of one we are already commissioned to make, you would earn a small percentage of the value of that commission. Would that be of interest to you?"

"I would be most privileged," said Robin with a slight bow.

"Some of those visits would take place here, much as it did yesterday. Our customers sometimes do wish to travel here to explore the Ironworks and enjoy my hospitality. But I also mean for you to call on them, when they are too distant or too busy to make the journey themselves. These are the very trips that I have been making myself, such as those that brought me to Rose Bank and David's shop where we first met. But I am finding it increasingly difficult to get away from the Ironworks. If I am away calling on customers, production here suffers. If I remain here to manage the day's affairs, then we lack for work. So I mean for you to do the traveling for me."

Travel? Have a day, or two or more, away from the smithy, away from the long, dusty, hot, stifling, smoky, gritty days of grinding and polishing? Days of doing nothing more than journeying from place to place? He might even, on such a trip, find himself nearing the Chalklands of his domain, or encounter a fellow traveler who might know something of what was happening at his kingdom. When do I start? Robin wanted to ask. He did not in the least want to discourage Oliver John from this notion. Nevertheless, he needed to be certain. "Sir, I am but the apprentice, as you have said. Shouldn't Franklin...?"

Oliver John nodded. "Yes, that would seem to be appropriate. But Franklin has not shown to have the aptitude that you seem to have for this. Besides, Franklin is a married man and you are single. I think the travel will be easier on you than on him."

Robin knew that Franklin was fond of Babs and had no great need or desire to be away from home for long periods of time. Still, neither the man nor his wife would balk at an opportunity to make more money. "If that would be your wish, sir."

"Although of course I realize that you cannot do your work while traveling, I would not want production to suffer unduly."

"I understand. I would endeavor to make every minute that I'm here count double. Sir, would I be taking samples to show?"

"Yes, I think that makes for a persuasive presentation."

"Well, sir, I don't know if you're aware... I have no horse." Robin tried to sound nonchalant about what was a source of embarrassment. "That would be quite a bit to carry."

Oliver John laughed. "Indeed. No, I don't imagine that you can go on foot shouldering a sack full of swords. I suppose that I can make a mount available to you for these trips."

"Very well, sir. Uh, sir, will you be telling Franklin about this?"

"Oh, indeed. I would have already mentioned it but I wanted to make certain first that you were prepared to accept the charge."

"I most certainly am."

"Fine. Then return to the smithy and your work but have Franklin report to me now."

The tread with which Robin climbed down the stairs from the tower was just as heavy as his steps up had been. His heart beat fast at the opportunities that this new development presented, but he did not at all relish facing the reproach that he was likely to get from Franklin.

Sure enough, when Franklin returned from meeting with Oliver John, his face revealed anger and resentment. "So, you have been granted a special opportunity, a privilege, one might say—"

"Franklin..."

"—such as is usually offered to a master after years of learning, achievement, and service."

"Franklin..."

Franklin turned his face away and took his seat at a grindstone. "I thought that we were partners, Robin," he said quietly.

"Franklin, I... we will be sharing in this boon. I will be bringing us more work, better work, better-paying work."

Franklin pressed the grindstone's treadle a few times. "Yes, I suppose that's so."

"It's going to be a lot of traveling, a lot of time away from home. Would you want that?"

"I wouldn't mind it."

"Babs might."

Franklin was not mollified. "She's a good wife. She would see that it would be for the best." Franklin looked at him and glared. "I could do this, you know."

"No one said that you couldn't," Robin replied, although in effect that was precisely what Oliver John had said. "Look, I didn't ask for this. It wasn't my idea. But it's a good opportunity, for us both. The shop will grow, and we will grow with it. We'll make more money, maybe have a penny or two extra at the end of the day. We could put some aside; maybe... maybe open our own blacksmith shop someday."

Franklin's glared softened and his eyes took on a faraway look. "You suppose?"

"I know so," Robin said with a conviction that he did not feel, and he felt a little queasy spinning this fantasy. He actually had been squirreling away a penny here and a penny there, gradually paying down the debt that he had amassed at the Ironworks' store. When that was discharged, he planned to devote every spare cent to building the war chest that he would need to reclaim his kingdom. Going into business with Franklin was not part of the plan, but the prospect seemed to restore Franklin's good humor. Robin smiled. Franklin would have that blacksmith shop. When Robin had regained his kingdom, he silently vowed, he would appoint Franklin as the royal blacksmith. "Are we still partners?"

Franklin grinned. "Partners."

If Robin thought that he had been working hard before, he was working even harder now, squeezing every bit of production out of every possible minute of daylight. He would work until evening approached which, as the summer days grew ever longer, came later each day. He did not notice how many hours he spent working until he returned to his hut, beyond weary in every inch of his being. Days when he made a presentation to a customer were even longer. When the customer's arrival at the foundry was announced, Robin would shed his workday clothes for a fresh shirt, splash water on his sweaty, sooty face, and rinse the dust from his hair. Then he would deliver what was now becoming a well-rehearsed lesson on the advantages of making a greater investment in the materials and workmanship that went into the crafting of a sword.

Then, late though it was, after the customer had left, Robin would light the lamps in the shop to finish the work scheduled for completion, or put the finishing touches on his secret project for his most important private customer: himself. At the very least, he did not want to be out on the road alone without adequate protection. And he harbored the faint but heartfelt hope that he might find himself in a position to mount a campaign to reclaim his throne.

He finished his sword in the nick of time as Oliver John approached him about a road trip.

"I wish for you to call on Lord Stanley Allen in Allenton. Lord Stanley is an important man there. A good customer, a good friend. I have enjoyed his hospitality and he mine." Oliver John's chuckle made Robin recall the time that William Haden had visited.

"You will be traveling to Allenton," Oliver John said. "That is two day's travel to the south and east. You can be guided by following the Cold River. Not all of that area is settled so you may not find any accommodations until you reach your destination."

Robin wondered if Oliver John assumed that he would take the opportunity to stop at every alehouse that he came upon.

"My weather prognosticators tell me that the day should be clear and well-suited for traveling. You shall leave on the morrow, so tonight you should pack whatever personal items you want to have with you on the trip." He handed Robin a bundle tied with string. "For you to wear to your presentation to Lord Stanley Allen. You will also find a barber in Allenton."

Robin felt his face grow warm and his temper flare, but he stamped out that fire before it burst into dangerous flame. He doubted that Oliver John intended to be insulting. The man was just being practical. Robin could hardly show up to make a persuasive presentation dusty and dirty from the road.

"Tomorrow, report to me at the turret instead of to the smithy and we will review your itinerary."

As the day's end approached, Robin dragged his feet. He wanted to leave the Ironworks well after dark. Tonight he would spirit his sword from the smithy. He planned to leave it at his hut and fetch it on his way out of town.

In the hut that night, Robin unearthed the ermine trim from its hiding place and shoved it deep into his rucksack. Should he come anywhere near his former kingdom, he would want the royal trappings.

Meeyoo sat in the doorway and watched. "I am packing, Meeyoo," Robin said. "Tomorrow I will start a journey that will take me away for many days. Shall you accompany me? You'll be alright here by yourself, I have no fear of that. And you may not care to be on the road with me. You would have to spend much of the day riding in the pack. Nor can I speak with any certainty at all about the reception that we can expect when we reach our destination, much less the welcome or lack thereof that I might receive should I find my kingdom. There may be a battle, I simply don't know. And if I do find it and reclaim it, who knows when I would be back this way." He chuckled. "Somehow I don't see myself being able to rule without your wise counsel.

"And, I would enjoy your companionship on the journey. Someone to talk to besides myself. Not that talking to a cat makes me look any less like I have taken leave of my senses than talking to myself might."

"Mee-you," said the cat.

"Yes, I get that. Me. You. Me and you. Anyhow, Meeyoo, you sleep on it. I will stop here to collect my sword before I begin the journey. You can let me know of your decision then."

CHAPTER TEN

In the morning, Robin rose eager to greet the day. Today he would not spend every daylight hour in the smithy. He would feel the sun on his face and breathe in fresh air that wasn't smoky, gritty, and superheated. And he would be getting a horse to ride.

A sword. A horse, even a new suit of clothes. Robin grinned. When the time came to retake his throne, he would be ready.

As instructed, Robin found Oliver John atop the tower. Almost too late, he reminded himself to greet the man with a bow.

Oliver John smiled. "I am relieved that it will be you on the road and not me." He passed an outstretched arm across the vista below. "There is so much to do here, I cannot see myself leaving. But Lord Stanley Allen whom you will meet is a very important customer and cannot be neglected."

"I am eager to get started, milord," Robin said.

Oliver John regarded him with narrowed eyes. "You do not have your pack."

"I mean to collect it on my way out, sir," Robin said. Along with his sword.

"Very well. Here is where you are headed." He unrolled a scroll on which was drawn a map. "Your route follows the Cold River, as I mentioned yesterday." Oliver John traced the line of the river with an index finger. "If you do not dawdle and make good time, you should reach Allenton by nightfall. You will find an inn there, and you can meet with Lord Stanley Allen in the morning." He proceeded to describe the other landmarks that would tell Robin that he was headed in the right direction.

"I'm an experienced traveler, sir," Robin said. Too experienced, as of late, he thought. "I'm sure I will have no trouble finding it."

"Excellent. Here is a small present for you to give to Lord Stanley as a token of my appreciation." Oliver John produced a small but ornately stitched scabbard that held a little bread-saw. He grinned. "These are proving to be an outstanding invention. My customers love getting them as gifts, and then so enjoy using them, they order several for their household and as gifts for their own friends and allies."

As Robin had suspected. He and Franklin had been making quite a few of them.

Oliver John handed Robin a small purse. "Some coins for the expenses: food and care for the mount, and yourself, of course."

Robin nodded soberly, although his spirits soared. He had packed dried meats and fruit for himself to eat en route, and had hoped to find enough forage on the trail for the horse so that he wouldn't have to pay for feed. As much as he would have preferred to find a bed for the night, he had planned to spare the expense and simply sleep outdoors if the weather favored him. Much of the per diem that Oliver John was giving him would go into Robin's war chest.

"Let's get to the stables then and get you on your way."

As they approached the stables, Robin's elation evaporated. He had gone to sleep envisioning himself astride a sturdy and handsome riding horse but what stood at the entrance to the stables, saddled and draped with saddlebags heavy with samples was a donkey.

A donkey. Robin tried to hide his disappointment.

Oliver John patted the donkey's rump. "This strong little fellow will give you many miles of service," he said. He handed Robin a portfolio of fine sueded leather. "These are your letters of introduction," he said. "Lord Stanley Allen is expecting me, and this will explain why I am sending you in my stead. These documents detail the decisions and agreements that you are authorized to make on behalf of the Ironworks."

"Thank you, sir. Put your mind at ease. I will do you proud," he said and at the last minute, remembered to bow.

The reins clutched in his hand, Robin set out on foot, leading the donkey away from the Ironworks. Though he had eagerly anticipated riding, he was reluctant to mount the animal within sight of his fellow workers. He realized that no one but he found the idea of riding a donkey the least bit embarrassing. Nevertheless, he hesitated. Donkeys had the reputation of being ornery and stubborn. Robin knew this to be untrue. Donkeys were genial and docile animals unless they were abused. Still, he knew that he was unfamiliar to the donkey and did not wish to start his first trip being thrown from the animal or kicked.

However, the donkey walked obediently alongside him. They exited the gate and Robin said, "Well, we are going to be together for many a day and I hope that we will get along. Oliver John did not tell me your name, and perhaps you don't have one. But I can't just call 'Hey' when I want your attention. Hay is for horses." Robin chuckled at his own joke. "I mean no offense. You are, actually, a rather handsome animal in your own right."

The donkey turned its head and looked at Robin with deep dark eyes and drew back its lips as if in a shy smile.

"So what say I call you Duncan?" Robin said.

The donkey dipped his head as if in agreement.

"Great. I'm Robin, Duncan."

People will think I'm a madman, talking to an animal, Robin thought. He knew that donkeys were sociable and liked the company of other beings. Nevertheless he was grateful that there was no one on the road to witness. "We've got a long way to go but I mean to enjoy the trip, so you should not find yourself overly taxed."

Duncan dipped his head as if to nod in acknowledgement.

At last they reached Robin's hut. "Wait here a minute, Duncan. I have just a few more things that we need to take with us." Robin opened the door to the hut and was grateful to find nothing had been disturbed. His pack sat on the bed where he had left it. He would not need to wear it on his back on this trip. Duncan could carry it. Robin reached under the sleeping pallet's straw mattress and retrieved his sword. He regretted that he had had time to fashion only the most minimal scabbard for it. He had thought to modify a baldric so that he could carry the sword across his back, but that creation would have to wait.

Through the hut's open door, he spied Meeyoo bounding towards him across the field only to come to a sudden stop when she spotted Duncan. Adopting a slinking stealthy crouch that kept her partially hidden by the grass, she drew cautiously near.

Robin stepped outside, stood beside the donkey, and called to her. "Meeyoo, it's OK. This is Duncan. He's friendly, he won't hurt you." At least, Robin thought, I don't think he will. Donkeys didn't like dogs and didn't much care for goats, either. But the barn cats and donkeys at Bell Castle always seemed to get along well.

Meeyoo crept closer. One tentative paw at a time, she drew in front of Duncan, her haunches and shoulders tensed for a quick leap back if she were threatened. Slowly, Duncan lowered his head until the two animals were nose to nose.

"Well, now. Duncan, this is Meeyoo. Meeyoo, meet Duncan. Duncan will be accompanying me on this trip. What did you decide? Are you coming?"

Meeyoo turned her back on the donkey and went into the hut. She leaped onto the bed and climbed into the pack.

"I guess I have an answer," Robin said. "Shall we be off?" He collected his pack and looped the straps around the pommel of Duncan's saddle. Meeyoo poked her head out of the pack and peered at him. Duncan fixed Robin with an expectant look. Robin sighed, shook his head, and climbed into the saddle.

Duncan proved to be as Oliver John had said: serviceable. Neither fast nor formidable, he plodded along at a steady pace without complaint, eliciting no unwanted scrutiny, which Robin had to admit would surely have been attracted had he, in the well-worn garb of a laborer, been seen on the road astride a war horse. Robin had to accede further that a donkey suited his needs more than a horse would. Duncan would be content to graze on grass and Robin could keep for himself the money Oliver John had given him for feed. Water shouldn't be a problem as their route paralleled the Cold River.

The road in the environs of Riverington was fairly busy with traders and travelers coming and going. It had been some many weeks since Robin had been away from the Ironworks and he found the sight of all that traffic stimulating. Some riders of humble animals would travel alongside him and Robin enjoyed the conversation, although he did not meet anyone who knew anything of chalk lands nor did he hear any mention of Bell Castle. Most of those outbound from Riverington rode horses or pulled empty carts and so moved along quicker than Robin did astride Duncan. As the morning stretched toward noon, Robin found himself with little company on the road.

At about midday, Robin decided that they had made good enough progress and could afford to take a break. He needed to stretch his legs and thought that Duncan could do with rest, a drink, and something to eat. He dismounted, led the donkey off the road, and stopped when he came upon a stream that fed the river. He lifted his pack off the saddle so that Meeyoo could get out and cautioned her not to stray, knowing that she wouldn't go far, not in strange surroundings.

Duncan contentedly munched grass and Meeyoo happily nosed little lizards out of the grass. Robin felt himself relaxing and feared to get drowsy. In the near distance and set back not too far from the road stood a small building, an alehouse or an inn. "I'm going over there," he told his companions. If it was indeed an alehouse or inn, he might meet a traveler who had useful news, either of Allenton or, with a great deal of luck, of the Chalklands. "I won't be long," he said.

The small wooden building was a public house, Sweet Water by name, one that served food and wine as well as ale. Robin didn't really want to order anything to eat, as he had packed sufficient provisions, nor did he want anything to drink, which would likely just make him feel lazy. But he did want an excuse to linger a bit and talk. The room was crowded with other patrons who, like Robin, were taking a break from their travels. Any one of them might have useful information, so he joined them at table.

The cellarer, who gave his name as Eian, asked Robin what he would have. Unlike the beefy, balding, apple-cheeked, red-nosed fellows that often worked an alehouse, Eian was a slender man with salt-and-pepper hair and sparkling eyes. His white shirt, black apron and neatly-trimmed beard lent him a refined demeanor.

Robin asked for a small beer.

"That we have. But wouldn't you like to try our specialty? It's a fortified wine. My own blend."

Robin had had fortified wine, although not in some time, and liked it, but knew well that it was not a beverage that promoted a long productive day of travel. He remembered, or actually did not so well remember nights when drinking fortified wine had loosened his tongue, his will, and his wallet, so he politely declined. He sipped his beer, talked with Eian and other regulars, and learned that to nearly everyone's knowledge, the road ahead was clear. A few reported encountering bandits and Robin found himself almost hoping some outlaw would give him an opportunity to test his new sword. He didn't put much stock in the tale though as everyone knew brigands rarely struck during the day. By nightfall, he would get off the road.

A priest who traveled to serve many small communities told the curious tale of finding that some settlements he was used to visiting seemed to have collapsed. He had noticed no signs of violence and was baffled at the disappearance of what he had known to be strong trade centers. "No violence" was pretty much the only part of his story that was of interest to his fellow travelers. Robin shrugged off the story. Small settlements perched precariously on the thin edge of Nature's favor, and rose and fell all the time.

No one said anything that led him to believe they had knowledge of the Chalklands, so Robin finished his beer and said, "I had best get back on the road."

"Sure you won't have a taste of the wine?" asked Eian.

"You're very fond of that wine, aren't you?"

"It is my pet project," Eian said.

"I didn't know that grapes were grown in this area," Robin said. Certainly, he hadn't seen any grapevines in his travels.

"It's a bit of a challenge, but it can be done. If you get off the road and nearer to the river, you will see grapes close to the water. Cultivating wine grapes takes some care and attention, but I do enjoy a nice glass of wine. I'd be happy to give you a sample. No obligation."

Robin laughed. "I can hardly turn down such a generous offer," he said, and accepted what amounted to a generous sip. "Oh, yes, that will put hair on a man's chest," he said.

Eian laughed.

As he reached into his purse for coin to pay for the beer, Robin got an idea. "Could you put up a measure of that fortified wine for me to take with me?" he asked, thinking he would treat himself at the end of what he intended to be a successful journey.

"Not a problem at all," replied Eian. "We have some already bottled and corked."

Robin returned to the grove where he had left Meeyoo and Duncan. Bundling Meeyoo and the bottle of fortified wine in his pack, he mounted Duncan and returned to the road.

Traffic thinned as Robin got further from Sweet Water until he was quite alone on the road. Despite the prospect of sleeping in the open, he found himself feeling relaxed and light in spirit, perhaps for the first time since leaving Rose Bank and David's shop for the hard life at Oliver John's Ironworks. Had he made a mistake in leaving? He had not been unhappy in Rose Bank. He had shelter, food, companionship — even affection.

"But that wasn't contentment," he said to his traveling companions. "That was complacency. "I could have stayed there the rest of my days, made a life, maybe even taken Dolores as a helpmeet. But that would have been the end of ever regaining the kingdom.

"No, this was the right choice. Look at us, Meeyoo. We have a little money now, a sword. With the help of Duncan here, we will have more to add to the war chest. We're out on the road, meeting people. Surely someone will know something of Bell Castle."

The next day as he neared Allenton, the landscape underwent a subtle change. The trees were not so tall, their leaves not quite as broad, and the wooded areas were somewhat sparse. The green of the grass and bushes had more yellow to it. The midsummer heat became even more intense and the air more humid.

The road that he traveled more or less paralleled the Cold River. At the point where the bed widened as the river traveled a bend, he found a small town. The town had no fortification although the tightly packed ring of three-story buildings that encircled it formed a sort of wall. A sign on the pergola arching over the road told him that he had reached Allenton.

It was much like Rose Bank, albeit larger. At its center stood the well. Ruts in the road disclosed where stalls and wagons stood on market days. Several permanent structures lined the main road through the settlement. As Oliver John had suggested that he might, he spied a traveler's inn with accommodations for both him and Duncan. He revisited his original plan to camp out overnight and decided against it. He had done that last night, had been riding all day. To make his most effective presentation to the lord Stanley Allen, Robin would need a good night's rest and a way to bathe and dress in the morning.

"Meeyoo, I think you had best stay in the stables with Duncan tonight. The innkeeper might not take kindly to cats," he said. At the stables, Robin dismounted Duncan and made arrangements with the stable hand. After the man had left, Robin piled up some straw in a corner of the stall. He took down his rucksack, lifted Meeyoo out, and set her on the straw. She burrowed in, making a little nest for herself from which she could survey her new surroundings. He shouldered the pack, hefted the heavy bag of samples, and lugged it to the inn. On the morrow, he would bathe and dress himself in the fresh outfit that Oliver John had given him. For tonight, he would partake of his provisions and make something of an early night of it.

Though the bed was comfortable enough and he was certainly tired from the long day's ride, Robin found that he could not fall asleep. His thoughts buzzed and his stomach knotted with anticipation about tomorrow's meeting, but mostly he missed the comforting weight and soothing purring of Meeyoo on his chest. He tossed and turned for what seemed like hours. Exasperated, he lay on his back and stared into the dark, despairing of getting even a few hours' sleep before dawn. Finally, he snuck out of his room, into the stables, and curled up with Meeyoo in the straw.

In the morning, Robin found that Allenton had a bath parlor where he took care of both breakfast and bathing. He dressed in his new suit: a pair of new leggings; clean, white bag-sleeved blouse, and a velvet-and-brocade jerkin with a bit of fine trim. He found the barber of whom Oliver John had spoken. At the stables, he transferred all the contents of his pack into the sack of samples except the ermine trimmings and Meeyoo. "You will have to stay with Duncan in Stanley Allen's stables while I meet with him," he told the cat.

Robin led a heavily laden Duncan down the road. A successful merchant, the Lord Stanley Allen lived alongside the river where he docked his boat. A modest curtain wall surrounded the property. Robin stopped at the gatehouse and handed his letter of introduction through a slot window to the chamberlain. Moments later, the chamberlain came around and opened the gate.

"Welcome," he said and handed the letter back to Robin. "You may leave your mount at the stables, then return here to meet Lord Stanley."

Robin thanked him and did as directed. At the stables, he hoisted down the sack of samples and handed Duncan's reins to the stable hand.

Lugging the heavy sack, he returned to the gatehouse where the chamberlain introduced him to Lord Stanley Allen, a tall man with fluffy white hair and an equally fluffy white beard.

Robin handed his letter of introduction to Lord Stanley who read it with a sober expression on his face.

"So, Lord Oliver John is not coming," he said.

"No, sir. He has sent me in his place." Robin gave Stanley a hopeful smile but the man continued to frown.

"You are Robin?" Lord Stanley asked.

"Yes, sir," Robin replied. Then with great deliberation he put his left arm, bent at the elbow, behind his back and resting at his waist, palm out. He brought his right arm, crooked at the elbow, to his front and with his palm against his body, and bent forward in the most ostentatious bow that he could manage, resisting the urge to peep up and gauge the man's reaction.

"Come," Lord Stanley said.

Robin hoisted the pack of samples and followed Stanley from the gatehouse into the manor's parlor. Like Stanley, the parlor was large but not showy. The furnishings were of good quality, but not forbiddingly formal. The room had an inviting warmth to it. Robin nodded in admiration of the hunting trophies hung on the walls.

"So tell me, what of my friend?" Stanley said.

"I have not been at the Ironworks all that long... sir," said Robin. "But just in the short time that I have been there, Lord Oliver John has been buying fewer stock blade blanks in favor of forging blanks to more custom specifications," he said. "He has added large, power-driven bellows to the bloomeries. This creates hotter flame and enables us to devote our attention to maintaining a consistent temperature, which results in a more even tempered metal, with fewer weak spots." He went on to describe to Lord Stanley Allen the other ways in which Oliver had expanded the Ironworks, most having to do with producing a finer, not to mention a more costly, product.

"Well, now, perhaps we should get to what you have come to show me," said Stanley.

"May I use this table?"

Stanley nodded and Robin spread out his specimens. "While it is possible and of course very common to build up the basic billet to the rough form that the sword will take, we can also make a sword using the stock removal method. That is, we forge a blank that's slightly larger than the finished product will be, but we bring the sword to its final size though filing, grinding, cutting, and polishing." In some ways, this was a more wasteful method as some raw material was lost in the process. However, it was faster than the forging method and it had the added advantage, at least to Robin, of keeping him and Franklin busy.

Stanley seemed unimpressed and, to Robin's dismay, a trifle bored. He had also brought to show Stanley one of the finer hilts that they could produce as well as their best pommel, guard, sheath, and scabbard.

"Yes, well, that is all very interesting," Stanley said, although to Robin the man did not sound the least bit interested. "I will give this all some consideration." He seemed prepared to leave the parlor and escort Robin back to the stables,

"Which Lord Oliver John greatly appreciates, as do I," Robin said quickly. "In fact, he asked me to give you this gift to thank you for granting me the courtesy of your time," Robin said. "He apologizes for not being able to come visit you himself."

"I too regret it," Stanley replied as Robin rummaged in his rucksack. "I have enjoyed visiting with him."

"And he you," Robin said. He reached into his sack for the bread saw and also withdrew the bottle of fortified wine that he had bought for himself at Sweet Water.

"Ah, what is this?"

"A newly discovered wine for which he has a special appreciation, much as the one he holds for a respected friend such as yourself."

Stanley gave a short laugh. "Good man, that Oliver John. Well, let me sample the lord's latest discovery." Stanley strode to the sideboard, selected a goblet, uncorked the wine, and poured himself some. He took a sip and paused, savoring the flavors. He nodded his head and took another sip. "Yes, I can see why he likes this. It's quite bracing."

Based on the sample Robin had had in the alehouse, "bracing" would not have been the word he would have chosen. "Dizzying" was more like it.

As Stanley continued to drink, he returned to the table where Robin's samples were still displayed, picked up a pommel, and hefted it.

"So, this serves as a counterweight, you said," Stanley said.

"Yes, sir," Robin replied, and measured out a little more information about the pommel's function.

Stanley tipped up his goblet and then frowned.

"Empty, sir?" Robin asked. "May I get you more?" Without waiting for an answer, Robin seized the bottle from the sideboard. Stanley held out his goblet.

Robin eased back into his presentation and displayed his own sword into which he had put the best craftsmanship of which he was capable. By the time he had finished, he had dispensed enough persuasive blandishments to propose a very fine sword indeed, and Stanley had had enough fortified wine to agree to commission it.

"My knights would benefit from finer armaments as well, would they not?" Lord Stanley asked.

"Oh, indeed," Robin replied, trying not to stammer at the prospect of outfitting all of Lord Stanley's troops. "If you would just sign here, milord," Robin said. He produced from his portfolio a parchment with language that authorized the Ironworks to fashion the sword "as presented."

"I can change the quantity?"

"Of course. Just mark through the quantity on the agreement, indicate the quantity that you require and initial the change."

"That's simple enough," said Stanley. "I will go fetch a writing instrument."

"Oh, I have one here," said Robin. From his bag he produced a quill pen and a small bottle of ink corked and sealed with wax.

"Well, you did come prepared, didn't you?" said Stanley.

"I did not wish to waste your valuable time, milord," Robin replied, trying not to pant although he could barely catch his breath from excitement. He threw in a quick bow for good measure.

"Certainly not," said Stanley. "Well, the sooner we complete these formalities, the sooner we can get back to the wine, isn't that right?" He laughed and clapped Robin on the back. "Join me in a toast to our friend, would you?" He hoisted his glass.

"I would be most honored," Robin said, wondering why Stanley did not offer him a glass and how he could join in a toast without one.

"To Oliver John," Stanley said and took another sip.

"To Lord Oliver John," said Robin. As Stanley inked the agreement and affixed his seal, Robin gazed wistfully at the wine bottle.

Robin replaced the sample pack on Duncan's back. He lifted the flap of the rucksack and whispered, "OK in there, Meeyoo?"

He got a meow and a warm raspy lick on his hand in reply.

"We're off, then," he said. Reluctant though he was to part with it, he gave a coin to the stable master and thanked him for his service. He expressed thanks to the chamberlain and led Duncan out the gate.

When he was far enough down the road for the mansion to be out of sight, he let out a whoop, drunk on success if not on fortified wine.

"We did it, my friends," he said to Meeyoo and Duncan. "Surely we are leaving our difficult days behind us." Astride Duncan, he rode back toward the town of Allenton as proudly as he ever had atop his most favored war horse.

It was now well past midday. Robin had intended simply heading back toward Riverington and the Ironworks, but he knew now that come dark, that would put him in the middle of nowhere. Had he not been weighed down with the valuable samples, he would not have been concerned. Instead, he decided to pass another night in Allenton. He had a meal at the inn and then returned to the stables. There he changed back into his work clothes and spent another night sleeping in the straw.

The next morning, he set out as soon as it was light enough to see. When he arrived back at the road that ran along the Cold River and led back to the Riverington and the Ironworks, Robin paused.

"We're making good time, I think, don't you agree Duncan? I think we can afford a little detour. Maybe we will pick up a hint of the whereabouts of the Chalklands. If we find such, we can explore further when we return to deliver Stanley's sword."

He steered Duncan in the opposite direction.

CHAPTER ELEVEN

Many hours later, Robin had traveled some distance from Allenton and no closer to Riverington but not, that he could see, any closer to his domain. Though his eyes strained for any sign of limestone or other familiar landmark, at last he had to accede that their current course was not taking them closer to the Chalklands. If anything, the foliage was even less familiar, the terrain flatter and the soil less rich. There was little traffic with few crossroads along this route and few signs of settlements. His kingdom was much more densely populated than this. He doubted this was leading him closer to his homeland and reconsidered the wisdom of the detour. Certainly, he did not relish the thought of finding himself alone at night in an isolated area. He didn't doubt his ability to defend himself, having had much training and practice in arts of war. But why invite trouble?

He decided to give himself and the animals a break, then turn back. If they made good time, they could overnight at Sweet Water and return to Riverington on the morrow. Despite his earlier resolve to spare expenses, he planned to treat himself to a bottle of fortified wine which he had earned and richly deserved.

Alongside the road, the groundcover looked more like weeds than grass. Duncan showed no interest in it and it did not look inviting even to Robin. In search of water and suitable grazing for Duncan, Robin headed down a side road that he thought might lead to creek or tributary. The road got ever narrower, ever more rugged the further he went until at last it wasn't a road at all but just a trail through ever deepening woods. This, he decided, wasn't taking them anywhere useful. Perhaps if they doubled back to the main road and ventured in the opposite direction they would find water and grass.

He turned Duncan around to head back the way that they had come. They had gone just a few paces when Robin heard unsettling sounds, crunching and crashing that he recognized but could not name and which filled him with a sudden, odd dread. Duncan stopped. Curiosity made Robin prod him to keep moving toward the sound. Duncan's bawling protest sounded more like "Nay!" than "neigh." Robin urged him forward but out of a compelling sense of self-preservation, at a slower pace. When he smelled smoke, Robin pulled up and turned Duncan to go back whence they had come which Duncan accommodated with an eager step.

An otherworldly roar brought Duncan to a sudden stop, set Meeyoo to howling, and raised the hair on the back of Robin's neck. He was about to spur the donkey into a full-bore retreat when he heard a woman scream.

His heart pounding, Robin turned the donkey toward the sound and urged it forward. Duncan neighed and shook his head in refusal.

"Just a few paces," Robin said to the donkey. "Just to get a glimpse of what's going on. If we can't be of assistance, we will run like the wind and get the hell out of here."

Duncan moved forward, his mincing steps speaking volumes about his opinion of this course of action. As the sounds grew louder and the smells stronger, Duncan moved even more slowly.

At last the cause of the uproar became visible through a veil of leaves and the sight was terrifying enough to frost Robin's limbs and turn his blood to ice.

Ahead, white smoke streaming from its flared nostrils, a dragon flung its long-necked head about, flinging fire from its mouth and setting the surrounding shrubbery afire.

At its feet, a human waved a lance and hopped from side to side, dodging the sparks. Although its form was obscured by the folds of a red hooded cloak, the figure's small stature and narrow shoulders led Robin to deduce it was a woman, a conclusion that was confirmed when her shouted imprecations carried over the dragon's roar.

"Go on, now!" she yelled. "Get gone!" She jabbed the dragon's leg with her lance.

The dragon lifted its head and roared. The smoke streaming from its nostrils became dark gray billows and the fire that it spat was more like flames than mere sparks.

"What does she think she's doing?" Robin said, more to himself than to Duncan, who shuddered beneath him. "She's just making it angrier. Why doesn't she run or hide?"

"Come on, now," the woman cried. "Don't make me mad."

As if in reply, the dragon lowered its head and spread its jaws wide, baring fangs that looked sharper than any sword. It spit a lick of flame close enough to the woman that her cloak caught fire.

"Oh drat! Now look what you've done," she said, swatting at the smoldering fabric. "This is my favorite riding cloak."

The dragon snorted smoke into her face, smoke that was now nearly black. Robin could hardly believe the woman's insouciance in the face of certain death. She ought to be scared out of her wits.

"We have to get her out of there now," he said, "before the dragon decides to stop toying with her and just finishes her off!"

Duncan shook his head and sat back on his haunches. Meeyoo howled from deep inside the rucksack.

"Right," said Robin, dismounting. He made certain the rucksack's strap was looped securely over the saddle horn. "No point in dragging you two into this madness. Duncan, get ready to run. I'll be back in a flash."

He drew his sword and thrashed his way through the undergrowth. "Stand back!" he called. "Take cover!"

The woman heeded not. Robin wondered if perhaps she couldn't hear him over the dragon's bellowing and the crackling of the burning foliage. She continued to berate the beast, jabbing at its legs with her lance. What did she think to accomplish with those puny thrusts except to exacerbate the dragon's fury?

The dragon swung its head skyward to the right and let loose a fearsome howl. Smoke all but blotted out the light that filtered through the forest's canopy. The dragon spewed a tongue of flame that ignited the leaves overhead and shed an eerie light on the terrifying tableau. Robin saw the dragon turn its head to the left, beginning an arc that seemed certain to target its helpless adversary.

"Oh, well, now you've really gone and done it," the woman cried. She pulled her lance back, thrust forward, and stabbed the dragon's claw-toed foot.

The dragon stamped its injured feet and let loose a thundering clamor that loosened the leaves from the trees and sent them showering to the ground. Robin wished for a spear or bow-and-arrow. Close-in fighting with a dragon would not have been his first choice and did not bring the promise of success. Nevertheless, he rushed forward. At the dragon's feet, he danced from side to side. The dragon swung its heavy head, trying to keep this new small prey in sight. Robin danced and jabbed with his sword. At last, intent on finishing off his opponent, the dragon raised its head, to build up another blast of smoke and steam, Robin knew. When he saw an opening, he aimed not for the dragon's heart, protected as it was by a thick scaly skin and a rock hard sternum. Instead he drove his sword into the dragon's neck and the large vessel that carried blood to the beast's heart.

The dragon's scream made the trees quake and the earth below Robin's feet rumbled. Robin withdrew his sword. The dragon's open wound drenched Robin in hot, malodorous blood.

Robin looped his free arm around the woman's waist, lifted her off her feet, and hauled her away as fast as he could move from the scene of the battle. Behind him, the dragon emitted high-pitched screams that made Robin's ears throb. Robin feared he'd been made deaf until he realized that he could hear the sounds of the forest burning behind him.

He kept bulling his way through the bushes, his arm tight around the woman. He didn't dare turn to see what transpired behind him. He hoped that he was headed in the right direction, back to where he had left Duncan and Meeyoo, but his main objective was to put as much forest as possible behind him and the woman as quickly as he could.

The dragon's roar became more of a keening. Robin heard tree limbs crack and clatter to the ground. The sound of whole trees splintering drowned the dragon's howls. An awesome crash seemed to echo throughout the entire forest and then all was silent save for the sound of wood burning.

Robin decided to risk looking back. He set the woman on her feet and turned to face the battleground. The dragon was down, not quite on the ground but rather speared on the spikes of torched and shattered trees.

Robin exhaled the breath he had held from the moment that he dismounted Duncan and lowered his shoulders from around his ears.

He turned to face the woman. She stood with her hands on her hips, a scowl on what otherwise was an attractive face.

"Now look what you've done!" she said. "You killed it."

Speechless, Robin gaped in amazement.

She threw her hands up in the air. "I didn't want to kill it. I just wanted it out of here." She let her arms fall by her side and glared, her lips pressed into a thin line.

"I... I... I thought you were in danger," Robin said.

She paced in a small circle. "I just wanted to make him irritated enough to leave."

"Oh, he was irritated, all right," said Robin, feeling his own irritation seething.

"I had him, you know," she said.

"You didn't have him!" Robin replied. "He was about to make a cinder out of you. What the hell were you trying to do, skewer him for your supper? Stabbing him in the foot, are you kidding? That's no way to fight a dragon. That will only make him angry."

The woman pouted. "Oh, and I suppose you know a lot about dragon-slaying."

"I've slain a few in my day," Robin replied. As indeed he had, although not singlehandedly. Serious dragon-slaying required an entire cadre of well-trained, well-coordinated, and well-commanded knights to have any chance of success. One such campaign was one of the last things he remembered doing as king. The lengthy expedition had him and his knights absent from Bell Castle for what seemed like eons. Though he could not have said now when that had been, the techniques polished in many battles came as naturally as breathing, and had stood him in good stead today. "And I'll bet you have a lot of experience in dragon-slaying?"

"As a matter of fact, I do. You might say I slay dragons every day. Anyhow, that isn't a dragon." The woman looked over her shoulder at the huge carcass.

"It's not? Well, it's not a housefly," Robin said.

"No, it's not a housefly. It's a wyvern. No front legs, see?"

"Right. Important distinction. Like that would have stopped him from turning you into toast?"

"Well, it would have, actually. If I had made his feet and legs hurt badly enough, he would have had to take flight."

Robin sighed and shook his head. The woman was clearly demented. He wondered if she might be so deranged as to be a danger to him. That was unfortunate, as despite the dirt, sweat, and dragon's blood that besmeared her face, he could see that she was attractive. Light brown hair grazed her shoulders. Deep brown eyes had a fire that Robin might have attributed to intelligence if he hadn't suspected that she might be insane. Her gown draped a trim figure that he could see now that her cloak was thrown back. The deep red velvet cloak bore a large area of black singe from the dragon's, or wyvern's fire, and a large heraldic emblem. He saw a red shield with a gold ribbon and silver chevron, silver hands held open in greeting, and a silver helmet, all symbols of generosity, peace, strength, sincerity, and justice. Above the shield, the image of the fox spoke of one who would use wisdom and wit as a means of defense. The slogan "certavi et vici" told of battles fought and won.

Robin surmised that the woman was a servant of a royal court. Odd that a ruler would send a woman out to battle dragons, even if they were wyverns which to him seemed equally dangerous.

"They're such pests," she said, "flying around, spitting flames, setting trees on fire. A frivolous waste of good timber if you ask me. Of which we have little enough at Sea Gate Fortress and have to import at considerable expense." She smoothed her hair back from her forehead and brushed cinders from her cloak. "Speaking of forest fires, we had best remove ourselves to safer surroundings, don't you agree? Our friend got quite the little conflagration going, blast him." She looked back at the distant fire. "How did you arrive here? On foot? Do you have a mount?"

Robin hardly thought of Duncan as a mount but in reply he simply said, "A mount, yes. He must be around here somewhere." At a safe distance, Robin hoped, and prayed that Meeyoo was with him.

"I as well. Shall we go look for them?" She removed her glove and held out her hand. "Alexandra."

Robin cut a slight bend at the waist, then took her hand in greeting. He noted that her skin was smooth and unblemished, the nails neatly trimmed. Robin guessed that Alexandra was not only in service to a court but possibly one of high ranking, a lady-in-waiting perhaps. The woman did have a certain confident bearing, in addition to one hell of an attitude, and had a refined manner of speech. It was his own courtly speech patterns that he had quickly learned to mitigate so as not to invite suspicion. "Robin," he said.

"Thank you for your help, Robin," said Alexandra. "Not that I needed it."

"You're welcome," he replied. "Not that you needed it. Shall we try heading this way?" Perhaps Duncan had gone back in the direction from which they had come.

"Seems as good as any," she said, and they set off walking.

After a few false starts, Robin thought that he recognized the area. He saw a trail that he and Duncan might have traveled. Twigs were broken going one way, and there were even fresher breaks hinting at someone or something having passed going in the opposite direction. "This looks promising," Robin said. "Let's head this way for a while. Duncan," Robin called. "Duncan, if you're nearby, make some noise."

Robin continued down the trail, but more slowly, growing ever more certain that he was on the right track, and continued to call Duncan's name. At last he heard a rustling and a familiar bray. "I think we've found him," Robin said and hurried toward the sound and the light gray-and-white shape he spotted in the distance. "Aye, we've found them!" he said. "Duncan, thank goodness," he said. He lifted the rucksack from the saddle horn and peered inside but the cat was not to be seen. "Meeyoo?" he said, his heart racing. "Duncan, where's Meeyoo?" Robin rummaged around in the pack. His heart sinking, he dug deeper and was rewarded when his fingertips met whiskers and a scratchy wet tongue at the very bottom. He moved his belongings aside and Meeyoo looked up at him with wide eyes. Robin at last exhaled the breath that he had held from the minute he'd spotted the dragon.

"Oh, my, your poor steed," said Alexandra.

Robin came around to Duncan's other side and saw Alexandra examining a burn on Duncan's neck and forequarters. Robin felt tears sting his eyes as he realized that Duncan had made an attempt to follow him into the fray and had gotten burned for his efforts.

"Don't move, Duncan... Duncan's his name, you said?" asked Alexandra.

Robin nodded.

"Don't move, Duncan. Give me a minute now." She took a few steps to the right, doubled back, and went to the left, stopped and then went further into the brush until Robin could make out only the red of her cloak.

"What are you looking for?" Robin called.

"Found it," was her reply. She emerged from the brush holding her index finger high. The tip gleamed with a dark golden substance: a dollop of honey. Gently she applied the honey to Duncan's burn. "That will help for a while but we need to get him some serious attention, and quickly," she said.

"We can ride —"

"No, no. You stay here. We shouldn't cause your Duncan any more exertion than absolutely necessary. I think my horse may not be far." She eyed Robin's rucksack. "Do you have your cup in there? There's a bit of a stream yonder." She pointed behind him. "You should get some water for the both of you."

It was true, he did need water, and so did Duncan. Nevertheless, there was no mistaking her imperious tone. This was a woman who was used to giving orders. Head of the kitchen, perhaps.

"I shall be back soon, I hope," she said. "Don't stray too far from this spot or we'll be circling around looking for each other for the rest of the day." She pulled her cloak closely around herself and set off in the direction where she had found the honey calling, "Charger! Charger!"

Robin set off to find the stream and some water for himself and his traveling companions.

He had long since returned, watered himself, Duncan, and Meeyoo, and was vacillating between impatience and concern when he heard a rider approaching.

"Meeyoo! Meeyoo, hurry! You've got to get back in the pack," Robin said but it was too late. Coming down the track at respectable pace was the woman Alexandra astride a gaited horse of robust proportions. The horse came to a stop, lifted its head, and neighed, which to Robin sounded a lot like "Hey, good day, my friend!" The horse stretched out its neck and tapped Robin on the chest with its nose.

What left Robin standing with mouth agape was the horse's livery. There was no mistaking the appointments were of the highest quality. The leather of the saddle, halter, bridle, and bit all gleamed from recent polishing and the royal crest that emblazoned the woman's riding cloak was everywhere, even engraved on the stirrups.

There was no question that this Alexandra was a very important member of the court. Robin had a hollow feeling in the pit of this stomach that she might, in fact, be the ruler herself.

Had he a hat to doff, he would have done so. Instead, he bent in a deep bow followed by a scrape with his right foot. The gesture still felt creaky and awkward. Yet something about Alexandra called for acknowledgement. As she drew up alongside Duncan, Robin said, "Your Majesty?"

Before he could offer to assist, she had dismounted. "Oh, thank you, thank you. Yes, Empress of Sea Gate Fortress, but such formalities are not necessary among fellow dragon-slayers."

Robin gulped. Empress? He thought of the Tarot card that had appeared in the reading David had done for him. True, David had said not to take the appellation literally and further, this woman had neither fair hair nor a rose-bedecked gown. Nevertheless, the coincidence was eerie.

Robin scoured his brain for what was the appropriate protocol for a person of his presumed status to observe in the presence of royalty, but he was too boggled.

She spotted Meeyoo. "Ah, I see you've made a friend."

Meeyoo twined around Robin's ankles.

"Oh, this is not a new friend but an old one. A traveling companion, eh?" she asked.

"Yes," Robin said hesitantly. Not everyone that he met was a cat lover.

Alexandra bent to scratch Meeyoo behind the ears. "And what's your name?"

Meeyoo responded by meowing and nudging Alexandra for more pets. "Ah, Meeyoo. Pleased to meet you." Alexandra straightened up. "She has the look of a fine mouser."

"How can you tell?"

"She doesn't look hungry. Or do you feed her?"

"A little of both," Robin said, not at all ready to relate the tale of the desperate morning that Meeyoo tried to feed him.

"Now, we should best be about getting poor Duncan some attention," said Alexandra. "I have a very fine physician who should be able to help Duncan recover completely. But I'm afraid he will bear no rider until then.

"I can walk."

"It's a fairly long way and we would make better time if we ride double. Duncan can walk behind."

The surprise and dismay that he felt at such an outrageous suggestion must have shown in his face because Alexandra said, "I know... it's somewhat unseemly. But we should be all right. We haven't seen a soul in these parts all day."

"Till we reach the woods' edge, then," said Robin, still uncomfortable with the idea. Should someone see them he would be taken for a kidnapper or worse. Nevertheless, he got Meeyoo back in the rucksack, shouldered the pack, and got a hold of Duncan's reigns. Empress Alexandra scooted to the far front of Charger's saddle. Robin climbed aboard behind her, reached around her, grabbed the saddle horn, and they set off down the track.

The going was slow. Duncan lagged behind, whimpering and grumbling. Robin talked to him over his shoulder, encouraging him to keep moving despite the pain and telling him that they would find him relief soon. "I know that you hurt, good friend," he said, "and I know that you were only trying to help me."

It seemed as though they had been riding for hours without making much progress when Duncan stopped altogether and refused to move. Robin and Alexandra dismounted.

"What's the matter, old boy?" Robin said to Duncan, stroking his neck.

Alexandra examined the wound. "Oh, I think he's just in too much pain to go much further. I wonder, do you think we could fashion him a palanquin of some sort, a travois? Charger's very strong, he could pull it."

Robin tried not to look too surprised. What did empresses know of travois? "I... possibly we could, but whether we could make one strong enough to support Duncan is doubtful. Even more doubtful is whether we could get him to lie on it."

Empress Alexandra pressed her lips together and sighed. "Good point. Well, we'll just have to get him to press on, won't we?"

"You ride," said Robin. "I'll walk along beside him. We weren't going that fast anyway. Your Majesty," he added as an afterthought.

And so they pressed onward, Robin feeling the pain of every one of Duncan's anguished steps as if it was his own.

The angle of the shadows suggested it would soon be dusk when Robin noticed that the trunks of the trees around them appeared to be thinner and spaced further apart. "I think we might be nearing the edge?" he said.

"I believe you're right," Empress Alexandra called from astride Charger. "Yes, I see clearing ahead."

They walked on a little further and then even Robin could see the landscape open before them, including the suggestion of a wagon way.

"I'm going to ride ahead and try to find help," Alexandra said. "I'll return as soon as I can." With that, she spurred Charger forward down the wagon way.

Robin continued to walk alongside Duncan, patting his head and murmuring encouragements. They made their own slow progress until finally they left the woods behind and were picking their way along the wagon track. Robin felt his spirits lift when he saw a small cloud of dust blur the horizon. Before long he could make out a rider approaching.

"Hang on, Duncan," he said. "I think this might be the Empress returning, but even if not, I will do what I can to get whoever is coming to help."

The rider was indeed Alexandra, nearing them at a gallop. Behind her and moving quite a bit slower were more travelers.

She reigned Charger to a stop and dismounted. "Great news!" she said, breathlessly. "I stopped at the first farmstead that I found and they had a cart to spare. I think that will do the job. They were kind enough to agree to help transport Duncan to Sea Gate Fortress."

Kind, maybe, Robin thought. More likely, obedient to their ruler or perhaps hoping for a handsome reward.

"Meanwhile, until they get here, I have some provisions." She opened a saddlebag and produced a flask and a small meat pie for Robin. "And look, here's a little something for Duncan that might give him some relief." She handed Robin a twist of parchment that proved to contain some orange powder. "See if you can't rub that into the wound without causing him any more discomfort."

Robin looked a question at her.

"It's turmeric," she said. "It's like ginger."

Robin had not heard of ginger being used to treat wounds but he did as directed.

The Empress took a long swallow from her own flask and unwrapped a wedge of cheese. "Oh, I didn't forget Meeyoo," she said, breaking off a bit of cheese and holding it out to Robin.

"She's in the pack," Robin said. "You can give that to her. She won't bite, not if you're offering her food."

They finished their repast and moved out slowly to meet the approaching wagon. Between the farmer and Robin, they managed to get Duncan loaded onto a cart hitched to the farmer's ox. The Empress mounted Charger and Robin and the farmer rode double astride the ox.

As they headed toward Sea Gate Fortress, Robin realized that his detour would never have brought him nearer to the Chalklands. The landscape here was totally foreign. What appeared to be willows had leaves thin as needles. Other trees were stranger still. Their tall trunks appeared to be covered in snakeskin. They did not form spreading canopies, but shot straight up and ended in the most unusual feathery flurry of branches. All were of a green that was almost yellow. Some had branches that ended in plumes. Still others had broad fans for leaves. Few shrubs grew higher than his head and most would have come up only to his waist. Though it was summer, not many bore flowers. Those that did seemed to be ablaze, so bright was the color of the orange- and purple-red of the blooms.

The crops grown on the farms that he could see from the road were equally odd. Some of the plants appeared to be sprouting wool. Robin wondered if these were the very "vegetable lamb" plants that produced the fiber called cotton. Other stalks ended in feathery red tips that made the field look to Robin as though it had been planted with paintbrushes.

The light paled and the air cooled as the sun moved lower in the sky. The road led them to a walled and gated settlement. Alexandra explained that this was the city of Sea Gate, part of her domain. Of course, once it was established that their party included the Empress, they were granted entrance and even offered an escort, which Alexandra declined. She asked, however, that a fast rider be sent ahead to bring word to the castle of her imminent arrival and need for medical attention.

The road took them through the center of the town, impressive in its size. Owing to the hour, the marketplace was deserted and they stopped only to water the mounts and check on Duncan.

It was night when later they reached a viaduct. Robin wondered if they were nearing Sea Gate Fortress, although he could see no tall structures on the horizon. As they approached the viaduct, he could see that it crossed a body of water wider than a simple moat.

At last the walls of Sea Gate Fortress came into view, outlined by torches. Robin did not know if the sentries on the ramparts saw them first or he them but moments later, the gates opened. Riders emerged, some carrying torches and lanterns, and charged towards them. One pulled ahead at a gallop: a woman, it seemed from the breadth of the shoulders. Going for a night ride had probably not been on the woman's agenda as she seemed to have dressed hastily. Emblems of the Empress's court emblazoned the cloak that no doubt covered night dress. She had put back the hood to reveal hair that had already been braided for sleep. Robin thought she might be the Empress's lady. She pulled up alongside the Empress and they had a short conference. The woman then brought her steed alongside the farmer's ox. The farmer gave Robin a questioning look and all Robin could do was shrug.

"Greetings, gentlemen," the woman said. "I am Leigh. I am a physician of the court."

Robin could not have been more surprised. The farmer bowed and Robin followed suit.

"Let's put on some speed and get the patient within the gates."

The farmer urged his ox to move as fast as he could without upsetting the cart.

Once within the gates, other attendants appeared.

By lantern light, the physician Leigh peered closely at Duncan's wounds and touched his flank. The donkey whimpered and shuffled his feet but otherwise bore the examination.

Leigh straightened and spoke to the Empress. "Honey and turmeric?"

The Empress nodded.

"Excellent emergency first aid for a burn. Analgesic and disinfectant. Good thinking, Sandy."

The Empress nodded in acknowledgment.

Sandy? Robin noted that Leigh did not bow or bestow any honors on the Empress, but was instead as familiar with her as she might be with a friend. Perhaps they were sisters.

Leigh turned toward Robin. "A burn like this... well, we do need to give him some care. The burn itself doesn't appear too severe. But we will need to debride the damaged tissue. He won't like that operation much but we will do what we can to lessen the pain of it. Then we will need to keep the wound area clean until it scabs over and new skin forms. He will need to rest and be idle until it does. You understand, you won't be able to ride him, and he won't be able to do any work."

"Oh, well, as long as he'll be better..." Robin said, wondering what to call the woman or how to behave.

"Yes, it might take some weeks but he will recover. May I take him now? I'd like to get him to a stable and begin. It would be good if you could come with us, sir," she said to Robin. "He might accept my ministrations better if you're there to give him confidence."

Robin did a double-take at the appellation. She was calling him "sir?" Who were these strange people of Sea Gate Fortress? He turned toward the Empress. "Is that acceptable?"

"Oh, yes, of course," she said. "Let's go get started."

Robin and the farmer helped unload Duncan from the cart.

The Empress directed the other attendants to see that the farmer received hospitality and a generous reward to pay him for the use of his oxcart and his time.

On foot, she and Leigh led the way to the stables. They handed off their mounts to stable hands. Leigh conferred with the stable master regarding accommodations for Duncan. The stable master led them to a free stall and he and a groom set about getting Duncan comfortable. Meanwhile the physician Leigh sent another attendant to fetch her tools and supplies.

Taking care of Duncan's burn involved cutting away tissue with fine, very sharp blades. Despite the dismal circumstances, Robin found a small part of his attention captured by curiosity about the physician's knives.

"I need to make a neat edge in the wound," the physician explained. "That will decrease scarring that might later cripple Duncan." For once, Robin had no interest in the details. He just wanted to know that Duncan would recover.

She went on to blot blood and serum, wash the wound with cleansing solutions, apply protective and healing ointments, and cover the damaged area. Duncan let it be known that he was in pain, and Robin tried to sound confident and comforting although his heart raced with anxiety and his shoulders ached with tension.

"That dressing will need regular changing," said Leigh. "Do you think you can do that?" she asked.

"Yes, of course," Robin replied.

"You're not going anywhere?" Leigh asked.

"Well, the animal can't travel, can he?" Alexandra said.

"Not until he heals, he shouldn't," replied Leigh.

"But you were bound for somewhere when you stopped to battle the wyvern, weren't you?" Alexandra asked Robin.

He had been, but the stress of the day had so thoroughly banished any thought from his head that for a moment he couldn't remember where he had been headed.

"Right now, the most important thing is to tend to Duncan," he said.

"Well, then, since you are clearly spending the night within our gates," Alexandra said. "I shall have prepared —"

"I'll stay here," Robin said.

"In the stable?"

"He's my responsibility," he said, and for the first time since the wyvern made his appearance, Robin thought of Oliver John. How would he explain all this to the lord? He felt the first prickle of dread. "I won't be getting much sleep anyway. Not until I know he's past the crisis."

"That's one well cared-for animal," said Leigh to Alexandra.

"Wait until you see the cat," said Alexandra.

"The cat?"

Alexandra chuckled. "I will have some food and bedding sent your way," she said to Robin. She took Leigh's elbow. "Come, I will tell you all about my day."

CHAPTER TWELVE

"And how is our patient this morning?"

Robin turned his head. Empress Alexandra stood at the entrance to the stall, holding two mugs. "Ale?" she asked.

Robin stood and brushed the straw from his clothing. "Thank you." He wondered why she hadn't simply sent a servant on this errand. The thought of servants reminded him to bow, something that wasn't getting any easier with practice although if anyone deserved the tribute, the Empress certainly did. He straightened, took the offered mug, and sipped. "Doing better, I think. Not any worse, at any rate. Poor guy, I think he may still be in some pain."

"Leigh tells me that should abate some by the end of the day but he'll be sore for a while yet." She sipped her ale. "Tell me, Robin... you're not from around here, are you?"

"No," he replied, wondering what gave him away. In the tumult of yesterday's trials, he had forgotten to alter his speech and sound more like a commoner. "I was traveling to Riverington from Allenton where I was visiting with a customer."

"Oh, I know of Riverington. Not far from there is Lord Oliver John's Ironworks, a huge enterprise. Very successful. You know of it, I'm sure."

"I do. Actually, I w-w-work for Lord Oliver John." In Robin's mind this was a temporary arrangement, like a role that he played in this strange drama in which he had been cast.

"Do you? Doing what, pray tell? Come, tell me about it."

He followed her from the stables toward the gatehouse. As they walked, Robin described his job in the smithy, first as a blacksmith's apprentice, then as design engineer, and his newest charge as an itinerant salesman.

"So, you are a peddler," said Alexandra.

His pride wounded, Robin felt his temper flare. "A bit more than a peddler," he said sharply. Or a bit less, since the goods that he sold weren't even his, and Oliver John kept the biggest share of the proceeds. The realization served only to humiliate him further. "Lord Oliver John had sent me to Allenton as his representative, to consult on the commission of a sword." He described how he turned Lord Stanley Allen from taciturn and disinterested into genial and extravagant, with a little help from the fortified wine he had bought from Eian's Sweet Water cellars.

"You got him drunk!" Alexandra said.

Robin felt his face grow warm. "I did not! I simply presented him with a bottle of wine. He didn't have to drink the whole thing."

Alexandra rolled her eyes. "The end result was that you got the commission."

"That's correct."

"And you have that signed agreement?"

"It's in the saddlebags."

"It's not doing you or Oliver John much good there, is it?"

"Well, no, but as soon as Duncan heals, I will —"

"Duncan will be a while healing," said Alexandra. "Meanwhile, Lord Oliver John may be wondering what happened to you. He may even be entertaining thoughts that you absconded with the money that he gave you, the donkey, and the samples."

"I... I hadn't thought of that." The prickle of dread that Robin felt yesterday enveloped him in cold fear. "That just isn't true. I would never do that!"

Alexandra regarded him with a puzzled expression. "The lands of Sea Gate Fortress are not exactly on the way between Allenton and Riverington. You were headed in the wrong direction when you came upon me and the wyvern."

"I had thought to find a more direct route than I had taken on the outbound journey. I got lost."

Robin gulped as Alexandra regarded him with a guarded look that said she suspected there was more to the story than he was telling.

They reached the gatehouse. Alexandra led them into the chamberlain's post. She settled on a window seat and bid him to do the same. He found himself studying the stone of which the castle was built, which if it was stone, was not any he had seen before.

"So, Empress, the Emperor...is he traveling?" Robin asked. He noticed that she wore no ring. Perhaps there was no Emperor at all. Why else would Empress Alexandra be out slaying dragons in the woods.

She sighed. "He died."

"In battle?"

"Sadly, no, although that would have been a fitting end for him. He was a fine man, a brave man. He had led many a charge and emerged unscathed." She sighed. "Charger was his horse." She sighed again. "No, it was an illness. A wasting disease so awful you wouldn't wish it on your worst enemy. Nothing even the best physicians could do anything about, not even Leigh. At least she was able to keep him pain-free for the most part."

"I'm sorry," Robin said, although it felt lame. What could he say? Not all married couples shared affection as those unions arose more often out of economic necessity than from love. He thought briefly of his own Queen. It seemed when he allowed himself to think of her that her affections had been estranged of late. It was clear the Empress had cared for her husband. Robin wondered at the enormity of her loss. Now the woman still lived in the same castle, surrounded by familiar people and things and wanting for nothing, yet in many ways she was as devastated by her loss as he was by his.

"It was a great loss, not just for me but also for the Empire. I've tried to run it as he would have, but it's hard to do the job of two people."

"Well, of course it is. Hasn't there been a king who would take you..." As wife? Robin had been about to ask, but the words withered on his tongue before they could fall from his lips. He pictured the Empress singlehandedly skewering the wyvern and realized that there would be no "taking" of this woman by anyone, for any reason.

He stopped. He was chatting with the Empress as if they were equals. Which they were, except that she didn't know that. It was getting harder, not easier, to remember his "place."

"Oh, there have been proposals, none with any merit. So I just keep soldiering on though I am not the person that the Emperor was. He's been gone for years but I am only now just grasping the enormity of what he accomplished." She smoothed a crease in her sleeve. "Even knowing what he did and how he did it doesn't mean that I can do it." She seemed to shake off her despondency forcibly. "The Empire is not what it once was. It is what I can make of it." She gazed into the distance, as if to read an answer in the sky. "I give it my best. That's all I can do."

"Are there no sons to help?" Robin asked, thinking of his own sons and how his disappearance would have catapulted them prematurely from boyhood to manhood.

The empress gave him a wistful look. "No. We came late into each other's lives. We were so busy building the empire we put off building a family. And then there was the illness." She spoke matter-of-factly about what had to be the source of much pain and sorrow. "So, have you always worked at the Ironworks? Are you from Riverington?"

"No, I sojourned In Rose Bank for a time. It's where I met Lord Oliver John."

"Rose Bank, you say. Where is that?"

"North of Riverington, near the Brave River."

The Empress gave this some consideration. She looked puzzled. "I think that this is not in the Empire, although I believe there are lords in that area who owe us allegiance. Is it a center of much production?"

"Not really. Just a small place. From what I saw, valuable mostly as a trade center, a junction of several well-traveled roads. We had visitors from many different realms. The farmers there are independent landholders."

"And you were a blacksmith there too?" she asked.

Robin felt his face grow warm. It had been difficult enough to describe his job at the Ironworks in terms glowing enough that he retained some dignity. He was loathe to tell the Empress that he had swept floors in a barbershop. "No. More an entertainer."

The Empress's eyebrows lifted in surprise. "An entertainer? You mean, like a mime? A mummer? A trouper?"

"More like a troubadour. A teller of tales, a singer of songs. I play the harmonica."

The Empress grinned broadly. "You do? How wonderful! Perhaps you will perform for us sometime."

"I would be delighted," Robin said, and realized that indeed he would be if it would bring a smile to the Empress's face.

Alexandra stood and paced the chamber in silent thought for a moment. Finally, she said, "You should go to Riverington and report to Lord Oliver John."

"The physician Leigh said that Duncan cannot yet travel."

"You could take Charger," Alexandra replied.

"But that's your horse!" Robin felt his pulse race at the prospect of riding the kingly mount.

"Well, I have lots of horses. And I'm not sure that taking a lady for an outing is the best use for him."

"When that lady is riding to a dragon-slaying it is," Robin said.

"Still, I've got other mounts that I can use, and Charger seems to like you. You could deliver the contract to Oliver John, then come back to return Charger. By then, Duncan should be healed and your life can return to normal."

If by "normal" she meant his life working for Oliver John, she couldn't be more wrong, Robin thought. "I am humbled by your offer which is beyond generous but I couldn't possibly accept it." She was right, though. He really did need to return to Oliver John before the man decided Robin had proved himself to be a scoundrel. He might even publish a notice ordering Robin's arrest, offer a bounty. Some overeager individual might decide it would be easier to deliver a corpse in exchange for the bounty. Robin felt chilled as he imagined ever more dire complications.

Yes, he did need to find a way to get back to the Ironworks. Walk, if he had to. Perhaps he could use the coins that he hadn't spent on the journey to Allenton to hire another donkey from one of Sea Gate Fortress's citizens.

Donkey. Oliver John would have to be told that his donkey was wounded. He might demand compensation. Robin saw the few coins that he had with great sacrifice scraped together for his war chest vanish.

"I... I couldn't. It would be a debt that I could never repay." And he had enough of that, now that he owed Oliver John for one donkey in addition to the account at the Ironworks' store.

"Ah, but I have an idea to press you into service on our behalf."

"What could I possibly do for you?"

"Riverington is not part of the Empire's domain. Oliver John owns the land on which stands the Ironworks, and the town is a commune, is it not?"

Robin wasn't sure and so did not comment.

"In any case, neither is fortified, correct?"

"That's correct. The town has a small lookout tower. The Ironworks has a fence and a gate, the factory has a small tower, and Lord Oliver John's manor has a wall, but that's it."

"Exactly. Not much in the way of barricades. Yet it's a thriving, growing area, sure to attract unwanted attention. To be honest, we would like to consider it part of our domain."

Robin felt a little queasy. Had he stumbled onto an imperialist plot to wage war upon Oliver John?

"Oh, don't look so shocked," Alexandra said. "I don't mean to send an army in to take the place by force. No, what I have in mind is a strategic alliance. We could provide defense. The citizens may not see a need for it now, but I believe that they will before long as word of Riverington's assets spreads. In exchange, we would ask Oliver John for favorable terms on metalworks."

"And taxes, of course."

Alexandra gave him an arch look. "Aren't you insightful? Yes, there would be taxation but it would be no great burden. I have never understood the point of draining the very people we are counting on to provide what we need. In any case, as my representative, I would like you to 'explore' whether Oliver John and the townsfolk would welcome such an alliance. Pave the way, so to speak, for future discussions on the subject.

"In exchange for this aid, I will give you the use of Charger for your journey, and tend to Duncan and Meeyoo in your absence. And give you a stipend for expenses."

Robin felt lightheaded. A horse, and more coins. "I would be honored to assist in this manner. I can't imagine that Oliv— milord would not be amenable to such an alliance."

"Fine, I will make the necessary arrangements." Alexandra clasped her hands together. "You should plan to leave posthaste. You have a long return trip since you have ended up so far out of your way. Go back to the stables and collect your belongings, then return here for your departure."

Trying not to rankle at the peremptoriness of her charge, Robin stood also and bowed.

CHAPTER THIRTEEN

Robin sat much taller in the saddle as he headed toward Riverington and the Ironworks than he had when he left. Then, he had feared being seen riding a donkey. How foolish that had been. Duncan had proved to be a brave, reliable, and companionable ally.

Still, astride Charger, Robin felt more like his old King Bewilliam self. Adorned in his Sea Gate Fortress livery, Charger attracted admiring looks from passersby, which became inquiring looks when their gaze came to focus on Robin. Garbed in his work clothes, he looked suspiciously ill-suited to be riding a royal steed. He feared not, as he had letters from Empress Alexandra authorizing him the use of the horse and empowering him to initiate important conversations with Oliver John and Riverington's residents.

But first he had Stanley Allen's commission to convey. The sooner he delivered that, the sooner Franklin could get started on all the work.

Franklin and not Robin? And what of Franklin? Robin was going to need his cooperation. How would he react to Robin's latest turn of good fortune? He had been none too pleased with Robin's last promotion.

Robin realized that he had hadn't given the smithy a minute's thought, as if his days of working there were already over. Oliver John no doubt expected Robin to return to his worktable and sharpening stones, churning out blades and taking a break from that labor only when the next visiting customer or road trip called him away. Robin needed to meet with the citizens of Riverington and to do that, he would need leave from Oliver John to be absent from the smithy.

For the first time, Robin thought less about how Oliver John might respond to Alexandra's alliance proposal and more about how he might react to Robin's association with the Empress. Having not met her, Oliver John could not be blamed if he were suspicious of her motives. He might suspect her of being intent on a conquest and regard Robin as an accomplice and a traitor. Robin realized that this presentation would be the most challenging of his sales career.

Robin smiled. In his pack was his secret weapon. He had stopped in Sweet Water on the way home and purchased another bottle of Eian's potent fortified wine. Once again, it didn't appear that Robin was going to get to enjoy any. Oliver John, however, was sure to love it.

Night had long since fallen but Robin had not left the road. Though the Empress had given him enough coins such that he could afford to rest at an inn for the night, Robin thought to add the money to his war chest. Charger didn't seem to be at all lagging. Robin felt his own attention flagging but wasn't terribly concerned. The road was clear. He was certainly making much better time on Charger than he had on Duncan. As long as he could keep Charger moving, he might make the hut at the Ironworks by daybreak.

He had, perhaps, even nodded off a bit because a rider was along his right side before Robin even realized it. Why had he not heard the tinkling of the little bell wayfarers carried to announce their approach?

"Where ya bound, stranger?" the rider asked in a gruff voice.

"Riverington," Robin replied. There was scant light but he didn't like what he could see. The man wore a leather arming jerkin. Sturdy leather gloves covered his hands, wrists, and forearms. His hat was pulled low on his brow, the jerkin's collar stood up against his neck, and the gruffness in his voice was due to a kerchief covering his lower face. With a suddenly racing pulse, Robin deduced that the kerchief was not worn as protection from the dust of the road, but to disguise the man's face. The warmth of the summer night vanished in a shiver of fear as Robin realized that had not heard the traveler's bells because he wore none. Robin now faced a highwayman. Only highwaymen snuck up on travelers like this.

With the most subtle of movements, he passed Charger's reigns from his right hand to his left.

"Riverington, aye. I'm bound there too," said the highwayman.

Robin felt the chill of horror penetrate his core. Highwaymen preyed on vulnerable travelers and rarely attacked villages whose defenders were likely to put up a good fight. Riverington, he knew, had no such defense and apparently this scoundrel knew it too.

Carefully, ever so carefully, Robin moved his right hand toward his sword.

"Nice horse," the rider said, but there was no pleasantry in his voice.

"Yes, he's —"

"Ya got some finery there, too. And I'm betting I'll find me some dandy things in them saddlebags." In the moonlight, Robin caught the gleam of a dagger in the man's right hand. "Methinks you should dismount and hand it all over."

"Methinks not," Robin said. He grasped his sword at the ricasso, pulled straight back, drove the pommel into the man's midsection, and was rewarded with a loud and startled breathless grunt. As the man doubled over, Robin brought the sword's blade up under the highwayman's chin. "No, sir, I think it's you who should hand over your weapon and dismount." He looped

Charger's reins around the saddle horn, sending up silent thanks to whoever had trained the horse to stand steady.

"The dagger, hilt first," Robin said. He took the weapon and slipped it under his belt. "Now, dismount. This side," he said, intending to keep the man pinned between the sword blade and the horse.

But the highwayman flung up a gauntleted forearm and knocked the blade aside. He made an ungainly dismount to the right and went lumbering into the bushes along the side of the road.

Robin considered giving chase but it was dark and he imagined he could spend the rest of the night crashing through unfamiliar thickets with little chance of success in apprehending the robber. The man was now on foot and unarmed. He would be unlikely to do any further damage this night.

Taking the reins to the robber's horse, Robin mounted Charger and continued on to Riverington at a considerably faster pace.

When he had left Sea Gate, he had planned to ride straight through to his hut, rest, and refresh himself there before reporting to Oliver John. He had stayed overly long in Sweet Water and the struggle with the highwayman had further delayed him. It was still night when Robin reached Riverington. He longed to continue on to his hut, to get something to eat, and rest. But now there was the matter of the highwayman to tackle. The need to speak to the village's burghers about defense had taken on more urgency. Though disarmed and on foot, the highwayman could still present a threat. Those bandits rarely worked alone and Robin didn't doubt that there might be a band of robbers with their thieving eyes on the settlement. The people of Riverington needed to be warned.

Not even the farmers of Riverington were up and about yet. He rode into the settlement to find it dark and quiet. At the center, he stopped by the well and drew some water for himself and the horses. He found a couple of somewhat-shriveled carrots still in the bottom of his rucksack and a bit of dried meat that amounted to little more than a wafer. He sat on the ground, his back propped up against the well.

He didn't know that he had fallen asleep until he felt a hand on his shoulder. His eyes springing open, he saw that day had dawned. He jumped to his feet and found he faced a sturdy woman in a rough dress and apron. Across her shoulder was a yoke from which hung two buckets. He recognized her as Mary, ale-wife and the mother of Jane who sometimes brought a lunch wagon to the Ironworks.

"Take it easy, Robin," she said. "I came to fetch water to start breakfast and beer and found you asleep. What are you doing here? Why are you not at the smithy? Are you ill? Do you need help?"

"No," said Robin. "But you might. I need to talk to your husband." Paul was as close to an alderman as anyone in Riverington got.

"Sounds serious," she said.

"It could be."

"Come then. He is getting the fires going. And you may say that you don't need help, but you look like you could use some."

"Here, let me help you," he said, and took the water buckets onto his own shoulders.

"Much obliged."

Robin followed her to her house. It felt like more than just a few weeks ago that he had enjoyed a rare night off from the foundry here.

A reedy, clean-shaven man, Mary's husband Paul stoked the outdoor cook fire. He stood as he spotted Robin. "Robin?" he asked.

"Yes, sir."

"A little early for you to be calling on us, isn't it? No work for you today?

"Not yet," Robin replied. "I have been on the road, returning from a trip on behalf of Lord Oliver John."

"And you look it. Mary, bring Robin something —"

"— to eat and drink," his wife said. "I've already thought of that." She collected the water buckets and went into the house.

"And on the road, I had an experience that I must tell you about," Robin said to Paul. He related the attack by the highwayman. "He was familiar with Riverington. I think he means to come here. He may have confederates. You must be on guard."

Paul looked concerned, and not a little frightened. "Do you think that attack is imminent? Do we need to raise a hue and cry?"

"I don't think so. I took his dagger, and his horse. That may have slowed him down. But I think it would be advisable to sound an alert, to be on the lookout, to ready your defenses."

At this, Paul looked even more troubled. "Of that we have little. We are just a small settlement." He looked about, and his expression became more aggrieved. "We would need a wall, a gate, a tower, guards. This is a little market town; we don't have the kind of money it would take to establish or maintain all that."

Robin felt almost guilty about taking advantage of this new threat but there was likely no better time than the present to bring up Alexandra's offer of an alliance. It would provide the village protection that it didn't have and now, apparently, sorely needed.

Over the very early breakfast that Mary brought out to them, Robin described Alexandra's offer.

"How come you to be in the service of this Empress, so far away?" Paul asked.

Robin gave him a brief telling of the dragon-slaying episode.

"Well," said Paul, "it sounds like you were passing through at just the right time. And the Empress's good fortune is now to be our good fortune." Paul promised to convene the burghers that very day. "Shall I send word to you at the Ironworks?"

"Yes. Whatever you decide, or even if you have no decision but only more questions. I will be returning to Sea Gate Fortress very soon.

"Now I have a question. What would you suggest that I do with the highwayman's horse?"

Paul looked thoughtful.

"It's probably stolen, wouldn't you think?"

Paul nodded. "Does it have any brands or marks that would suggest who is the rightful owner?"

"I don't know. It was so dark. It's only now light enough to get a good look," Robin replied.

"Let's go see what we can see."

Robin and Paul returned to the market square where Robin had left Charger and the highwayman's horse at the well. The robber's horse was somewhat old, too-well ridden and too little fed, and fitted with worn tack. Neither the horse nor the tack had any distinguishing marks.

Paul shrugged. "I say you keep him, as compensation for the fright you received. We can call it high justice. I suppose if you should ever encounter the rightful owner—"

"I would be prepared to surrender him," Robin agreed.

"Sounds fair enough to me."

Robin paid for his meal, bought some feed for the two animals, and continued toward the Ironworks. As he rode along, he marveled at finding himself now with not one but two mounts, when not long ago he had to get where we wanted to go on foot. He considered what name to give his newly acquired horse and decided on "Thief." It was a bit pompous for the old animal, but Robin told himself that maybe with good care, the horse would grow into it.

He stopped at the hut where he tied up Thief, cleaned himself of the road dust, and put on a clean shirt and leggings before proceeding on to the Ironworks. It was odd to arrive at the hut and not have Meeyoo come bounding across the grass to meet him. It would be a lonely night here indeed and he would be glad to be back on the road headed for Sea Gate Fortress.

No gatehouse, no chamberlain, Robin observed as he rode into the Ironworks. He had never given the absence of either any thought. Today, however, he saw how vulnerable was the establishment. Anyone could ride in unchallenged, from the lone bandit bent on making off with the first valuable he found, to an invading force. And yes, the Ironworks was even more of a prize than it had been the day Robin first traversed this road. The Ironworks produced more than just swords now, some of the credit for which rightly belonged to himself, Robin thought with a bit of ire. Bread saws and scissors and even frames for eyeglasses had proved to be popular and Oliver John sold more of them every day. At first they were ordered by the wealthy who had the extra coins to spend on items that worked just a little better and made life a little easier. But the sheer utility of the items soon proved to be attractive even to the commonfolk. Oliver John had directed new models to be crafted of less expensive materials so that more people could afford to buy them.

Yes, the Ironworks would be an attractive acquisition.

As a man emerged from the mill Robin realized that he had come within sight of the factory's tower battlement. He found himself considering how the tower might play into a plan for increased fortifications. True, it was at the center of the Ironworks. Defenses would have to be erected closer to the entrance. Still, the tower would make a good secondary lookout.

As Robin drew closer he recognized Oliver John. Robin dismounted and taking Charger's reins in hand, went to meet him on foot, thinking "I need to speak with Oliver John about the wisdom of going about without a personal guard."

"Who be you?" Oliver John called, and then he stopped. Sticking his neck out he said, "Robin?"

"Yes, milord," said Robin, and he bowed, somewhat dismayed at how much easier this was becoming and at the same time somewhat proud at his presence of mind.

Oliver John circled Charger and studied the Sea Gate Fortress crest. "I think you have some explaining to do," he said.

"Yes, sir," Robin said, "But first, I bring good news from Lord Stanley Allen, and a gift, milord." Robin produced the bottle of Sweet Water wine and the parchment bearing the signed agreement.

Oliver John eyed the bottle and said, "What have we here?"

"It's a fortified wine," Robin said. "Lord Stanley Allen thought that you might enjoy it."

"Indeed, I might. Let's see." Oliver John set off in the direction of the mansion. "Come along, Robin." For all the time that he had spent at the Ironworks, Robin had never been inside Oliver John's manor. He nodded with approval at the appointments in the parlor. Oliver John was a big man and so was the furniture. Commodious high-backed chairs bracketed a substantial table upon which stood robust candlesticks. A window alcove accommodated a writing desk heaped with parchments, scrolls, bottles of ink, and quills. In one corner, two cushioned armchairs flanked a table draped with an embroidered cloth. Above, plates and goblets stood on shelves mounted on the wall.

Oliver John took down a goblet. "Sit," he said, indicating a bench along the alcove window. He uncorked the bottle, poured himself some of the wine, took a seat at the desk, and removed the parchments from the portfolio. His expression was stern as he read, but then he started to chuckle. The chuckle became a laugh. "Stanley... he said. He lifted his goblet. "To Lord Stanley Allen."

As he had with Lord Stanley Allen, Robin waited a moment to be offered a glass of his own, only to be disappointed. It rankled. He was good enough to come into their homes, to do business with them, but not good enough to merit even the simplest hospitality. Had they known he was a king, they would have been honored to have him in their presence, would have bowed to him instead of expecting him to bow to them. Instead, they tolerated him only insofar as he could do something for them. When he regained his throne, Robin promised himself, neither man would get any favors from him.

"To Lord Stanley Allen," Robin said carefully, wondering what was amusing about the parchment.

"So, we are to make the sword, 'as presented,' and 'anything else' you think he needs?" Oliver John said.

Robin felt his face grow warm. "Yes, sir," he said, trying not to sound surprised. Lord Stanley Allen must have added that language to the scroll when he signed it.

"Clearly, he was impressed with your presentation," Oliver John said.

"I did my best, milord," Robin replied.

Oliver John turned his desk chair so that it faced Robin. "Excellent. I am pleased. I see that sending you was the right decision. Lord Stanley Allen is a good friend and longtime customer. I fully expected you to be successful. Having passed this test, you have given me the confidence to send you as my representative to more prospects."

Robin felt his anger abate slightly. More trips? With any luck, he would never see the inside of the smithy again, and might yet find himself in the Chalklands.

"Now, would you like to tell me how you transformed a donkey into a warhorse?"

Yes, I would, Robin thought, but first, Oliver John, you need to drink a little more wine. "I had set out on the return trip to Riverington." Robin said, "I was coming away from Allenton and sought to find a more expeditious route." There had been no need to tell Empress Alexandra that he had really been taking a detour to search for the Chalklands, and there was no need to tell Oliver John, either. "I did not find it, but I came upon a damsel in distress."

"Oh?" Oliver John said, taking another swallow.

Robin cleared his throat. He had told the Empress that he was a teller of tales, and indeed he was. He had kept alehouses open past last call and had kept David's restless customers entertained with his amusing stories. This was going to be the most engaging tale he ever told. He recounted every snort, snarl, gnashed tooth, torched tree, and ear-shattering bellow of the savage wyvern that threatened the imperiled lady, whose beauty

Robin spared no detail in describing. Oliver John seemed engaged, so when his cup ran dry, rather than break the spell, Robin fetched the bottle and poured, talking all the while. At last, he came to the fatal sword thrust and the swooping off her feet of the —.

"Sword? You had a sword? How came you to have a sword?" Oliver John asked.

"I... I..." Robin felt queasy. "I made it, sir. From scraps and —"

"From scraps? From my foundry? In my smithy, with my tools, on my time? Let's see this sword!"

"Not your time, sir," Robin said as he drew the weapon and handed it to Oliver John. "I stayed late and came in early and —"

"It's all my time, you arrogant insubordinate!" Oliver John bellowed. "I should cut off your head with this sword!" He swung the weapon in wide arc.

Terrified, Robin ducked into a crouch. When his head did not separate from his shoulders, he dared to glance up.

Oliver John twisted the sword about. "Handles very well, good balance —"

"It's the addition of this fuller here, sir." Tentatively, Robin stood. "It lightens the blade without weakening it."

"Good grip here," Oliver John continued.

"The guard is just the right size, not too big so as to add unnecessary weight.

"This engraving on the pommel—"

"—is not simply decorative, sir. Let me show you." He took the sword and turned it pommel-forward. "You see the sharp edges here? If the sword is used as a striking instrument, the pommel can not only deliver a blow but also cut."

Oliver John glared. "You know your sword making. We've established that. That doesn't give you leave to use my resources to make your own. Did Franklin authorize that?"

"No, oh, no." Robin wanted no trouble to fall on Franklin. "He knew nothing of it. It was my idea. I thought it advisable to have a finished sword that incorporates all the optional features we have to offer, to demonstrate. Not to mention, I thought that I might need protection on the road. Which as it turns out, I needed."

Oliver John hefted the sword. "You have made a good case for this. So you may keep it, and your job. I will deduct the value of it from your wages."

Robin blanched. "The value of it" was likely to be high, very high. He had put everything he had learned about sword-making into the weapon, and every useful option. But he simply said, "Thank you, sir. Who knows when I may next need to save myself, not to mention rescue an Empress from a dragon? Speaking of which, in answer to your question about the horse, since the donkey had sustained an injury in her service —"

"He what?"

"He suffered a slight burn. He's going to be fine!" Robin rushed to explain. "He's getting the best of care. He simply needed some rest while his wound heals. The Empress gave me the use of one of her horses, so... so... so that I could continue on my way and deliver to you this contract from Lord Stanley Allen, since she recognized that this is an important commission worth considerably to you."

"Thoughtful of her," Oliver John groused.

"Yes, she was most gracious. She thinks very highly of you, by the way."

Oliver John's eyes brightened. "Does she? The Empress of Sea Gate Fortress?"

"Yes. You've heard of her?"

"Oh, indeed. Ruler of a strong, prosperous domain. A widow, quite reclusive. Some say the evil spell that sent the Emperor to his untimely death also turned her into an old crone. But you found her to be attractive."

"Oh yes, milord. Very."

Oliver John took a thoughtful sip. "And you say she was complimentary of me."

"That she was. In fact, she gave me this letter to present to you." Robin produced the second important missive.

For the second time that day Oliver John's brow wrinkled as he perused a document. He looked up at Robin.

"What know you of this?"

"That you should enter an alliance to provide the Ironworks with a system of defense?" Robin wondered if, having heard of the Empress's charms and widowhood, Oliver John was contemplating an alliance of another sort. "Milord, it's a suggestion that merits your consideration." Robin stood. "I was attacked on the road. An armed highwayman apprehended me, seeking to take the horse and all I carried. Had I not had that sword, I would not be here talking to you now. The brigand has his sights set on Riverington and I don't doubt that there are more of his ilk with similar designs. And as I rode up just today I found myself observing just how vulnerable the Ironworks, and you, milord, are, out here in the open, with no fortifications, no defense force, no soldiers, not even a personal guard. We have been fortunate indeed to have enjoyed peace here but I fear that may not last. It's a violent world out there. Look at what almost happened to me. The Ironworks is an attractive plum and without defenses, it would be easy enough to pluck. You should —"

"Are you telling me what to do?"

Robin felt his temper flare. And why shouldn't he? Clearly, he knew more than Oliver John did. Hadn't Robin shown him how to make better scissors and eyeglasses? Hadn't Robin shown him how to make a bread-saw? All of which were now popular items that had expanded the Ironworks' product line and fattened Oliver John's purse. Had he not taken many of Oliver John's good customers and made better customers out of them? And what thanks had Oliver John shown? An extra coin here and there?

Was Oliver John now going to reject an attractive arrangement simply because it wasn't presented by a gold-braided royal emissary? What was wrong with these people, with Stanley Allen and Oliver John? Robin had had enough of being told that he was arrogant, that he didn't know his place. Couldn't they see who he was? Perhaps they could and didn't want to face the fact that he was in fact better than they were.

Now the Empress, the Empress hadn't stood on ceremony. From their first encounter, she had taken his measure and recognized his true merit. She had entrusted him with almost the same responsibility as had Oliver John. More, one might say, as there was certainly skill called for and more at stake in the enlarging of an empire than there was in increasing the value of a sword-making commission.

"I am suggesting that you take the offer seriously," Robin said, barely able to control his temper. "If you were smart —"

"*If* I were smart!" Oliver John slammed down his goblet. Wine sloshed out and splashed on some documents. "Are you saying I'm not? Was it a mistake to endow you with greater responsibilities and more latitude? I can see that it was as it has simply fed your inflated sense of self-importance." He snatched up the Empress's letter in his big hand and for a moment Robin feared that he meant to crush it, but Oliver John simply gestured with it, saying "I will call on the Empress myself regarding this matter. You on the other hand should report back to the smithy immediately. A hot summer spent in front of that furnace should burn the insolence out of you."

Not a chance, thought Robin. He would not spend another minute in the employ of this haughty ingrate. Why should he when he could be an emissary for the Empress who had already shown herself to be a grateful overseer who rewarded a good effort handsomely?

"I think not," said Robin. "You will have to find some other slave to do your bidding."

"Are you mad? Do you think I offer the opportunities that I've extended to you to just anyone? Where else do you suppose you will get a chance like this to make something of yourself?"

Robin said nothing. If he told Oliver John that he would make his own chances, the man would not believe him.

Oliver John scowled and turned so red that Robin expected steam to billow from his ears. "That being the case, you will remove yourself from these premises immediately and not return!"

"I will be glad to, if you will give me my final wages," Robin said.

"Your final wages will be going to your debt at the Ironworks' store, your rent for your lodgings, and the damage to the donkey," Oliver John said.

Robin felt lightheaded with anger and dismay. It was as though all the months that he had worked here had been for naught. "I will collect the horse I rode in on and be on my way."

"You will not," Oliver John said. "I told you to leave immediately and you will. I will return the horse when I go to convene with the Empress and collect my property."

"No, sir. I have been given safekeeping of the horse by its rightful owner," he produced Alexandra's letter to that effect. "I mean to discharge that responsibility."

Fuming, Oliver John said, "Go, then. If you are as smart as you seem to think you are, you will not let me see you again."

Robin directed Charger back towards the hut. He would have like to have spoken with Franklin, who would no doubt hear of Robin's dismissal from Oliver John, and come to an incorrect and unflattering conclusion, but Robin feared the action that Oliver John might take were he discovered in the smithy. He stopped at Franklin's home thinking to explain what had happened to Babs. Instead, when she opened the door, he found Franklin at his supper.

Franklin pushed away from the table and rose to give Robin a quick embrace. "I am so glad you are back," he said. He peered out the door and spied Charger. "What have you here? Did Lord Oliver John give you this? I heard you had gotten the use of a donkey."

Before Robin could begin to describe what had transpired, he had to be patient and accept Babs' hospitality. He should have been both hungry and thirsty, but the clash with Oliver John had robbed him of his appetite. He barely sipped at his ale and only nibbled at the cheese while Franklin described the strain of trying to keep up with production without Robin's help. Robin bit his lower lip. "I'm not going to be of much help there, I'm afraid."

"What?"

So there was no telling of the battle with the wyvern and the rescue of the Empress. Instead, Robin had to tell of his dismissal.

"But why?" Franklin sputtered.

"Well, see, I had made this sword —"

"You what?"

Robin threw up his hands in protest. "Well I wasn't going to go out on the road defenseless!"

"And you took stock from the smithy?"

Robin nodded.

"And the lord found out about it." Franklin's face became stormy. "I told you! How many times did I tell you? Do not help yourself to the materials."

"I know, I know! You told me, you did. It's not your fault. I thought he would understand my need for protection."

Franklin rested his forehead on the table. When he looked up, his expression was pained.

"Never mind about me. I have good news for you," Robin said, and described the huge commission from Stanley Allen. The smile that he thought this would bring to Franklin's face did not manifest.

"And just how am I to get all this work done singlehandedly?" he asked.

Robin pushed the cheese bits around his plate. "I suspect Lord Oliver John will hire someone else."

Franklin clasped his hands and sighed. "He'll have to if there's to be a prayer of fulfilling this commission."

"See? You will have work aplenty. Extra coins —"

"And there I will be, after all this work is done, with the stake for our own smithy and no partner."

Robin felt his face grow warm. Yes, he had said something about the two of them opening their own shop, but he had never been serious about it. Regaining his kingdom was his only ambition.

"So what will you do now?" Franklin asked. "Where are you bound next? Will you go back to Rose Bank?"

Robin thought about telling Franklin about his new appointment as Empress Alexandra's representative. Somehow, in the light of Franklin's chagrin, it didn't seem wise. "All I know is that I have to leave here tonight. Now." Which although it wasn't quite the truth, wasn't entirely a lie.

At the hut, he looked around with a heavy heart. He would have to abandon the bed that he had built, the latrine that he had dug. The next occupant would enjoy those improvements. He was, however, taking the cook pot, the shovel, the crockery, spare clothes, and other items that he had bought, just as the occupant before him had done.

He would miss the blooming of the rosebush that he had tended. One thing that he would not miss would be spending the night here alone, without Meeyoo. He decided that he would not stay here another minute. He would head into Riverington and find a bed there. There he would find feed and water for his two horses. There he had friends.

CHAPTER FOURTEEN

As Robin approached the Sea Gate Fortress gates, he felt queasy. Since leaving the Ironworks, he had thought about little other than how to explain what had happened between him and Oliver John.

It wasn't as if he had failed. In fact, the expedition could be considered a success. The merchants of Riverington were eager to entertain a proposal from Alexandra's that would result in protection for the settlement. Robin felt only a little guilty about it. It wasn't as if this wasn't a wise move for them. The threat of attack was out there. It was only a matter of time before bandits raided the settlement. If someone held his toes to the fire, he might admit that he may have exaggerated the urgency to act just a little bit.

And, Oliver John too seemed favorably disposed toward uniting with Sea Gate Fortress. True, he might have ulterior motives. However, Robin was confident that Alexandra could handle that.

He felt proud to be bringing the assets of Riverington and the Ironworks into Alexandra's regime. She had been more than generous, in providing care for Duncan and hospitality for him and Meeyoo. He was honored by her faith in him in not only sending him on this mission, but entrusting him with Charger. The weight of the responsibility and the obligation had weighed heavily on him. Now, the scales were back in balance and he felt good about that.

Yet while he had made a new friend in Oliver John for Alexandra, he had made an enemy for himself. On the face of it, his actions might have seemed rash, even short-sighted and ill-conceived. Yet he realized that his resentment had been brewing for some time. It had never been his plan to make working at the blacksmith shop his life's work. It had always been a means to an end, the end being to find and regain his kingdom. He would just be getting about that a little sooner than he had planned.

The gate's chamberlain recognized Robin, of course, yet requested to see his papers nevertheless, which didn't surprise Robin. Everyone that he had met at Sea Gate Fortress seemed devoted to and protective of the Empress and were dedicated to the meticulous performance of their tasks.

"What of these horses?" the chamberlain asked.

"I'll be returning Charger to the Empress. This other mount is my own."

The chamberlain nodded. "Take them both to the stables, then. I will send word that you have arrived."

At the stables, Robin was greeted by the head groom who handed off Charger and Thief to stable boys.

"How is Duncan?" Robin asked.

"Much improved," said the stable master. "Go see him."

Robin found the donkey in his stall, munching a carrot. At the sight of Robin, the donkey lifted his head and gave an enthusiastic bray. Robin felt warm with delight and lightened in spirit to see the animal standing and looking clear-eyed. His delight became despondency as he realized that he and Duncan would be parting company. At least Duncan seemed to be on the mend. Robin was already in enough trouble with Oliver John without adding the loss of property to the man's list of grievances.

"How's that wound?" he asked. The burn was covered with a bandage and Robin hesitated to remove it.

The straw rustled and Meeyoo emerged. With a loud "Meeyoo!" she came and rubbed her jowls against his ankles. He picked her up and scratched her behind her ears. "I missed you, Meeyoo. It's just as well that you weren't with me, though, as I had some terrible adventures. And I'm afraid we need to find a new home."

"How's that?" came a voice from behind him. Robin turned to find Alexandra had entered the stall, carrying a tray that held a tankard, half a loaf of bread, and a candle. He remembered to bow and upon straightening took note of her costume. She wore light slippers on her feet. Her hair had been plaited for bedtime and he suspected that the long cloak that she wore covered a nightgown.

"The chamberlain sent a messenger to tell me that you had arrived. I thought that after your travels, you might be thirsty or hungry."

"Indeed, I am both. Much obliged," he said, discomfited that his arrival had interfered with her retiring.

"So, tell me about the journey," she said.

"Aye, well, it's a long story but the short of it is that you have good prospects for two new alliances. I will tell you all about it but first, what of Duncan here?"

"Leigh tells me he's mending well. She still has the wound bandaged as you can see. She wants to keep it covered until a bit more of a scar forms. But apparently it's healing over. In any case, he has good appetite and good humor."

"That is good news. I am greatly in her debt."

Alexandra discounted that with a wave of her hand. "She is just doing what she loves: healing."

"Be that as it may, Lord Oliver John will collect him when he comes to speak with you about the alliance."

Alexandra clapped her hands together. "Excellent! Come, tell me about it and why it is that you need a new home."

She led him from the stables and they strolled across the bailey toward the castle.

"I... resigned my position at the Ironworks," Robin said. "Lord Oliver John and I had a parting of the ways."

Alexandra arched a brow.

"Not to worry. That will not negatively affect any agreement that you might strike with him. He is well aware of the need for fortification, especially in light of what befell me on the road." Robin related the encounter with the highwayman. "That incident also impressed upon the people of Riverington the need to establish defenses. So they as well wish to discuss an alliance."

"Great news! Success on both counts. I believe we have cause to celebrate. I will declare a feast."

"Whoa, wait. No agreements have struck. All I have accomplished was to get the parties to consider it."

"And that's all you were charged with doing. So you have succeeded. That's good news. I believe in celebrating good news whenever it comes as there is no shortage of bad news," said Alexandra. "I do regret that my good fortune came at the expense of your calamity. How frightening for you to be attacked."

"I'm none the worse for wear. I got the better part of the bargain out of it. I gained a horse. Old and swaybacked, but a horse nonetheless."

"So, you are in possession of stolen merchandise? No doubt the horse was stolen by that highwayman from someone else."

Robin felt his face grow hot.

"I thought so too, as did the alderman at Riverington but neither of us could find a clue as to the rightful owner. The alderman thought I might as well keep it. I pledged to return him if the true owner is ever discovered."

Alexandra chuckled. "I was just having a fun at your expense. Truly, that sounds fair enough. If you are not returning to the Ironworks, where are you bound?"

Excellent question, thought Robin. What was left to do but return to the road and continue to search for the Chalklands? He had a few coins and could raise some more by selling off the tools and household items that he had purchased for the hut. "I really hadn't given that much thought. I was focused on getting here, seeing Duncan and Meeyoo, returning Charger to you, and telling you about the prospects for alliances."

Alexandra was silent for a moment. "Well, then, I have an idea. Since you are, at least for the moment, at loose ends, perhaps you would consider one more foray on my behalf. To Allenton?" She looked a question at Robin. "To hear you tell it, Lord Stanley Allen is more prosperous than I had thought."

"He's quite the successful merchant. Prosperous, yes. I would say on a par with Lord Oliver John. They have a business relationship, and I believe are friends as well."

"Then perhaps also should Sea Gate Fortress be a friend, would you agree?"

"You are asking my opinion?" Night and day from yesterday when Oliver John had almost cut Robin's head off with a sword for voicing an opinion.

"Well, you just came from there."

"Then yes, I would have to say he would be a worthy league."

"So, would you wish to return there and discuss it with him? I would make you an offer similar to the previous mission: expenses for the journey and compensation if you are successful."

"Compensation?" A return visit to Allenton would not bring him closer to the Chalklands. He had already determined his kingdom must lie elsewhere. But his parting of the ways with Oliver John had depleted his war chest, which "compensation" could replenish. "Such as?"

Alexandra tilted her head and thought for a moment. "You can have the use of Charger again. You can hardly ride a swaybacked horse any distance. You can leave him here. I don't doubt that Leigh will want to see if there's something she can do for him."

Robin scratched his head. Wherever he was going from here, he would get there faster with a mount like Charger. "I would be honored to be in your service," he said with a bow, already planning to revisit Eian at Sweet Water on the way to Allenton. This bottle of wine, he vowed, he would himself enjoy.

"I'm delighted to hear it. But tonight, you should rest. We do have accommodations in the castle keep, unless you truly prefer to sleep in the stables."

Robin chuckled. Between sleeping in the stables here and at Allenton, he had had quite enough of that lately. "Not to seem ungrateful, but what about Meeyoo?"

Alexandra waved her hand. "Oh, she can stay with you, of course. We have several domesticated animals in the castle: cats, dogs, caged song birds, fish in bowls. It sounds like a regular menagerie but they all do have their little jobs, their place in the scheme of things."

"In that case, a proper bed would be most welcome," he said.

At their approach, the guards spread wide the doors to the castle. "Then, I shall have a chamber prepared. If you will return to the stables and collect your things, I will have a chambermaid meet you there and show you to your room. And tomorrow night, you will be our honored guest at the celebration." Alexandra handed him the candle. "If you will excuse me..."

To his amazement, she cut him a curtsy. He returned a most sincere bow.

The chambermaid that met him at the stables surprised him by honoring him with a bow and calling him "sir."

As they crossed the inner bailey and entered the castle's great hall, Robin felt the stress and strain of the recent months drain from his head and shoulders. He felt strangely at home. Perhaps it was owed to being in a castle. Though it was not Bell Castle, it nevertheless felt familiar. He thought that might be because all castles were similar in purpose and design. For whatever reason, the volume and layout of the great hall just felt right. He could guess at what rooms occupied the wings: kitchen and barracks to one side, perhaps; guard rooms and bathhouse to the other.

On the castle's second floor, he followed the chambermaid along a gallery overlooking the great hall. This would be a busy floor: not quite as public as the floor below but not nearly as private as those above. Likely, top ranking military officers and castle managers were accommodated on this floor where they would have quick access to the wall walk and the watch tower.

The chambermaid led him up a winding staircase and then to a chamber. She touched the flame of her candle to one on the dressing table and Robin could see that though the room was small, it offered all the accommodations an overnight guest needed: bed, table and chair, clothes chest, dressing table with a bowl and pitcher, chamber pot. The brazier for heating the room would not be needed this warm night. The furnishings, while of an obvious high quality, were not elaborate, and in that, Robin found something that was both comfortable and comforting. The linens encasing the fluffy pillows and covering the mattress were not linen at all, but cotton, cool, soft and damp, almost clammy to the touch. The humidity of Sea Gate Fortress's location was pervasive, he was discovering. The candle's stick was made of a wood that was pocked in many places and of a weathered grey color. The same type of wood framed the mirror that hung over the dressing table.

"Driftwood, sir," the chambermaid said when he fingered it.

"Driftwood?"

"Yes, sir. Scoured from our shoreline. It's anyone's guess from what distant land the wood originated." She flung out an arm as if to indicate the far reaches of the Earth.

Robin looked across the room and out the chamber's small window but all he could see was a starlit night sky.

"If you require anything else, sir, just ring the bell," said the chambermaid. "Also, you will find the castellan's quarters on the floor below."

CHAPTER FIFTEEN

When she had gone, Robin opened the rucksack and let Meeyoo out to make a careful circuit of the room. Having satisfied herself that no threats lurked in the corners or under the furniture, she leaped onto the bed. She signaled her approval of the bedding by rolling around on her back and stretching.

As he transferred his few personal possessions to the chest, Robin regarded his clothes with dismay. His shop clothes would never do for appearances at court. Over the past months, his own royal cloak had taken a beating. The only thing suitable that he had were the clothes Oliver John had given him and which until now he had forgotten that he still had. Robin wondered if Oliver John realized that the garments had not been returned and was even now levying a charge of theft?

Robin sank into the bed thinking the worry would keep him awake. When Meeyoo roused him before morning's light, as was her wont, he was surprised to find that he had actually fallen asleep and slept through the night.

"Meeyoo, there is no work today," he muttered. "You didn't need to rouse me so early." He lay there for a moment with Meeyoo stretched out on his belly. The moist breeze that wafted in from the small window was cooling. He heard a steady low rumble that he thought must be the wind and which he found relaxing.

When next he opened his eyes, it was well past dawn. Meeyoo was on the chamber floor mewling and nosing the door. When Robin opened it, he found that what had attracted her attention were the aromas coming from a tray of food. It was what he had been used to having for breakfast before his morning repast became hot water with herbs and, if he was fortunate, a piece of dark bread. He recognized sliced ham and turkey, mild cheeses, smoked herring and whitefish, white bread, and ale.

Alongside them were two items that he did not recognize: both egg shaped, with bumpy skins, one green and the other amber orange. The orange one smelled fruity and sweet while the green one had a vegetable aroma. He devoured the bread and shared pieces of the meats, fish, and cheese with Meeyoo, then tentatively poked at the colored eggs with his knife. Neither turned out to be any sort of egg at all. The orange one was juicy and tartly sweet, with a center of black roe that tasted not like fish eggs but almost like pepper. The green one had flesh that was soft and buttery, and a hard pit. He decided that he liked both of them and wished he hadn't eaten all the bread; he would have spread some of the green egg stuff on it.

One thing that the tray hadn't included was a bread-saw. Robin resolved to craft one for Alexandra at his first opportunity.

Having enjoyed the best meal that he had had in recent memory, he could have easily gone back to bed. But there was the matter of getting himself outfitted for tonight's feast to address. It seemed he had no choice but to wear the only suit he had, purloined though it may be.

"Might as well be hanged for a sheep as a lamb, right Meeyoo?" he said. Still, even these garments were in need of freshening. Intending to find the castlellan or a laundress who could give them some attention, he got himself cleaned and shaved and dressed in the newer of his work clothes. Tucking the garments under his arm, he set off in search of the castellan. He found him not in his chamber so Robin headed next for the first floor and the kitchen. As he traversed the gallery overlooking the great hall he saw an audience in progress.

Alexandra sat on her throne. The sight of the Emperor's throne standing empty next to hers touched Robin's heart. A heavy crown sat atop her head and a weighty purple robe covered her from neck to ankles. Robin stood in the gallery for a few moments and listened to a lord petitioning for loan to fund the bolstering of his domain's defenses. Robin sighed. How often had he heard such pleas? Often enough to know that the answer was never an easy yea or nay. He had enjoyed weighing the pros and cons of such decisions. Who today sat on his throne, making these judgments for his kingdom? His wife? His sons? An interloper? Robin gripped the gallery's railing, inundated by a sudden wave of estrangement so strong that he felt faint.

"Are you all right, sir?" came a voice at his back.

Robin blinked away tears and turned to face the chambermaid who had assisted him yesterday. "I'm fine, thank you."

She curtsied. "Is there anything I can do for you, sir?" she asked.

Robin took a deep breath to collect himself. "Regarding tonight's feast: how formal is it?" he asked. "When I set out yesterday for Sea Gate Fortress, I had not planned for an extended stay."

The chambermaid smiled. "Oh, you needn't be overly concerned, sir. We're not formal people. This is an island. We often end up making do with what we have right here."

Island? He was closer to the sea than he imagined, and so far from the Chalklands that he felt lost. Despair again threatened to overtake him. "Will this do?" he asked, shaking out the suit.

"I'm certain that will be fine, sir," she replied.

"It could use some freshening, though," he said. "I was on my way to inquire about that."

"Allow me to take care of that for you, sir." she said. "I will have it returned to your chamber this afternoon."

She took the garments and left him in the gallery, his forearms propped on the railing. As he stood listening to Alexandra conduct the business of Sea Gate fortress, his thoughts and emotions fluttered about as though they were leaves in a stormy wind.

When at last the audience was concluded and the great hall had cleared, Alexandra stood. A lady-in-waiting appeared and stood at attention while Alexandra removed the heavy robe and exchanged the crown for a simple short veil to cover her hair, held in place by a lightly-jeweled circlet. The clothes that she had been wearing beneath the royal robe were startlingly simple. Her linen gown's foreshortened sleeves left her forearms bare and the raised hem grazed the top of ankle-high boots. She wore no jewelry or other finery.

She spotted him in the gallery and with a wave beckoned him to join her.

"Well, good morning," she said. "I hope you passed the night well."

Robin laughed. "I think I could have slept the entire day away."

"I can imagine. It has been a few trying days for you."

You have no idea, he found himself thinking.

"And your breakfast?"

"Fit for a king," he said, trying to keep wistfulness from coloring his speech.

"I suspect that you are eager to get started on your latest campaign. However, I thought it might be helpful if you were more familiar with Sea Gate Fortress. And I do hope you will stay for tonight's feast, which, if it weren't for you, we wouldn't be having."

"I am looking forward to it."

"Well, then. Let's take a short walk, shall we?"

She led him out of the castle and in the direction of the fortress wall at the rear. Over the top of the wall, Robin could see only sky. The absence of trees or hills in his view gave him a strange detached feeling of floating in space. He wondered if this was how birds felt as they flew. As they drew closer, the horizon came into view, but that was simply a line where the lighter blue of the sky met the darker blue of the sea. There was nothing else; no buildings, no land, no trees. At a distance, far beyond what he could see, he imagined lay foreign lands of which he had heard but had never visited. He was suddenly struck by the staggering bravery of the first sailors to board a vessel and head out to sea, confident that they would reach a land that they could not see and knew of only in theory or by rumor.

They reached a narrow lookout tower that stood taller than a tree.

"From the tower you can have an all-encompassing view of the fortress and our surroundings," Alexandra said. They climbed to the top. Indeed, on three sides, Robin saw the tops of the trees, buildings, and walls that encircled the fortress, and the lands beyond. Within site of the castle's towers, an inlet led to the fortress's dock. At a distance he could make out the viaduct that linked the island to the mainland. He turned back toward the ocean and looked down. To anyone approaching from the sea, the fortress wall presented a sheer face of stone that was somehow not stone. Robin asked about it.

"Ah, no, it's not stone, of which we have little, just as we have little timber. So we make our own stone, of sand and crushed oyster shell. Of that we have plenty."

At the fortress's base, sandy soil bearded with groundcover and stubbly bushes sloped sharply down to another wall. Below that, another steep slope ended in a narrow stretch of sand lapped by the waves of the ocean.

"Sometimes I think I'd like to build a staircase so that I could simply climb down from here to there," said Alexandra, drawing a line with her finger down the slope to the water's edge.

"Why?"

"I like to walk on the beach. It relaxes me and helps me to think clearly. As it is, to get to that spot is a major undertaking. I have to dress to ride, put together an escort, have horses saddled, go all the way out to the gate... it's a half-day's ride."

Robin snorted. "Not quite half a day."

"Well, in any event, it's not an easy spot to get to."

"That's as it should be. To build a rear gate or stairs or other access to this spot would simply undermine your defenses," Robin said. "It would create a vulnerable point that would have to be guarded continuously. Here at least any attacker would first have to risk a sea approach past two towers to reach the dock and attempt a landing at a very narrow spot, in full view of sentries and soldiers, with no cover whatsoever, then try to scale the walls. The chance of any kind of success at all is very slim and few would attempt it."

Not for the first time, Alexandra regarded him with suspicion and Robin realized that he had spoken with way too much erudition and confidence.

"Of course you're right," said Alexandra. She turned towards him and with narrowed eyes said, "How know you this?"

Robin felt his face grow warm. "I... I talk to people. I've had a beer with guardsmen."

"Likely you have, but that's not the truth of the matter." She propped her right hand on her hip. "You are not exactly who you say you are. You are not a blacksmith, a cutler, an itinerant salesman, or a troubadour."

"I am!"

She shook her head. "Perhaps you can do all those things and more besides, and perhaps you do them well. But that's not who you are. Who are you, Robin?"

He gazed out at the sea. He stood at the end of land. Without boarding a boat and going out into the ocean, he could not get any farther from the Chalklands than he was at this moment. He took a deep breath. "I am... that is, I once was... I mean..." He sighed. "I am a king. I am King Bewilliam, ruler of the Chalklands."

"The Chalklands?"

DEVORAH FOX

"Far from here. North, I think." He laughed. "I doubt it's across that water. I'm not sure. In all my travels of late, I have approached nothing like my home realm. I'm beginning to think it is of another world entirely."

"You mean, like of a spirit world?"

Robin did not reply, deciding it best not to pursue that theory lest Alexandra think he had taken complete leave of his senses.

Alexandra pressed her lips together and cocked her head to the right. "What happened?"

"You believe me?"

"That would explain much: your bearing, your speech. Your confidence and competence. Your leadership abilities and mettle in a crisis. That you'll take counsel and direction but not an order. The way you don't seem to know how or when to bow and the reason that you don't seem to know your place. I thought at first that it must be simply your arrogance and pride —"

"Arrogant? I am not arrogant!"

Alexandra grinned. "But it's more than that. You truly are not accustomed to recognizing anyone as your superior." She curtsied. "King Bewilliam."

Robin felt his blush deepen. "Please. Such formalities are not necessary between fellow dragon-slayers," he said.

Alexandra straightened. "What happened? Were you deposed?"

"No, I don't think so."

"You don't think so? Don't you know?"

"No, I don't." Robin took a deep breath, then described finding himself alone and destitute in the cow pasture a half-day's ride from Rose Bank.

"And you don't know how that happened?"

Robin shook his head. "I have come to suspect a spell, an enchantment."

Now it was Alexandra's turn to snicker. "An enchantment," she echoed drily.

Robin arched an eyebrow. "You don't believe in enchantments?"

Alexandra shook her head. "Not really. Do you?"

"I don't know what to believe any more. I can't come up with any other explanation. One minute I was king, the next minute, POOF!" Robin flung his fingers wide.

"Do you remember anything?"

"Not much, and the longer that I am away, the dimmer my memory becomes."

"Well, I have an idea then. Come with me."

He followed her from the tower back inside the castle. Alexandra waylaid a servant. "Run ahead please and tell Ruth that we are on our way to consult with her briefly," she said. The servant bowed, then hurried ahead while Alexandra mounted the stairs in a more leisurely fashion and led Robin down a corridor.

They paused outside the entrance to a chamber. The servant emerged, bowed, and said, "She is ready for you."

"Thank you. Follow me," Alexandra said to Robin and then entered the chamber.

The room, while not overly large, was somehow inviting. Richly colored wall hangings and draperies glowed with warm reflected light. Sunlight refracted through colored glass lanterns that hung like gems from the ceiling. Chairs and benches upholstered with velvety cushioning invited the visitor to sit and relax.

A woman with golden hair wearing a light yellow gown seemed to float more than walk towards them, her gentle smile and sparkling eyes as warm as the light that beamed through the open chamber window and glinted off a gold goblet encrusted with jewels.

"Alexandra," the woman said, bowing slightly and taking Alexandra's hands in both of hers. She straightened and said, "So nice to see you. But this is not a social call? You have something that you wish to discuss. Not a problem, I hope."

"A problem, yes, but not mine."

"I am glad to hear that." She turned to Robin. "Hello, you must be Robin. Leigh told me of your bravery. I am Ruth."

Who was Ruth? Royalty? A servant? Robin looked a question to Alexandra. Bow? Not bow? and finally decided that there was nothing to be lost by honoring a charming and gracious lady.

She returned the greeting with a curtsey. "You have our most heartfelt gratitude for coming to our lady's aid."

"Not that I needed it, Ruth," Alexandra said.

The woman looked at Robin for confirmation.

"Not that she needed it," Robin said.

"Of course not," Ruth replied with a hearty laugh. "Well, how can I be of help to you today?"

"Ruth is a counselor," Alexandra said to Robin. "She has helped many, young and old, rich and poor, with baffling problems that have defied other solutions. They were ever so grateful. Look, one merchant gave her this as a thank-you." Alexandra picked up the bejeweled goblet.

"Robin appears to have lost his memory," Alexandra said to Ruth. "Not of everything, just of some things that are nevertheless very important. He thinks he might be under some kind of spell."

Ruth nodded. "Yes, when we have problems with how our mind works, it can be very perplexing, very disturbing. It's so mysterious, and we can't imagine how something like that could have happened unless some outside force has interfered with us. Please, sit down." She indicated that Robin should take one of two armchairs that flanked a small table atop which were a clear glass sphere, a deck of cards, and a faceted chunk of rosy-colored quartz.

Robin had seen these objects in the chambers of fortune-tellers and soothsayers. Was Ruth a magician, or even a witch? Weren't all witches supposed to be ugly, with long warty noses and scraggly black hair? Perhaps Ruth wasn't a witch. Or maybe she was, and was already using magic to appear as a lovely golden-haired woman. Robin felt a twinge of dread, but then again, who better to counter an enchantment than another witch?

"Let me ask you a few questions and please be honest. It won't serve you at all to prevaricate. That will just keep the truth hidden. Before you discovered the memory loss, had you had much to drink?"

"No, not any more than usual."

"And how much is usual?"

"Not... I know what you're asking and no, this was no 'morning after.' I had not been on a bender. I've done plenty enough of those to know, and this wasn't one of them. I had none of the other symptoms, the headache, the dry mouth, nothing like that. "

"Had you had anything unusual to eat or drink?"

"I don't honestly remember but I don't think so. I felt fine in every other way except that I was disoriented. I found myself in an unfamiliar place with no knowledge of how I got there."

Ruth looked at Alexandra. "Does not sound like a medical problem or a poisoning." She turned back to Robin. "Some foods and drinks have hypnotic agents that can make us feel as though we have been bewitched."

Robin chuckled. "Believe me, I know. As a youth, I did sample some that left me feeling, well, more cursed than bewitched."

Ruth smiled. "Well, then, what is your most immediate memory prior to your finding yourself disoriented?"

"That's the thing. I don't have an 'immediate' memory. What I do remember goes back much further and doesn't provide any useful clues."

Ruth clasped her hands in her lap and looked down, lost in silent thought for a moment. When she again looked up, she said, "This memory that you seek to recapture may be hiding behind another truth that you wish to avoid. You may have to confront the one to attain the other. I can help you cut through the veil that clouds your mind, but you must be prepared to face whatever it is that hides behind that veil. The fact that you have such a complete blankness leads me to suspect that you are avoiding dealing with something very painful. I would not blame you for not wanting to revisit it."

Robin glanced at Alexandra, then back at Ruth but neither woman spoke.

"Give it some thought. I will help you if you wish it. But for me to be able to do you any good, you must be committed to the process," Ruth said.

She stood, and Robin took that as a cue that the audience was over. He stood also and Alexandra rose from her seat.

"Thank you, Ruth," she said.

"I hope to see you again, Robin," Ruth said.

"Thank you," Robin murmured, at a loss for anything wittier. Ruth's words had left him with an uneasy feeling, not unlike heading down a dark road on a moonless night.

As they walked along the corridor leading from Ruth's chamber, Alexandra asked, "Well, what do you think?"?

"I thought that you said you didn't believe in enchantments."

"I don't, really."

"But your counselor, Ruth, with her crystal? You believe in her, in what she says."

"Ruth is no soothsayer, privy to cosmic secrets. What she is, is a very astute judge of character. A good listener. The crystal is just a device. It gets the questioner to relax and be open. Then Ruth can discern truths the questioner has been hiding, not only from others, but from himself."

Robin thought about David and his Tarot cards.

"And she is good at seeing things from many angles, at perceiving options and possibilities that others may not. And if they are avoiding an advisable course of action, either out of ignorance or fear, she uses the 'magic arts' as a way to persuade them to consider a different approach by telling them that Fate has opened another way for them.

"So, no, Ruth is not a soothsayer or sorceress. Instead, she believes that many of the tribulations that besiege us are of our own doing. The result of poor decision-making or not paying attention or selfish motives. And that we can make our own good fortunes."

Alexandra chuckled softly. "I know, it isn't welcome news to hear that what you wish to recall is blocked by a painful memory you would rather avoid. But perhaps it's not as bad as you fear. Let's ride down to the beach. You might find, as I do, that a walk along the beach loosens the chains that bind your thoughts."

Robin shrugged. "If that be your wish."

He followed her to the stables. Alexandra had Charger saddled for Robin, and chose a handsome walking horse for herself. They exited the fortress's front gate. Alexandra led them to a trail that by its somewhat overgrown appearance seemed to be infrequently used. They rode in silence single-file along a narrow track that switched back twice as they worked their way around the tiers of protective walls. Grass gave way to plants that bore small goblet-shaped flowers and vined across ground that was more sand than soil. When they at last arrived at the shore, Alexandra said, "This is the spot that I wanted to reach."

Robin looked back up at the fortress walls which now loomed formidably far above them.

"Looks impenetrable, doesn't it?" Alexandra said.

"As it should."

"But even the most formidable obstacle will yield to a strong will." She punched Robin lightly on the arm. "Listen to me, now I sound like Ruth. It's beautiful here, don't you think? Let's just put our cares behind for a moment. May I suggest that you take off your boots lest you ruin them with salt water."

Alexandra unlaced her own shoes and, reaching beneath her skirt, rolled down her stockings. They set their footwear on a rocky ledge well away from the surf's spray. Robin saw now how well the short length of her gown suited beach-walking. They set off barefoot along the damp sand.

Robin had often gone for long rides about his kingdom and found that indeed, getting away from the bustle of the court and castle freed his mind. Here, he found the unbroken expanse of sea and sky almost unnerving, as if he were no longer sure of what he knew to be true. He kept having to look at the sand, shrubs, and trees that climbed toward the reassuring solidity of the fortress walls. He found that if he stood too long in any one spot, the tide would seem to suck the sand right out from under his heels. It was uncomfortably like having the royal rug pulled out from under his feet.

He had noticed that Sea Gate Fortress was normally a windy place. Sometimes it was merely breezy while other times it was gusty, but in all cases, the wind seemed never to be still. Here, the wind coming off the water pushed at his hair and dampened his clothes and had an aroma unlike anything that he had smelled before. It smelled salty — he hadn't realized that salt had an odor. He thought that he could smell the fish that lived in the sea. And the air had a green smell, something like but not quite the same as hay or grass.

He was unprepared as well for the sound of the ocean. At first it seemed like the wind in the trees, a loud, continuous, and steady roar. After a few moments he realized that it wasn't as regular as it had at first seemed. There were several notes — whispering, sighing, splashing, and crashing — that alternated in a sort of rhythm. There seemed to be an inhalation as the tide drew back, followed by the most minute of pauses, and then an exhalation as the surf rushed to the sea. He decided that the sound of the ocean breathing was not unpleasant.

Birds worked the shoreline in search of food. Robin saw plump birds that were somewhat pigeon-like in size, but had feathers of pure gray and white. They didn't sing or chirp but instead had a cry that sounded almost like laughter. Tall birds with long necks and long beaks had even longer stilt-like legs. Smaller, sparrow-sized birds skittered about on skinny little legs.

Along the strand were scattered brilliant sapphire jewels the size of his fist that glowed in the sunlight. They looked like tiny toy boats with fluted sails. Robin was amazed that precious jewels simply washed up and lay about on the beach. Had there been a shipwreck along this shore? But he saw little other debris, not the merest scrap of fabric and only a few pieces of what the chambermaid had called driftwood. Was there a cave or underwater lode nearby and the gems simply washed up onto the beach? Were such riches part of Sea Gate's wealth? Did servants ride down here every day to harvest them? He reached to pick one up.

"Don't touch that!" cried Alexandra.

Struck with sudden dread, Robin turned to look at her. Were the jewels cursed? Maybe that explained why they were lying on the beach and no one had collected them. The presence of magic charms so near him unnerved him, as if he were especially vulnerable to enchantments and might fall even deeper under a spell.

"Poke it with a stick if you must, or your knife, but don't touch it with your fingers, and don't let those strands get near your skin," said Alexandra.

His arm outstretched, Robin jabbed the jewel with his knife and was startled to find that it wasn't solid but quivered like jelly. He jumped back. "What is that?"

Alexandra chuckled. "It's a sea creature."

"That? That's an animal? But it has no eyes. No mouth, no ears, no legs."

"But it does have a tail, after a fashion. See those streamers? Or maybe those are legs. Whatever they are, they are poisonous. There are stingers on those strands that have venom, like a snake or a bee. The sting is very painful and will leave nasty red welts on your skin that will last for days. We have seen people die from the stings although not often. Mostly the stings don't kill but they do cause great discomfort. We have found that these creatures can sting even after they are dead. So we keep our distance. After a few days, they dry up and disappear into the sand or get washed back out to sea."

"Incredible!" Robin said. "But it is so beautiful." Cautiously he poked at the puffy body below the fluted sail. "It looks like a little sailing ship."

He stepped well back and they continued to walk. After going a few paces, Robin said, "I do have one somewhat recent memory. The fight with the wyvern brought it to mind. I recalled a campaign that I led to get rid of a dragon. We had to journey far, very far, to fight not only the dragon but to demolish his lair.

We were gone for several seasons, maybe even a year. When I returned to the castle, things did not seem the same."

"How did you find them to be different?"

"My ministers and courtiers seemed confused. They seemed hesitant to respond to my orders."

"They didn't defy you?"

"No." Robin kicked at a shell with a bare toe and sent it skipping into the water. "They were tentative. I don't know how else to explain it. In many ways, it felt as if I wasn't even there. As if I had never come back from the campaign. Maybe I didn't! Maybe it was all a part of the enchantment. Maybe I had gotten bewitched at the dragon's lair. Maybe I thought I had returned but I hadn't, not really."

"Had you met any magicians at any point during the campaign?"

"Not that I recall. But what else would explain that it felt like no one really seemed to hear or see me? What else could?"

Alexandra lowered her head and fixed her gaze on her steps as she ambled along. "What indeed? That is curious. I don't know. Perhaps there had been an uprising of sorts while you were gone. Perhaps your ministers were plotting some kind of coup and hadn't quite completed their plans, weren't quite ready to pull it off. Maybe they hadn't expected you to return from dragon-slaying so soon, or even at all."

She looked at Robin as if to ask, what do you think of that idea? "So there they were. You had returned and resumed leadership. But there were those who were uncertain as to who really was in control."

Robin shrugged. "That makes sense on some level. Except that before I left I hadn't even the slightest hint that anyone was unhappy with my leadership or wanted to usurp the throne."

"Oh, you know, someone always does. If you think that idea has merit, give it some thought. Maybe you will discern the seeds of resentment in one of your staff that you had overlooked. Personally, I think it makes a lot more sense than some magic spell, especially since you don't recall encountering any wizards or witches."

What could have turned his trusted ministers against him?

"What had you thought to do?" Alexandra asked. "Where were you bound when you stopped to help me fight the wyvern?"

"Help that you didn't need," Robin said with a smile.

"Right. Were you on your way back to your kingdom in the... where did you say?"

"Chalklands. Not precisely. I was to visit that customer of Oliver John's in Allenton, Stanley Allen. I had hoped that I might find that I was nearing my kingdom, or perhaps make the acquaintance of some wayfarer who might have knowledge of the area. But I did not. I think I might be too far south. If I am in fact in an earthly realm at all."

Alexandra glared. "Of course this is an earthly realm and there is no other. We should return to the castle and confer with my cartographer. You can tell him of your travels, describe the lands through which you have passed. At the very least that will contribute to his knowledge and enrich his maps. If you tell him of the Chalklands, maybe he can figure out where they are, how far you are from them, and how you might get there. He's very learned, very wise."

This did not surprise Robin in the least. Alexandra's court did not lack for talented people. Leigh the physician, Ruth the counselor, and now a learned cartographer.

As they drew near the cartographer's chamber, Alexandra said in a whisper, "How do you want to be called?"

Robin stopped in his tracks. That was a good question. "I don't know that it serves for people to know I'm a king. They may be puzzled by my appearance. It might raise more questions than it answers."

"Good point," said Alexandra. "But I would also like to see you accorded some respect or at least head off the expectation of a bow that they'll get too late if they get it at all."

Robin felt his face grow warm.

Alexandra tapped her lip with the tip of her index finger in thought. "I know," she said, raising the finger. "We will call you Master Robin. You are a Master Cutler."

Robin chuckled. "Let's hope that doesn't get back to Franklin or Oliver John. I don't think either of them would be pleased that you awarded me a promotion."

"We'll worry about that at some other time. Here we are."

Robin followed her into the chamber. Lit by lanterns, the room was crammed with tables, stools, shelves, and desks piled high with parchments, and baskets filled with scrolls. Tapestries and drawings, all depicting lands and waters, covered the walls. Some of the maps were monochromatic and consisted of lines with numbers and writing. Others were lavishly illustrated in colored inks.

Small globes stood atop desks and large ones stood in stands on the floor. A telescope in a stand pointed out a window. Inkwells, tumblers filled with quills, sticks of chalk, short measuring sticks, and straight edges littered the desks.

Standing at one desk, a small man peered closely at a document through a looking glass. Wispy blonde hair poked out from under a well-worn blue cloth cap unlike any other that Robin had ever seen. A narrow band encircled the entire cap and attached to the front was a short piece like a small shield that extended out over the forehead.

"James," said Alexandra but the man did not respond. "Oh, James," Alexandra said, a little louder and more insistently.

The man looked about him and finally faced in their direction. "Oh!" he said. He grasped his cap by the shield piece, and lifting it from his head, swept it to his waist in a bow.

"Oh, James," Alexandra said. "You do me such an honor."

"It's always a delight to have you visit, Madame."

"Sorry to interrupt you, James, but I have someone very special that I want you to meet. This is Master Robin."

James stepped out from behind the desk and offered Robin his hand, which Robin gladly shook, assuming this meant that the cartographer James wasn't expecting any more elaborate obeisance.

"Robin is a master cutler," Alexandra said, "and an itinerant merchant and the veteran of many land travels."

"Indeed!" said James, his eyes growing brighter. "Have you time to tell me where you've been?"

"That's why I'm here," said Robin. He couldn't help but remark on the man's unusual cap. "Unusual headgear, sir," he said. "I don't believe that I've ever seen anything like it.

"Well, you probably haven't. It's of my own design. Inspired by something I spied on one of my travels. I was a sailor once."

"Robin also needs your help, James. He has been to a land to which he'd like to return, but he isn't certain where it is."

James chuckled. "You misplaced an entire land?"

"It would appear that way."

"Well, that isn't all that hard to do. I often misplace my reading stones, only to find that I've buried them under the very parchment that I wanted to examine."

The man could use a set of eyeglasses, Robin thought, and put a pair alongside "bread-saw" on his list of gifts to make for his new Sea Gate Fortress friends.

"Is this land across the sea?" James asked.

"I don't think so. I think it may be north of here, but by many days' travel."

"Ah, well at least that tells me what map we need." James beckoned Robin to follow him to a long table covered with stacks of books and documents. He gestured at a stool. "Sit, please. Madame, will you be joining us?"

"We may be at this a while," she replied. "Let me see about getting us some refreshments." She stepped outside the chamber and Robin heard her call, "Clarissa! If you would be so kind, would you fetch us a pitcher of cider and some cups please?" She crossed the room and joined them at the table. "Proceed."

"When did you last see this land?" James asked Robin.

"It was late winter, early spring."

"Describe the weather to me. What was the temperature? Was there precipitation?"

"It was mild, with the daytime requiring a light outerwear. Nights were cold."

"Freezing?"

"Sometimes."

"Was there snow?"

"Not this last winter, although there have been winters when there has been snow. Not a lot, though."

"We rarely get snow here," said Alexandra. "In fact, it's so rare, it's quite an occasion when we do. A few years ago we had several inches and it was so unusual, we made a festival out of it."

Robin tried not to chuckle but it was clear that the people of Sea Gate Fortress were fond of their festivals.

"So," James said, "not so far north as to have snowy winters. And the summers? Have you been there for the summer months?"

"Oh yes. It can be very hot. It's usually quite humid too."

James nodded. "That could describe the summer weather here at Sea Gate."

"Yes, but we don't have the sea breeze. I think it must be quite a distance from the ocean. There are waterways to be sure: creeks, lakes, even a river. But I don't ever remember seeing the ocean."

The cartographer James scouted about the room, seized upon a thin slab of slate and a stick of chalk, and made some notes.

Robin pointed at the man's writing instrument. "We called the area the Chalklands. We have much limestone, lying in exposed areas or jutting out of the earth's surface."

"Ah, this is indeed useful information. What type of foliage is there? Are there trees?"

"Of course there are trees," said Robin.

James shrugged. "Not all lands have trees. I have seen some desert lands where nothing grows at all. There is only sand."

"Oh, yes, of course, that would be true. No, there were trees: oaks, elms, and cypress."

James wrote on his slate. "What else grows there?"

"Grasses. Laurels. Roses. Cattails in the marshy areas."

"Excellent," said James, adding to his notes.

A young maidservant entered the room with a heavily-laden tray. Robin watched as she managed a low curtsy without upsetting the contents.

"Just put that on that table over there," Alexandra said. "We'll help ourselves, thank you very much. That will be all."

The maid did as bidden, curtsied again, and backed out of the room.

"Now that's how to bow," Alexandra said to Robin in a whisper. "Cider all around?" she asked.

"You are too kind, m'lady," said James but remained focused on his slate. Absentmindedly, he scratched the side of his head with the stick of chalk, leaving white dust in his hair. "And people. Were there people?"

"Of course there were people."

James said, "There's no 'of course' about it. Like trees, there are lands that have more animals than people. Describe the people."

Robin was puzzled. "They were just people. Men, women, children —"

"Of what color?"

Again, the question puzzled Robin. "Color?" He held out his arm and rotated it back and forth. "This color."

"So, not yellow or black?"

"Oh, I understand the question now. Yes, there were dark-skinned and golden-skinned people. Also red-skinned and olive-skinned and brown-skinned... people-colored people. I thought maybe you meant something like purple."

"Purple? Have you ever seen purple-colored people?" The man seemed especially intrigued by the possibility.

"No! Have you?"

James gave that some thought. "No, I guess not." James wrote on his slate. "Tell me about the industry. What did the people there do?" And he continued to quiz Robin about the Chalklands until he asked a question that Robin would have dreaded had he anticipated it. "How was the land governed? Was there a principal ruler?"

Robin felt his face grow warm. If he lied, he might never learn what he needed to know to find his way home. If he told the truth —

"I understand that there was a king," said Alexandra.

"Ah. Again, useful information. Some settled areas have no monarchy but instead have a plutocracy. The owner of the land is effectively the ruler."

Robin thought about the Ironworks, which was the likes of a small city with Oliver John as the supreme authority.

"Or, a theocracy, where the ruler is the religious leader, like an abbot or a bishop. Or there may be a dictator, one who had simply seized power and rules the land."

Robin felt a chill come over him as he wondered if in fact such a dictator now controlled the Chalklands in his absence.

"Others have no ruler. A monarchy is a challenge to manage and expensive to maintain."

"That it is," said Alexandra, and had he been able to comment, Robin would have agreed. He took as a personal responsibility the health, welfare, and prosperity of every one of his subjects. But it required many men and resources to ensure that everyone was looked after properly. No one decision met the needs of everyone concerned. It took many ministers, knights, and scouts to collect the necessary information. Many conferences and compromises went into arriving at decisions that would benefit the most and harm the others the least.

"In some areas, we are seeing the growth of communes," said James. "There is no ruler, and the citizens swear a mutual allegiance to provide protection from bandits or marauders. The residents will unite to put up defensive walls. In a public ceremony, they swear an oath to defend each other in times of trouble, and to maintain the peace within the city walls."

Like the settlements at Riverington, and at Rose Bank. "But who makes the law? Who enforces it?" Robin asked.

"The citizens agree amongst themselves. I do use the term 'agree' loosely. As you might expect, there are disagreements as to what is the best course of action, and constant power struggles as some citizens strive to have more control. Not everyone is content to let someone else make decisions for him. Still, these communes, as they are called, are becoming more numerous."

"We have several such communes in our realm," said Alexandra. "At the far reaches of our domain. There, because of the distance, it is difficult for us to provide effective protection. We can of course install an outpost but even the most trusted commander sometimes gets drunk with power and forgets to whom he reports.

"No, sometimes it's best simply to accommodate the self-rule. We can then form a strategic alliance with the commune. The Empire grants them the right to build a defensive wall and some fortifications and to conduct trade in exchange for the payment of taxes or some other form of tribute. This increases our wealth and our reach without overly straining our resources."

Robin wondered if Rose Bank and Riverington were communes. They seemed to consider themselves part of no particular realm.

At last, James laid down his chalk and slate, took up a mug of cider, and sipped. "I think I have enough information for now to get started. If I need further information, or have an answer...?"

"Send word to me," said Alexandra.

"Do you really think you can figure out where the Chalklands are?" asked Robin.

"If they are on this earth, I can find them," replied James.

If they are on this earth. That, Robin thought, was not something that he could confirm with any certainty.

CHAPTER SIXTEEN

"What do you think, Meeyoo?" Robin turned from the mirror and faced the cat who been sitting on the bed, observing his preparations.

Meeyoo yawned and stretched out on the bed.

Robin turned to study his reflection in the mirror, rearranged his curls one more time, and then threw up his hands and decided he had done all he could to make himself presentable. Equally challenging had been the problem of how to come up with a suitable gift. He was loathe to arrive at the feast empty-handed, even if the celebration was in honor of his achievement. But he had not the time nor the wherewithal to fashion a bread-saw. At last he had hit upon an idea that he thought had merit. It had better; it was the only thing he could think of.

From below he heard the sound of the horn announcing that the feast had begun. With a promise to bring her a tasty tidbit from the feast, Robin left Meeyoo sitting on the sill of the chamber's small window and went downstairs to the Great Hall. This morning, the room had been minimally furnished. The Empress had been comfortable enough on her throne, with ladies in waiting standing by with fans to keep her cool and supplying her with ale or food as she desired. Other than that, few seats had been provided and no refreshments offered. Robin had found that not at all surprising. In his experience, requiring petitioners to stand helped to keep their speeches short. Woe betide anyone who was late as he was then condemned to be on his feet the longest. As the morning wore on, the room would become warm and petitioners tired, thirsty, and hungry. Some would reevaluate their needs as being not quite as demanding as they had originally thought, and they would leave to satisfy the more urgent need to sit, eat, and drink.

Noise from the festival preparations had wafted up the stairwell all afternoon so he was not surprised to find the hall transformed. It was not, however, laid out as he would have anticipated. For a feast, he would have expected to see a long trestle table arranged to accommodate the Empress at its center flanked by the most prominent members of her court and honored guests, and tables for lesser royal staff and guests set perpendicular to it. Instead he found chairs, lounges, and benches grouped around smaller tables that held lanterns and candlesticks. A long trestle table held lanterns that would later keep the festival lively after sundown. The light sparkled in the ceramic glaze of the wine jugs standing on the tables. Vats of ale flanked the table. Trenchers of food had already been laid and perfumed the air with the aromas of roasted and smoked meats, fish, fruits, and pungent spices. Next to the food, stacks of large seashells stood ready to serve as plates and bowls. The tall windows had been hung with drapes of a light fabric. They wafted in the breeze, seemingly beckoning arriving guests to join the gathering. Door wardens in dress uniforms escorted visitors from the hand-washing station at the main entrance to join those already in the hall.

Although he had expected to see a throng of unfamiliar faces, Robin discovered that he recognized a number of people. The chamberlain, stable master, and castellan were in attendance. He crossed over to them and they exchanged greetings. He thanked them for the assistance that they had rendered and inquired about their lives at Sea Gate Fortress.

He recognized the third-floor chambermaid. Even though she was there not as a guest, but to serve, her presence made Robin feel more at home. He stopped her and with a bow, thanked her for making him feel so comfortable. She demurred but her delighted smile told him that she appreciated the acknowledgment.

He spotted Ruth the counselor and James the cartographer, Leigh the physician, and of course, Empress Alexandra. Ruth's gown was almost as ethereal and draping as the window coverings. In her pale colored dress and golden jewelry, she glowed like a sunbeam. Although James still wore his unusual cap he had changed into clothes much like Robin's, which he found reassuring.

Leigh, the physician, wore not the white gown and veil in which Robin was accustomed to seeing her. Her jeweled green silk gown skimmed her trim figure and her diaphanous veil floated over her dark hair like a layer of fog.

He was surprised to see Alexandra already in attendance. Had he somehow missed the fanfare announcing her entrance? She had changed from the simple gown she had worn to walk on the beach. Tonight she wore a gown of seashell pink that made her cheeks look especially rosy. Strings of pearls hung around her neck and the gold bangles on her wrists were studded with what appeared to be green and blue glass that somehow bore frost. Her light brown hair cascaded in waves held off her face only by a light tiara.

He joined them and was greeted with smiles.

"Ah, our special guest," Alexandra said.

Robin bowed to the party. "You do me such an honor," he said. "I haven't accomplished anything, only brought news of potential."

"Nevertheless, it's an excuse to have a celebration," she said.

"We love to party," said Leigh. The way her eyes glittered suggested to Robin that she had gotten an early start.

"I must ask about the gems on your bracelets," Robin said to Alexandra. "I have never seen gems like those. What are they?

"They are not gems," said Alexandra. "They're sea glass. Bits of glass that have been tossed in the waves, the edges rounded and the surfaces etched by the sand and salt."

What had the chambermaid told him? That the islanders made do with what they had? Shells for bowls, platters, and building stone, driftwood for furnishings, glass transformed by the sea for jewels. Though the guests were all dressed in fine clothes, their attire lacked the stiffness and severity of formal courtly attire. "Your island kingdom continues to amaze me."

His hosts smiled proudly.

Alexandra said, "I have arranged for the documents and supplies you will need so that you can travel to Allenton tomorrow. Tonight though we will not talk of business, but simply enjoy ourselves." With that, she excused herself to greet new arrivals. The castellan and chamberlain crossed the room to join Robin, Leigh, James, and Ruth. Plates of food were passed and cups filled and refilled. Jugglers and mimes, lutists and flutists weaved throughout the room, pausing to entertain the various clutches of guests.

His tongue loosened by more ale in one night than he had consumed in months, Robin told a story about a poor zoo that, lacking the funds to have a variety of animals, hired an even poorer mime to pretend to be a monkey. The mime was successful in entertaining the customers, the zoo became more popular, and the zookeeper generously rewarded the mime. But the mime noticed that the lion in the adjoining cage got even more attention than he did. Afraid to lose his job, the mime took to dangling from the top of the lion's cage and taunting the savage beast below. This gained much favor with the crowd and the mime's earnings increased until one day he fell. At the feet of the snarling lion, the mime abandoned his monkey persona and begged for mercy.

"'Be quiet,' said the lion, or we will both lose our jobs," Robin said.

Robin's audience applauded and the mime at his elbow doubled over in a fit of silent laughter.

Next Robin told of an advocate who, in his travels, frequented a particular inn where he began a dalliance with the innkeeper's daughter. When he next visited he learned that she had borne a child.

"The advocate asked, 'why didn't you send word that you were pregnant? I would have returned sooner, we could have married and the baby would have my name'," Robin said. "The innkeeper's daughter replied, 'when my parents found out about my condition, we sat up all night talking and decided it would be better to have a bastard in the family than an advocate.'"

Since there were no lawyers in his audience, this tale got a hearty laugh.

Robin took a long swallow of ale and said, "Once, there was a woman who got a magic potion that made her look very much younger than her real age of 50. She would work the crowd at alehouses and bet men that they could not guess her age."

His audience looked interested.

Robin continued, "She approaches two young fellows playing darts and challenges them. One accepts, studies her face carefully, and guesses that she is 39 but she says, 'No, I am 50' and he has to pay up. The second says that he will accept her challenge. This second young man looks her up and down, pays close attention to her hair and face, and guesses that she is 41 but she says, 'No, I am 50' and he has to pay up.

"She takes some of her winnings, gets herself an ale, and sits down at a table. An old codger is sitting there. The man's eyes are rheumy and the woman thinks this will be easy money, so she challenges him. He says, 'I am an old man and my eye sight is poor. But I would like to take up your challenge. When I was young, there was a sure way to tell how old a woman was. I will bet you double that I can tell exactly how old you are.'

"The woman agrees. The old man says, 'It sounds very forward, but it requires you to let me put my hands in your dress.'"

James wore an expectant look on his face, while Leigh appeared skeptical, and Ruth uncomfortable.

"The woman is not pleased. 'You should have asked about my terms before you accepted,' he tells her. Still, she is confident that she can win the doubled bet so she says, 'Oh, go ahead, then.' The old man slips both of his hands down the neck of her dress and begins to feel around very slowly and carefully. He bounces and weighs each breast. He gently pinches each nipple. He pushes her breasts together and rubs them against each other."

James's eyes were bright. Leigh's expression had become disapproving and Ruth looked almost fearful.

Robin continued. "After a couple of minutes of this, the woman says, 'That's enough.' The old man replies, 'Madam, you are 50.'"

Behind him, there was a cough and a voice asked Robin, "And just how did he know?"

Robin turned to find Alexandra behind him wearing a stern expression and his own face got hot.

CHAPTER SEVENTEEN

Her hand propped on her hip, she asked, "Well? How did he know?"

Robin took another swallow of ale. Finally he said, "The old man says, 'My eyes are dim but my hearing is fine. I heard you tell the other men.'"

For a moment, no one said a thing. Then Alexandra's lips quivered. She sputtered and then broke out in laughter as at last, so did everyone else.

Alexandra said, "Oh that is so dumb it's funny. We should have figured that out! That was very clever, Master Robin. I thank you. I haven't laughed like that in some time."

The look in Leigh's, Ruth's, and Jim's eyes told him this was so. He told a few more stories, each one sillier or more ribald than the last, which no one seemed to mind but instead enjoyed. Even Alexandra was entertained, laughing until she cried at a story that at the outset seemed to be about a maiden losing her virginity when instead it was about having a tooth pulled.

He bowed to Alexandra and said, "I beg pardon if I have offended. Your fine libations have loosened my tongue." He straightened and said, "Perhaps I should find something else to do with my mouth." That didn't sound right either, so he quickly produced his harmonica. "You had invited me to play," he said.

"I did indeed. Please, do."

Robin performed the first tune that he had played in David's barbershop which had proved to be well-known and popular. He followed it with a couple that were quite lively and set people to dancing.

He took a moment to wet his parched mouth with a swallow of ale and then announced, "This next tune I dedicate to Alexandra, Empress of Sea Gate." He proceeded to play a tune that had bright, lively phrases alternating with thoughtful, almost melancholy ones. The tune ended with a joyful and victorious flourish.

His charmed audience applauded and Robin bowed as might a performer at the end of a well-received play.

"That was absolutely delightful," said Alexandra. "I can't say I'd ever heard that last tune before."

"No one has before today," said Robin. "I composed it myself, as a gift for you, to honor you."

Alexandra rewarded him with a blush and her guests nodded their approval.

Better than a bread-saw any day, Robin thought, finding that he cared very much that Alexandra should approve of and like him.

Alexandra clapped her hands and a trumpeter blew a flourish. Robin would have thought this was to introduce the entrance of the domain's ruler, but Alexandra was already here.

Once everyone's attention was captured, Alexandra introduced Robin as the guest of honor. The entire assembly bowed and curtsied, and Robin felt as though he were back in his own court.

The musicians launched into a carole. Alexandra's guests joined hands and formed a circle. Alexandra held out her hand. "Shall we?" she asked Robin.

Leigh took his other hand and around they went. Those who knew the words sang as they danced. Somewhat stiff at first, Alexandra soon skipped and swayed with the best of them, her eyes bright and her cheeks flushed. Robin was pleased to see her shoulders shrug off the weight of her sorrows and responsibilities, if only for a night. When she turned up her face to smile at him, he felt that all was right with his world and that anything would be possible.

The danced ended but before Robin could make another move, Leigh pulled him aside. She regarded him with a stern expression. "I'm just wondering what you're trying to do." Without waiting for an answer, she said, "Just because Alexandra is a widow doesn't mean she's fair game for any man who takes a fancy to her. Everyone else here thinks you're a Master Cutler of some repute, but remember, I saw you when you arrived with the donkey."

"I'm not trying to 'do' anything," he said, "except perhaps to make her smile. It's clear that she has many burdens, many who depend on her, and she expects a lot from herself. I just thought I'd try to introduce a little gaiety."

Leigh narrowed her eyes. "Yes, you are doing that well enough. Just know that her welfare is our primary concern. We will not abide anyone trying to take advantage of her."

Robin held up his hands. "On my honor, that is not my intention." Until he had met Alexandra, his only intention was to recover his kingdom. It was now doubly his desire, so that he could prove himself truly worthy of her affection.

"See that you stay true to that," Leigh said.

She had no sooner flounced off than he was joined by James.

"I've been working on your problem," he said. "I think I may have something that will be of help."

CHAPTER EIGHTEEN

Already breathless from performing, dancing, flirting with Alexandra, and sparring with Leigh, Robin felt his breath catch in his throat. "You know where the Chalklands are?"

"I can't give you a map, but I might be able to help you find them."

Robin followed James to the ale vat and waited impatiently while the man refilled his cup.

"I think your suspicion is correct," said James. "I believe the land you seek is north of here."

"So you believe it's real?" Robin said, his pulse racing.

"I have no reason to suspect it's not," James said. "Here's what I would suggest. I would suggest that you go back to where you were when you last remembered seeing it. You said late winter, early spring, is that correct?"

Robin nodded. That would be the cow pasture outside Rose Bank. Go back, James was saying. Robin remembered David telling him to look to his past, and so had Ruth. The problem was that Robin couldn't seem to remember the past.

"I would suggest returning to that last spot that you remember, then head north. I have a list of clues that you can follow that might lead you to terrain that you recognize. I'm afraid there might be some false starts and backtracking."

"Still," Robin said, "it's encouraging. To have a plan and a direction. How can I thank you?

James smiled. "I would appreciate a souvenir of the Chalklands for my collection."

"Consider it done," said Robin. He went in search of Alexandra and found her on the esplanade outside the great hall. The way her face blossomed into a smile as he approached warmed his heart.

"This has been just a wonderful evening," he said. "I can't remember having such an enjoyable time."

"That doesn't say much when you claim not to remember anything," Alexandra replied.

"True. Yet I feel more optimistic that I will be able to recover my past." Once James had spoken of Robin's returning to where his nightmare began, he had found himself thinking of Rose Bank. He could recall in great detail his sojourn there, could remember his ride in the farmer's wagon, and even his waking in the cow pasture. When he tried to picture beyond that, all he saw was blackness as dark as if someone had thrown a hood over his head. But now he was eager to plumb that darkness. It was as if James's words were a torch that he could shine into that darkness. And with Alexandra championing his quest, Robin felt as eager to charge into the fray as a young knight at his first jousting tournament. "Meeting you, I feel, has turned my life around. I now see possibilities that were not there before."

"I must confess, you have helped me to see new possibilities as well," said Alexandra. "I thought that I would never laugh or dance again."

Robin found himself touched by the anguish and longing in her voice and realized again the tragedy that she had suffered. "Ah, lady, don't despair," he said, and put his arm around her shoulder. To his surprise and delight, instead of chastising him for such impertinence, she leaned into him and put her arms around his waist. He was struck by how easily and well their bodies fit together.

"Or kiss," she murmured into his chest. "I thought that I would never be kissed again."

Tenderly he tipped up her chin. "That, I can also help with."

When he returned the next morning to his chamber, he found that again, a breakfast tray had been left for him. Meeyoo had apparently decided that these were the tidbits that Robin had promised to bring her from the feast and had already helped herself. She looked up from the scraps of nibbled meats and fish with a guilty expression.

"That's OK, Meeyoo," he said. "I have already breakfasted with the Empress."

The night of passion had left them both spent and she had sent for reviving fruits and beverages to be brought. She seemed unconcerned that the staff would find him in her chamber, news that would surely spread throughout the castle before they finished their meal.

In their coupling, Alexandra had been by turns needy and playful. Robin had surprised himself with how much he had missed not so much the pleasures of the flesh but the sweet salve of intimacy.

He filled his pack with necessities for his trip to Allenton. "Meeyoo, I expect not to be gone long. Only overnight, perhaps. But I want to be light on my feet so you should remain behind. I think you should stay in the stable and keep Duncan company while he recovers."

With his pack and cat, he reported to the stables. The head groom had directed stable boys to ready Charger for journey. "You should check in with the chamberlain on your way out," he told Robin. "He has the necessary documents.

The head groom granted Robin's request to leave Meeyoo in Duncan's stall. There he found Leigh tending to the donkey. She regarded him with a disapproving glare. "I heard harmonica tunes emanating from the Empress's chambers very late last night. I was not aware that playing the harmonica was one of her talents."

"I —"

She jabbed his chest with an index finger. "I told you not to take advantage of her, did I not?"

"I did nothing of the sort," Robin said, trying not to sound as defensive as he felt. "You can ask her yourself."

"I will," Leigh said. She stalked from the stall, then turned and said, "If you hurt her, I will visit pain upon you and believe me, I know many, many ways to do that."

Of that, Robin had no doubt.

This time he rode even more determinedly toward Allenton, making only one stop at Sweet Water for the one item that would ensure a successful presentation to Lord Stanley Allen. Eian, who now regarded Robin as an important repeat customer, was dismayed to learn that out of three bottles, Robin was unlikely to enjoy even one sip.

"My friend, the least I can do is pour you a cup for yourself," Eian said.

It was an offer Robin could hardly refuse. He practically owed it to himself. It was as he sat enjoying what Oliver John had called a "bracing" beverage that Robin overhead a wayfarer's report that caught his interest.

"Very curious," the man said. "I had often stopped there on my travels. Really, it was hardly more than a crossroads with a well, an alehouse, a baker, and a blacksmith. The villeins were good people, all right, but you know how it is. Life is hard. They can barely put food on their own table, and they also have to put in weekwork labor on the lord's behalf. Then I began to notice changes. The blacksmith had new tools. The villeins that I met at the alehouse had new clothes, new shoes. They spoke of having new plows, an ox where they hadn't had one before. The transformation was almost magical."

Robin felt the hair on the back of his neck rise. He had left off thinking there were bewitchings and enchantments afoot and had decided his own twist of fate was due to something far more prosaic. Now, as he resumed his quest, here was talk of magic again. He didn't like it.

The traveler paused to sip his ale. "I asked if the farming had been especially good but they said, no, these were all gifts."

"Gifts from whom?" Robin asked imagining some witch who sought to beguile an entire settlement.

"Some lord. Not theirs, some other one."

Eian leaned his forearms on the table. "Now why would a lord distribute gifts to villeins on someone else's domain?"

"To woo their allegiance away," replied the traveler.

"Well, that makes no sense," said Robin. "They would still owe the same labor to the lord who owned the land to which they were bound." He had no sooner said this than he realized that he had spoken with way too much authority and was relieved when no one seemed to notice.

"From what I understood, the villeins were told that this lord intended to take over the lands that they worked. He vowed that they would be free. They would still owe rent of course, but would not have to work the new lord's own lands as well. The gifts were a pledge of faith."

That didn't sound at all right to Robin. A domain couldn't be run that way. There was too much work to be done and it was reasonable to expect it would be done by those who enjoyed the fruits of land that they did not own. He wondered if the traveler had misunderstood.

If the traveler were right, though, and the villeins' allegiance had been bought with promises of an easier life, they perhaps could be called upon to support this new lord in battle. Nevertheless, it was curious. It sounded expensive, and not likely to succeed. Robin thought about his campaign in Allenton. He, at least, was not stealing peasants from some lord but rather seeking alliance with the lord himself.

Speaking of which, Robin decided, he had best get back on the road to Allenton. He thanked Eian for the wine and resumed his journey. Although he missed the companionship of Duncan and Meeyoo, he sat much taller astride Charger as they arrived at the Lord Stanley Allen's gatehouse.

The chamberlain regarded Charger with his Sea Gate livery with suspicion. "Were you not here just days ago on a donkey?" he asked.

"Indeed I was. I have news for Lord Stanley Allen about that, and another matter of which to speak." Robin handed the chamberlain letters of introduction from Empress Alexandra. "And I have a gift that I think he will enjoy."

Still perturbed, the chamberlain told Robin to stand by while he went to see if Lord Stanley Allen would meet with him. Robin didn't know if it was curiosity, persuasive documents, or the hope there was another bottle of fortified wine in the offing that got him the audience. Before long, however, he was again meeting with Lord Stanley Allen in the parlor.

Robin remembered to bow. "Lord Oliver John sends greetings," he said. "He thanks you for the confidence that you have shown in him and wants you to be assured that work has already commenced on your commission." At least, Robin assumed that it had.

"And you came all the way here to tell me that?" Stanley Allen asked.

"I have come even further," Robin replied. "I have come from the ends of the earth, if you will. From Sea Gate Fortress. On a matter of great importance to you and your domain."

"I don't understand," Stanley Allen said.

"It's complicated," Robin said. "Perhaps you would prefer to make yourself comfortable." He bowed slightly and indicated that Stanley Allen should sit. Robin then took a goblet from the sideboard and produced the bottle of wine from his pack. "May I?"

Stanley Allen's eyes brightened. "My good friend Oliver John has sent me another gift?"

"No, sir, this one is from me. I observed how much you appreciated it the last time and thought to bring you some more, should you be so kind as to spare me some of your time."

"Oh, I did appreciate it. I'll try not to appreciate so much this time," Stanley Allen said. He accepted the goblet from Robin. "So, what is this other matter of importance?"

Robin suppressed his annoyance at once again not being offered any hospitality. Soon, men like Stanley Allen and Oliver John would be treating him differently. They would come to know him as King Bewilliam and they would rue the day that they disrespected him.

"I have found in my travels that threats to your safety and the safety of your domain, of which you may not be aware, abound."

Needing to buy a little time so that Stanley Allen could enjoy a sufficient amount of wine, Robin told his tale of being ambushed by the highwayman. That the telling took longer than the actual attack had was something only Robin would know.

Stanley Allen looked concerned. "How frightening for you. Yet you prevailed."

"I was spared, sir, for which I am grateful. I can only assume it was so that I might spread the news and so innocent people could take action to protect themselves.

"These threats have impressed upon your friend Lord Oliver John and the people of Riverington the need to erect defenses, and speedily. Empress Alexandra of Sea Gate, who holds you in high esteem, would like to offer you the same assistance she offered to Lord Oliver John and to Riverington, which they have accepted."

"Does she now?' said Stanley Allen. "I think that here we have little need for such assistance. If we find that we need additional fortifications and defenses, we have the means to provide them. After all, we have just ordered new armaments to be manufactured. And if we find that we need further assistance, we have already had a very generous offer that we are disposed to consider."

Robin felt queasy as he realized that this campaign was not coming to a successful conclusion. He found himself thinking about the tale the traveler had told at Sweet Water. It would be a strange coincidence indeed if the competing offer

Stanley Allen had received was from this same mysterious lord. Indeed, Robin did spy some new finery in Stanley Allen's parlor including the glittering jeweled goblet from which Stanley Allen drank his wine. "Sir, if you would—"

"Do tell Oliver John how much I appreciate his prompt action on my commission." Stanley Allen rose from his chair and started for the door. When Robin did not follow, he turned and looked at him questioningly.

"Sir, I humbly request, before you enter into an alliance with anyone, that you hear what the Empress Alexandra has to offer."

"I'll take that under advisement," said Stanley Allen. He opened the door and Robin understood that he was being shown out. With a heavy heart, he stepped through the open doorway.

"Thank you for the wine," said Stanley Allen. "I assume you will be returning when my commission has been fulfilled. I certainly would not turn away another bottle of this fine blend."

His smile was friendly enough but Robin burned with the shame of being so summarily dismissed. He gave Stanley Allen the most token of bows and headed back for the gatehouse.

Robin urged Charger along at a much slower pace as they headed away from the manor than he had set for their arrival. Though the horse moved slowly, Robin's thoughts raced. He hadn't quite failed. Stanley Allen had not entirely dismissed the idea of allying with Alexandra. Perhaps the man simply needed to review the other proposition that he had received. Robin could make another visit, with perhaps more compelling incentives, incentives such as those that had been offered by this predatory lord. Robin wondered what gifts he could bring that would be sufficiently persuasive. Certainly nothing that he could afford. He would have to borrow them with hopes of repaying the loan after successfully completing his mission, or convince Alexandra to provide such enticements.

One thing was for certain: Robin was loathe to return to Sea Gate Fortress with so little to show for his effort. As Charger ambled along, he wondered if he should stay overnight in Allenton and try again on the morrow.

"No, that would be too soon," Robin said. "I would still need to enrich our offer somehow."

At the sound of Robin's voice, Charger turned his head slightly.

"No, I have another idea."

CHAPTER NINETEEN

Charger stopped.

"Nay, Charger, we will keep moving," Robin said. "But I am setting us a new direction." He would not go back to Sea Gate empty-handed. Instead, he would go to Rose Bank. He would talk to David about an alliance. When Robin had left his employ for the Ironworks, David had said that he was welcome to return any time. Robin knew he would get a fair hearing from David, and could then return to Alexandra with at least one clear success. She might then be amenable to making a larger investment in pursuing Stanley Allen.

There was but one small problem with the plan. He did not quite know where Rose Bank was. He might be able to retrace the route that he had taken from Rose Bank to reach Riverington. He was not certain he could remember how he had come to Sea Gate from Riverington without revisiting the site of the fight with the wyvern. Would that he had Alexandra's cartographer with him to help with this problem.

Robin led Charger to the inn in Allenton. There he ordered something to eat and an ale to compensate for the glass of wine that Stanley Allen had not offered him. He quizzed the innkeeper and other wayfarers but no one had ever heard of

Rose Bank. Less confident of the wisdom of his plan than he had been, he nursed another ale while he considered his next move.

Perhaps if he backtracked toward Riverington, he would find someone who could direct him. It would be a long and uncertain way to reach his destination, but he could think of no other way. He sighed. The dark of night would not aid him. Even this revised plan would be best undertaken in the morning light. Dispirited, he took a room for the night knowing that he would get little sleep. Charger at least would be rested and refreshed come morning.

The next day, luck was with him. He did not have to go all the way to Riverington, but only as far as Sweet Water. There Eian gave him a warm welcome, one that became even warmer when Robin decided to buy a bottle of wine for David. Eian had heard of Rose Bank and was able to suggest the direction Robin should take.

He thanked the sun for staying with him as long as it did but when it finally gave way to night Robin found himself well distant from Sweet Water and not near any settlements that he could see. He feared not to meet violence on the road, for he trusted his sword and his fighting skills. Still, he was wary and alert. It was wearying and he knew he would be glad to see daylight or civilization, whichever came first.

They arrived almost simultaneously when at daybreak he found himself nearing Victory Fortress. He found it heartening as he knew the fair-sized city was between Rose Bank and Riverington. He knew he was on the right trail. The foliage and terrain was not that of the Chalklands. He hadn't expected it to be. It did tell him that he was far from the coast and nearing lands that he had come to know well, though it seemed a lifetime ago that he had last been here. Then he had been only slightly more than a vagabond, on foot carrying a pack and a tiny kitten. Now, his nobility acknowledged if not restored, he was astride a regal horse and Meeyoo, while not quite an adult, had grown from a kitten into a bold and frisky cat. Robin smiled. He would stop at Victory Fort to feed himself and Charger but would not stay overly long. He was eager to get to Rose Bank and to see David. He had so many adventures to relate.

His pulse beat faster as he recognized the road that he had taken from Rose Bank. Whereas before it simply led through the center of the settlement to the market square, now the road ended at a half-built timber palisade wall lacking a gate. It looked to Robin that the people of Rose Bank had started building fortifications but had been unable to finish. That boded well for the offer he brought from Alexandra. Rose Bank clearly already saw the need for additional defenses. An alliance with Sea Gate would enable them to complete them.

Robin guided Charger slowly through Rose Bank. Everywhere were signs of change. In addition to the new wall, a bench stood beside the well where there had been none. Structures that had been in disrepair had been mended, with roofs showing fresh thatch. But the settlement was strangely quiet for a summer afternoon. The street was empty of people. Robin remembered that merchants did not close their stalls nor did farmers move off their wagons until daylight began to wane. Perhaps business had been so good that sellers had quit early.

No smoke billowed from the baker's ovens or the blacksmith's forge. Robin cast a hopeful glance at the home of the ale-wife for whom Dolores sometimes worked, but no flag flew nor did the interior appear to be lit. Robin proposed to himself several logical explanations, yet could not shake off the eerie feeling that something was not quite right.

Puzzled, he guided Charger down the road toward David's shop. Though Robin set a certain pace, his thoughts wandered to Dolores. When he left Rose Bank, he had pledged to return and better her life yet in all the months that had passed, he had not given her a minute's thought. Certainly she had not been a factor in any of his plans to aid Alexandra and to regain his kingdom. What would he say to Dolores when he saw her?

He arrived at David's shop. The structure stood dark and quiet. Robin was saddened to see that the rosebush had suffered for lack of attention. Perhaps this was one of those days when David would close the shop and spend the night with his family. Yet the leaves piled up against the door made it appear that no one had gone in or come out in some days.

He turned Charger away from the settlement and toward David's farm.

The fields were as filled with people as the settlement had been empty. Robin told himself that the citizens had abandoned village business in favor of getting the most production out of a long summer day.

About the same time that Robin saw David and his family in their field, one of David's sons looked up from his work and spotted Robin. He shouted and pointed. They all stopped their work and remained where they stood. Baffled by the lack of the warm reception that he had expected, Robin quickly realized that Charger would be unfamiliar to them and that they might not know him atop such a horse. He dismounted and drew closer at a respectfully slow pace. At last he saw David's expression register recognition. He stepped across the field, his wife and sons close behind.

"Robin?" he said, and surveyed him from head to toe.

Robin reached out his hand which, after some hesitation, David took. "Are you a lord now?"

"No! David, it's just me, Robin."

David's sons gawked at Charger.

"Going to work for Oliver John turned out to be a good decision," David said.

"It's a little more complicated than that," Robin said. "I see I've interrupted your work. Let me help."

"But you would ruin your nice clothes," Carolyn said.

Robin pulled off his tunic and shirt and tossed them over Charger's saddle. "No I won't. Give me a tool. I can work as we talk." He had found that a tale told well made even the most onerous task easier to do, so he spared no detail in telling David and his family what had transpired since he saw them last.

David leaned on his scythe. "So you are now a knight for this Empress of Sea Gate?" he asked.

"Not quite a knight," Robin replied. "More a sort of ambassador."

David's son fingered Charger's livery. "This is the crest of the Empress?"

"Yes," Robin said. "Her castle is right up against the edge of the sea."

"The sea," murmured David's other son, his eyes wide. Robin understood his awe. Until a few days ago, he too could only imagine what the sea looked like.

"Boys, see that Robin's horse is fed and watered," David said. "And let us go into the house and get fed and watered ourselves."

"I would like that, especially as I have a matter of which I wish to speak with you."

Over ale and bread, Robin asked, "So why were you not at the shop? It looked to me like you haven't been there for a while."

David nodded. His expression was somber. "I have no time for that any longer but must devote myself to farm work, mine and the lord's. We all do. Even the baker and the smith have week-work that must come first."

"I don't understand. I thought you owed no work to any lord. I thought that was true for all the farmers around here."

"Things are different now," David said, sounding weary. "We owe a heavy debt to the Lord Bernard."

"Bernard... I think I know that name." It was familiar. Robin raked his memory to recall when and where he had first heard it.

"You remember the caller that came to the shop one night?" David asked.

"That was Bernard?"

David nodded. "He offered to advance us loans and assistance to better Rose Bank and our farms now, in return for repayment later when our yields were greater."

"But you turned him down. You said 'it wasn't in the cards.'"

"That night. He came again several times after. He made a compelling offer and we were persuaded to agree."

"That explains the palisade. The mended roofs and the bench at the well. But the wall is not complete. The shops were empty. And you say you and the neighbors are working harder than ever. I don't understand."

David sighed. "We had no sooner begun the wall, and started using our new tools and oxen to improve our fields when one of Lord Bernard's knights came calling, demanding that we repay the loan."

Robin felt a chill. He had heard this story before, from the farmer who had brought him from the cow pasture to Rose Bank many months ago.

"Of course, we had no cash. We hadn't even harvested our first crop yet. So we were pressed to supply labor for the lord's work, to give up our first fruits, and to pledge to remit a percentage of everything that we produce. It's a heavy debt. Some don't have an able wife and sons like Carolyn and my boys. Those of us who do help the ones who don't to meet their obligation. So the baker and the smith hardly have time for that work, and I have no time to spend in the shop." David's expression was sorrowful and almost piercing. "Would that you were still with me."

Robin's mouth went dry. He had no idea when he accepted Oliver John's offer that he was leaving David in the lurch. Had he remained, could Robin have prevented this disaster? He thought perhaps he could have. Should anyone had sought his counsel, he might have advised against the loan. But would his advice been sought? And had David not encouraged him to pursue his dream? "What are you going to do?"

David shrugged. "What can we do except the lord's will?" He gazed out the door toward the field in which his wife and sons still worked. "I should get out there soon. We have much to do before sunset. What was the matter that you wanted to discuss?"

"It's... it's of no import," said Robin. He did not know for whom he felt sadder: David and the hard-pressed people of Rose Bank, or himself who now would have to return to Sea Gate having completely failed his task.

He and David pushed away from the table. "I thank you for the food, for myself and the horse." He rummaged in his pouch for some coins.

"I can't take those," David said.

"I think you must," Robin replied, and pressed them into David's hand. He mounted Charger but before heading him away from the farm, he said, "I do have a question. What do you know of Dolores?"

CHAPTER TWENTY

Davⁱd hung his head. "Ah, that is a sad tale indeed. I am sorry to say she passed away."

Robin felt lightheaded. "She's dead? How?"

David sighed. "No one seems to know, exactly. No one had seen her around for a day or two. Then she was found lying by the side of the road leaving Rose Bank. She didn't appear to have been attacked, or poisoned. It was as if she had simply lain down, perhaps to sleep, and didn't wake up." David shook his head. "She was not the most robust of women. Methinks she fell victim to her frailty."

If by that David meant that the woman seemed to live on not much more than ale, he was likely right in his assumption. It was what Robin had foreseen and dreaded. Perhaps if he had taken her with him, or returned sooner to take care of her, she would still be alive.

He could barely make himself ask. He knew he would regret hearing the answer. And yet something prodded him to say, "You say she was found on the road leaving Rose Bank. Going in which direction?"

"South," David replied.

Robin swallowed hard. Had she inquired about my leaving, he wanted to know. Did you tell her where I went? But those questions he kept to himself. He already felt as sick about her death as he could bear.

"I will speak to the Empress Alexandra about your plight," he said. "Maybe she can help."

"Perhaps she can," David said, but without much conviction.

Alexandra. David. Dolores. And for that matter, Franklin. Under the weight of their expectations and disappointments, Robin felt rooted in place, unable to go back, unable to go forward.

Charger twitched. Without much determination, Robin steered him toward Rose Bank. He stopped the horse at the rose trellis that marked the entrance to the settlement and looked at the road that would take him back to Sea Gate. If he started for Sea Gate now, night would find him on the road. Were it not for the need to return his borrowed horse and fetch Meeyoo, Robin felt that he might not even go. He could picture Alexandra's bright eyes and expectant smile but could not imagine what he would say to her. He couldn't bear to imagine the crestfallen expression that would follow his news of failure.

He turned and looked at the road that had led him to Rose Bank many months ago. He had cadged a ride in a farmer's oxcart, having awoken that morning in the middle of a cow pasture. He remembered that. He thought he could even find the very spot where had spent the night. What had happened before that? Though he tried to visualize it, his past was still as murky as the peat bogs at the Ironworks. Now, however, so was his future.

He recalled the cartographer James telling him to return to the last place that he remembered and travel inch by inch back into the past. Robin was certain that he was not far from that spot. Riding Charger, it would not take him long to get there.

The plan had formed in his mind before he was even fully aware of it. He would find that spot, that patch of grass, that oak tree. Then he would take one more step, and one more step after that, and one more step after that. He would find the

Chalklands. And he would return to Alexandra not with a settlement or a village for an ally, but an entire kingdom. He would make things right for David, for Rose Bank, for Franklin, and even, somehow, for Dolores.

He took the road that he remembered traveling with the farmer John. In the waning daylight, farmers and shepherds worked the distant fields. Far off he spied a small herd of cows making their slow way from a tree-lined pasture. Though he thought it might be wishful thinking, the scene did feel familiar. The timing was right; he had been riding about half as long as he remembered walking before meeting the farmer. He steered Charger toward the trees separating the pasture from the road.

"Slow, Charger," he murmured, nudging the horse along the line of oaks. "OK, stop here." Robin dismounted and with Charger following slowly behind, approached an oak. It was of course leafier than it had been those months ago when it had arched over him, yet he was certain this was the spot where he had spent that night. Robin stood beneath the tree for a moment, then dug his folded cloak from his pack. He didn't need it for warmth as the air still held the heat of the day, but having it might help him to remember better.

He gazed up at the stars. Those were no aid as they were different from those that had shined on him when he was last here.

Still, it all felt familiar, and at the same time terrifying. So much was at stake. His next step would take him into both his past and future.

His heart pounded, his breath came short, and his pulse pounded in his head. Yes, he was afraid, deeply afraid. The last time he remembered feeling like this was on that final dragon-slaying campaign. That was odd since he did not recall that particular beast as being the most formidable he had ever battled. While something about that campaign seemed important to know, thinking about it made him tense and cold as if facing mortal danger.

What had the counselor Ruth said? That he must be brave and confront the memory, painful though it might be.

Robin took a deep breath and closed his eyes. He gingerly poked at the memory as though prodding the poisonous blue jellied fish on Alexandra's beach, fearful that a venomous tentacle would lash out at him.

A distant king had sent word that he needed Robin's unique talents. Robin had not wanted to go. The kingdom was miles upon miles away; it would take him weeks, months, just to get there. Robin would be absent from his own court and kingdom for longer than he ever had been in all of his rule.

But the beleaguered king offered a handsome reward. The proceeds from the Chalklands' farmers, shepherds, millers, miners, weavers, and merchants had been poor of late, the worst they had ever been under his rule. Outwardly Robin demonstrated confidence that he could, as he had in the past, restore the kingdom to the level of prosperity that it usually enjoyed. Privately, the state of the royal treasury had been a concern to Robin, and to Queen Daya, who did not hesitate to be vocal about it.

Had he declined the commission, he would have expected Queen Daya to support his decision. Never very supportive of his dragon-slaying exploits, she had become even less enamored of them after the sons had been born. But she had agreed with him that this commission would be of great benefit to the kingdom and had assured him that the kingdom would not falter in his absence. She reminded him that she was a competent administrator in her own right and he had to agree.

"It can be your last campaign," she said.

He thought of taking his sons with him but Daya protested. Better they should stay at home and assist her. It would be an excellent opportunity for them to get hands-on experience in the business of the kingdom, something that they needed more than dragon-slaying skills.

So Robin accepted the commission and left his wife and sons behind.

The journey proved far longer than anyone had expected. Robin and his retinue ran out of provisions and had to procure food from local farmers, food that proved to be just different enough from what they were used to as to seem strange.

After the overly long and taxing journey, Robin and his knights finally reached their destination. Their host welcomed his royal guests with a feast. The plentiful food and drink was a boon after the deprivations of the road, and Robin and his men enjoyed more than their fill. His blood heated by the rich food, wines and ales, and the anticipation of the battle to come, Robin also delighted in the lusty attention of one of the queen's ladies.

Robin opened his eyes and blinked until the stars above Rose Bank came into focus. So far the remembered events, though fraught with stress, were not overly uncomfortable although he did feel a prick of guilt recalling his dalliance with his hostess's lady. If this was the hurtful recollection behind which his memory hid, it was certainly bearable. He closed his eyes and took several slow, deep breaths.

The dragon-slaying expedition had begun on the following night, one such as this, clear and still. Encamped in a clearing in a pine wood, Robin grouped the knights around a fire. He had more than enough manpower, for the host king had insisted that his own knights be included in the raiding party. Robin didn't care for the idea. He didn't know these men, their capabilities, or their mettle. When it came to a fight, could they be trusted or would they run? But there was no arguing with the king who was financing the campaign.

Robin stood and addressed his troops. "Tomorrow, we must be prepared for any eventuality. The dragon may fight back. It might retreat and try to take shelter, in which case we will have to root it out. It might flee and we will have to pursue it. You must have one eye on the dragon, one eye guarding your own position, and one eye watching me for commands."

"Beg pardon, sire, but that's three eyes," said one of the king's men. "I have only two."

Robin's men chuckled. They had heard this speech before and knew that Robin meant only that they should be on high alert.

"Then keep those two eyes of yours sharp," said Robin. "Remember, dragons are not cattle. They are smart. They have grown to be centuries old by learning from their mistakes and not making the same mistake twice. They don't act rashly. They size up their opponent and consider the best course of action. Though they are big and bulky they are nimble.

"Know that though we are a team, each man must perform to the best of his ability." Robin circled the fire and looked each man in the eye. "Never let your attention falter. Be flexible. We will have several strategies at our ready depending on what moves the dragon makes but you must also be inventive so that you can meet whatever situation presents itself. You must be adroit at adopting a different course. Always watch your back and make sure you have an escape plan. If need be, we can return and fight another day but only if we survive the skirmish.

"Let me assure you though, that's not likely to be necessary. We have never had to retreat, have we, men?"

Robin's knights loudly and enthusiastically concurred.

"Now, on the morrow, we will bathe, put on clean clothes, and our best armor. We don't want the dragon to be able to smell us before we can see him."

The king's knights snickered.

"I'm serious," said Robin. "Dragons have a highly refined sense of smell, much like a dog. In addition, being properly outfitted shows the dragon that we are men to be reckoned with. That in itself can plant a seed of self-doubt in his mind. If there are chinks in your armor, the dragon will see it and take advantage of your weakness. When you are ready for battle in body as well as mind, you will have the confidence you need.

"Don't be overly bold. Don't hesitate to use your shield for fear it will make you look less manly. If as a result of your bravado you are injured or killed, you hobble the team. You may cost us victory.

"Don't be cocky and assume you know what the dragon's going to do. Dragons are inventive and full of surprises.

"Above all, you must be confident. So if you wish to spend some time before we retire practicing parrying with your sword, do that. However, do not stay up overly long or drink too much ale. The morning must find you rested, alert, and ready."

Once again, Robin opened his eyes. He found that he was smiling, and his pulse had quickened. Yes, he had fond memories of his dragon-slaying exploits. There were few other occasions when he felt so challenged, and so competent. He never doubted that he would be victorious.

The next morning, he remembered, he and his troops had set off for the dragon's lair. The sun glinted in the highly polished armor worn by each man, and Robin was glad that the king's men had taken his words to heart. The reflections alone could help to blind the beast just long enough for them to strike a blow.

They approached the cavern that they believed to be the beast's lair. The mouth of the cave opened to a space so dark that its depth and breadth could not be fathomed. From its bowels emanated billows of smoke. That made it difficult to see or breathe, and was meant to strike fear in the hearts of the attackers as they imagined themselves being incinerated. It was a common dragon distraction play and Robin was not fooled.

An unearthly rumble rattled their bones. Brave men though they might have been, the king's knights hung back a step or two as Robin advanced. As if it were contagious, their fear prickled the back of his neck, pinched his gut, and stopped his breath. But before he allowed himself to be afraid, he would first see the beast and take its measure.

They stood poised at the mouth of the cave but the dragon remained deep in its recesses. Another dragon ploy, Robin knew. The longer the delay, the more time their fear had to build. They might decide to turn and run. If they stayed, their impatience would lead to inattention or rashness.

Sure enough, one of the king's men cried, "Let's call him out!"

"Nay," Robin whispered, "and hold your tongue," for impatience could also prey on the dragon, who at some point would have to leave the cave to hunt.

When at last the dragon did emerge, the wait had taken its toll on both the hunters and the hunted all of whom were tired, lacking focus, and impatient. Despite its three heads, the dragon was not the most formidable that Robin had ever faced, but it was cranky and overwrought. It roared louder, stamped harder, and spewed more fire than was warranted by the threat he and his men represented. Robin saw the dragon's lack of self-control to his advantage but the fearsome display shattered the courage of the king's inexperienced knights. They fled in all directions.

Robin wasted no time railing at the desertion. The fleeing men drew the attention of the dragon's right- and leftmost heads. It was just the opening Robin needed to command an assault on the critical, center head of the beast.

Robin lifted his head and regarded the sky over the outskirts of Rose Bank. The moon had shifted position. Charger had fallen asleep while Robin had been so deeply immersed in the recollection.

His muscles clenched and his pulse raced as if preparing for an assault. Robin considered. His memory was accurate. That dragon had not been all that fierce an opponent. Yes, the taxing journey, the day's long wait for the fight to begin, and the defection of the king's knights had sapped Robin's men and he had ended up dueling with the dragon with little support from his knights. It still wasn't the worst dragon-slaying he had ever undertaken.

So why, Robin wondered, did the feeling of dread remain? Had something else happened, something that made him fear for his life? He had the uneasy feeling that he had yet to recall the painful incident that blocked his memory. He summoned up the counselor Ruth's instruction that he would have to confront that pain to pierce the veil obscuring his memory. With a deep breath, he plunged back into the past.

It had been night when Robin and his men returned to the king's castle, tired, hungry, dirty, bloodied, and bearing three pairs of dragon horns as trophies of the kill. The king greeted their return with effusive gratitude. A celebration feast would be held in their honor the following night, and Robin would then receive the promised reward.

The king's faint-hearted knights were nowhere to be seen. Robin wondered if they had been imprisoned or banished for their cowardice.

That night, alone in his chamber, Robin was visited by the lady who had shared his bed the night of the welcoming banquet.

"Lady, your attentions are flattering and under other circumstances would be desirable but tonight —"

"You must flee, now," she said.

"What? Why?"

"You are marked for death! Our knights have poisoned our majesty's mind against you. He resents the bargain that he made and begrudges you your reward. You must leave now!"

"But my men..."

"I will warn them."

Robin scrambled into his clothes and flung his cloak about his shoulders. He reached for his sack, his crown, and his sword but the lady grabbed his arm. "No time for that. You must go now!"

The lady scurried away from the chamber. Now not trusting anyone from this kingdom, Robin ran to warn his knights but their chamber was empty. Praying that they had indeed been alerted and had already escaped, Robin skulked through the shadows across the bailey. His knights were nowhere in sight and Robin hoped that they had already managed to escape, a possibility that seemed even more likely when he found the castle's gate already ajar. Hoping to converge with them on the road, he slipped through the gate. In the dark, he slid down the bank of the moat, swam to the other side, and escaped into the deep shadows of the pine forest.

He was well and safely away from the castle when he realized that he had been duped. No doubt the king had indeed come to regret the deal that he had made, may have never intended to honor it in the first place. His knights may have even been planted on the raiding party to ensure that Robin did not survive the dragon-slaying. The lady's maid too could have been part of the plot, paid or coerced to make Robin flee not only without his payment, but without his horse, crown, or sword.

Robin slowed to a walk. And what of his own knights? Were they, too, complicit? Their performance in battle had been uncharacteristically lax. During the welcoming feast, while Robin had dallied with the lady's maid, had the king colluded with them to leave Robin vulnerable?

Or did the conspiracy go back even farther? He recalled his discussion with Daya about the mission, her unexpected support of his undertaking the campaign.

"Your last one," she had said.

Chilled to the bone, unable to move, he had stood alone, unarmed, deserted in strange wood, listening to the pine needles rasping in the wind.

CHAPTER TWENTY-ONE

"And that's when I lost my mind," Robin said.

The innkeeper regarded him with more dismay and disbelief than sympathy. It was the look Robin had gotten every time he told this tale, and he had told it to every fellow traveler and innkeeper that he had met since leaving the oak tree outside of Rose Bank. Robin hoped that with repeated tellings the story would become less painful, that he would arrive at some understanding of how or why his wife betrayed him. So far, no number of retellings eased the pain.

But they had cemented his conviction that she had betrayed him. He had told Alexandra that when he returned from the dragon-slaying campaign, it had been as though he were invisible. Now, he knew, that had happened before he left. He already detected alienation from the Queen, confusion on the part of his knights as to whom to obey. It had been part of his reason for taking on the commission. He would return a hero. He planned to replenish the treasury and travel no more, but would stay and focus on his kingdom and his family, reconcile with his wife. Why her affections had flagged, he did not know, then or now, but there was no mistaking that they had. His ambition for the dragon-slaying campaign had been to return victorious, proof that he still was the man and ruler that he had been.

Instead he had wandered foreign lands for weeks, benumbed, as though under a spell. He could not have returned to Bell Castle even if he had wanted to because he could remember nothing of who he was, where he had been, or what he had done. The first rending of the veil obscuring his memory had come that morning when he awoke in a cow pasture, aware that who he appeared to be was not who he was.

Robin paid for his ale, collected Charger, and resumed his journey to the Chalklands. He had no better notion of where they were than before, but he followed the advice given him by James the cartographer: go forward, look for clues, ask for directions, double back if necessary, and try a slightly different route.

Today, he felt the thrill of anticipation. Somehow, he felt he was nearing his destination. Something felt familiar. Perhaps it was something about the landscape, the trees, and other foliage.

No, it was the earth itself. Peeking out from grassy and shrubby concealment was rock. White rock. Not the rusty iron-rich rock of the Ironworks or even the sandy soil of Sea Gate, flecked white with bits of sea shells. No, this white rock was white as chalk. He had arrived at chalk lands. Were they his Chalklands? Would he soon find Bell Castle?

He continued on, becoming more certain each step that he had reached his homeland and would soon reach his home.

"Let's stop for a moment," he said to Charger, and reigned him in. Before he went any further, he wanted to revel in the joy, however fleeting, of having arrived, at having achieved that for which he had so long quested and struggled, hoped and prayed.

He imagined riding on, reaching the castle, and being welcomed by family, staff, and subjects who had missed him, who had worried and feared for him. He would take up again his place on the throne. Robin pictured himself, cleaned, groomed, and once again robed in comfortable fabrics, refreshed and restored by a restful, dreamless sleep and decent food. His mind clear, his body strong, he would take charge. Poor decisions may have been made and ill-advised actions taken in his absence, and he would have to right them. He saw himself sitting on his throne, conferring with his ministers, commanding his soldiers. He saw himself riding through his domain, returning the waved greetings of his smiling subjects.

With a sigh, he acknowledged that none of that was likely to happen. Instead, he would have to confront Queen Daya and her betrayal. No good could possibly have become of Bell Castle and his kingdom in his absence. So acute was the sense of despair that he cried.

Underneath him, Charger twitched and turned his head as if to inquire about his welfare.

Urging Charger forward, Robin felt his shoulders slump and his heart weigh heavy in his chest. This would be a bitter and contentious reunion. Likely, some kind of a battle would have to be waged. He hoped to be able to get close enough to Bell Castle to assess the situation, then pull back and make the necessary preparations.

He continued on. The countryside was eerily quiet. There had been great farms on the land surrounding the castle. At this time of year, people should be out working the fields, but Robin saw no one, nor did he see any farm animals about. Ragged crops appeared to have grown wild untended, and haphazardly harvested by animals and vagrants as only the low-hanging fruit had been taken.

Robin found his sense of dread growing strong. He had at times allowed himself to entertain Alexandra's suggestion that there had been a coup, that he had been deposed, and that the shock had been so great, it had obliterated his memory. In nightmare moments, he imagined that he would near the castle and see an unfamiliar flag flying from the ramparts. Sentries would be wearing different colors and soldiers would be astride horses with strange livery. A foreign coat of arms would hang on the gate and an alien figure would sit on the throne next to Queen Daya. Now he knew that would very likely be the case and steeled himself for what he was about to see.

Though he liked to think of himself as a compassionate and beloved ruler, he knew now that loyalty could indeed be bought. His knights, his wife could have easily been persuaded to cast their lot with someone else.

He remembered the woods outside the walls of the realm as inhabited by the poorest who lived in caves or hovels that provided the most minimal shelter, even less than the hut that he had at Oliver John's Ironworks. They scraped whatever living they could from the land or plied noxious and lawless trades like begging, thievery, and prostitution. Since they lived outside the precincts of the realm, they were not counted as citizens. Neither were they provided for nor did they derive any support. Most citizens gave them nary a thought except for when they became a problem. Should a citizen stray from inside the protective walls, he could well expect to be preyed upon. Their mean and dismal life made them desperate and fearless and it was only their small number and relative powerlessness that made these savages inconsequential. Robin saw that their service easily could be had for the smallest improvement in their circumstances.

Peasants worked the farmlands surrounding the royal domain. They too had a hard life and kept only a small percentage of their work and earning. Some of their profits went to the kingdom but that never seemed unfair to Robin as it was his land that they worked. He had heard tales that his own knights would exact tributes to provide the peasants with protection from roving bandits. He didn't find that unreasonable but perhaps some found the price exorbitant. They may even have blamed Robin if they felt the pressure applied by his knights was excessive and been easy targets of someone who promised them better treatment.

Just inside the gates he was used to seeing the dwellings of the serfs who worked the mines and the mills. They had a hard life, it was true, and now that he had had a taste of it himself, he understood just how harsh their life was. For many there was no escaping it for they and their heirs were bound to the land and thus to the owner of the land. He had always assumed it was a fair trade. In return for their labor they were afforded the protection of life inside the kingdom's outer wall. Yet, maybe their bondage weighed more heavily on them than he had realized.

He would next pass the homes of villeins, farmers and laborers who paid rent and could aspire to owning their own property or business, much like the arrangement that he had with Oliver John. Unlike serfs, they were free men in the eyes of the law. Robin had always greatly valued the villeins' contribution to the overall prosperity of the domain. Maybe he had not made that sufficiently evident. But they were obliged to use the domain's sawmills and grindmills, and perhaps they felt burdened by this obligation, much as Robin's debt to Oliver John's Ironworks' store weighed ever on his spirit.

As he would near the inner gate he would pass the more commodious residences of the merchants and craftsmen, teachers and scholars, lawyers and accountants that ringed the main square, followed by the market stalls, the halls of public learning and of entertainment. Robin had not been aware of any discontent among this class of citizens. Had there been, and his ministers had simply not advised him well but instead delivered the malcontents to a new prospective ruler?

Finally, he would pass through the gate in the inner wall and enter the grounds of the castle itself.

Had there been rebellion amongst any of these people, he would have expected to find chaos, lawlessness, and mayhem. Or, had a new ruler taken over and established order, there would be signs of a new regime.

What Robin hadn't imagined was what he found: nothing. As he cleared the woods and drew near the kingdom he saw no habitations at all, although he thought that he could make out their ruins. He saw the outer wall, but not a single flag flew from the ramparts, not his or anyone else's. No sentries manned the turrets of the lookout towers or stood guard atop the gatehouse.

He had thought simply to approach the outskirts of the kingdom and assess what kind of challenge he faced. Having gauged the strength of the opposition, he would then amass whatever reinforcements he would need by whatever means possible and return to lay claim to what had been his.

Cautiously he approached, taking cover behind whatever tree or bush he could in the event that hidden sentries would at any minute call for soldiers to burst forth from the gates.

But none did, nor did any emissaries emerge to greet the unannounced visitor. He passed under the arched entrance of the outer wall without incident.

Just inside the outer wall he passed crumbling habitations and abandoned fields. Instead of the wailing of hungry infants, the cries of little children at play, the calls of women tending to washing or to family plots, or the shouts of men at work he heard only Charger's hoof beats and the rustle of small animals and birds in the weedy overgrowth. He looked up toward the towers of the inner wall and still saw no one. Not only did a troop of soldiers not come charging out, not even a single emissary emerged from the castle grounds to greet the uninvited visitor.

Robin found it almost more frightening than facing an army of inimical defenders.

Where had everyone gone?

The drawbridge was down and the gate open. It felt to Robin like a deceptive invitation to a certain hell, but he crossed the bridge and passed through the entrance anyway. He directed Charger across the bailey. Once a lawn so carefully tended it looked like green velvet, the grass was now a parched brown dotted with dandelions and sticker burrs. The well stood open but the bucket was gone. Robin sighed. He had hoped to get some water for Charger and himself. He charged himself with keeping an eye open for a suitable vessel and some rope.

He led Charger around the castle keep. No groundskeepers worked the landscape; no cooks manned the outdoor kitchen. The stables were empty. All the animals, tack, and feed were gone. For Charger he would be able to scrape together only the few bits of straw and a handful of grains that the rodents hadn't eaten.

He approached the castle entrance. He dismounted but held onto Charger's reins, though he did not know why. Did he think that like everyone and everything else here, Charger would simply vanish, or was he simply afraid to be completely and utterly alone? For whatever reason, he kept one hand on the reins as he laid the other on the great iron door handle and pushed the huge door open.

He led Charger into the great hall. The horse's hoofs resounded on the marble floor, or what was left of it. As if a sledgehammer had been taken to it, huge chunks of marble were simply missing. Weeds had sprung up in the voids. The candelabras and lanterns and sconces were gone; the upholstered benches that had lined the walls, gone; the rugs and tapestries and draperies, gone. In the draft from the open door, leaves skittered across the vacant space and collected in corners, snagged by spider webs.

Ahead, across the vast expanse of dusty shattered marble, atop a dais and sheltered by an alcove stood what was left of his and his Queen's ruined thrones.

Empty.

Robin gulped but his mouth was so dry there was nothing to swallow. The late summer day was bright and with no attendants to wield the huge fans, it was hot, yet Robin felt a cold so pervasive it made him sick. He pulled his cloak from his pack. Ragged though it was, wrapping in it gave him comfort. From the very bottom of the pack, he unearthed the ermine pelts that had once trimmed the cloak.

He led Charger across the floor to the dais, mounted the steps, sat on the stump of his throne, and fingered the ermine. Dead animal skins were all they were now. His eyes smarted with tears.

Gone. All gone. How could that happen?

It had to be an enchantment.

He wished now that he had first gone back to Sea Gate and arranged for some kind of entourage, at the very least, the company of Alexandra or James or even Meeyoo. All right, maybe not Alexandra. For her to see what had become of his kingdom would be mortifying. James at least would approach it with a sense of scholarly curiosity. Meeyoo would at first peer cautiously from the safety of the rucksack, then one paw after the next, slip out, and, keeping low to the ground, would slink around and explore. Just the idea of it made the scene seem somehow for a moment less alien.

But he hadn't expected this, this barrenness.

His heart pounding, he blinked away his tears and looked about him.

"Well," he said to Charger, breaking the eerie silence with his own voice, "I could simply restore it all. Start over. Apparently there is no one here to stop me."

Yet the moment he said it, the impossibility of it all became clear. Had there been a takeover, his challenge would have been to wrest back command. The ministers and courtiers, the soldiers and knights, the merchants and serfs and peasants would all continue about their business, just at his behest rather than someone else's.

But with the infrastructure completely gone, where would he find all the workers? How would he persuade them to do his bidding? It would almost be easier to put together an army than to repopulate an entire city.

And where was Daya? What had become of his sons?

Perhaps he would find some clues in the private areas of the castle.

Robin looped Charger's reins around a broken pillar and started up the grand staircase.

As had been the case throughout, anything of any utility that could be removed had been. Books, musical instruments, articles of clothing, hairbrushes, tables, chairs, beds, linens, candelabras, all were gone. Any glimmer of hope that he would find any of his clothing or weapons was extinguished.

He found nothing that shed any light whatsoever on what had become of his kingdom, his family, or any of the castle's inhabitants.

Of course the royal treasury was empty. Not a single coin, bar, note, title, or deed remained. Robin realized with a sinking feeling that if he wanted to try to reassert his dominion, he would have more than a difficult time without even the documentation that attested to his ownership of the land.

Furnishings and possessions did not show signs of having been removed by force. The draperies and tapestries had not been ripped down, but rather all the supporting hardware had been dismantled. Had the castle been attacked by an inimical foe, Robin would have expected to see signs of vandalism. A marauding force would have taken anything useful, of course, but would also have demolished as much as possible what couldn't be carried away.

Robin wandered back downstairs and to the kitchen and food stores. As in the stables, little remained except the odd moldy or dried ort. Every utensil and piece of cookware or serve ware was gone. Robin realized that he'd have to use his own cup to dip water from the well. For rope, he braided together some of the weedy vines that had invaded the inner bailey. It took several cups to fill the horse trough enough so that Charger could have a drink.

Robin returned to the stump of his throne as there was no other place to sit. He was beginning to think that the occupants had not been taken away by force along with the castle's furnishings. Scrapes and scratches on floors and disturbances in the dust seemed to imply that objects had been picked up rather than pulled or dragged from their places.

So if not a violent sudden siege, what then? A planned and orderly exodus was implied.

He could come to only one conclusion. Daya had united with another ruler. They had packed up and moved, and they had taken with them his sons and everyone who had an obligation to or depended on the kingdom.

Why would she do that? This kingdom was their sons' inheritance. Even had she wanted to take the throne in another domain, she could easily have appointed an earl and some knights to manage the Chalklands while she ruled from a distance. He couldn't imagine what her reasoning had been, but it didn't matter. Even knowing why she had done what she had wouldn't change anything.

Robin thought that he would weep had he any tears left. Instead, he felt hollow, insubstantial. Everything, lo these many difficult months, had been about getting his kingdom, his very life back. Now, none of that was there to be regained. Bewilliam, King of Bell Castle, ruler of the Chalklands was gone. He had ceased to exist.

Robin did not know what to do next. Fine dragon-slayer you are, he told himself, with no backup plan. Yes, those days were clearly over. The battle in the pine woods had indeed been his last.

He was loath to go back the way that he had come. The thought of traveling another day through the ruins of his life was more than he could bear. And why should he, anyway? There would be no partnership with David in a barbershop that was no longer in operation. No helping Dolores to a better life. There would be no partnership with Franklin in a smithy neither of them could afford. There would be no uniting of kingdoms with Alexandra, for he had no kingdom to offer.

He found himself astride Charger letting him go where he would. The afternoon light thinned, but so too did the forest. Robin thought he saw in the distance the myrtles, birches, and maples that suggested the presence of water. Before long he spied a track, then a trail, then a wagon way. The further that he went, the more the way showed signs of being well used. At a crossroads where several trails met the wagon way, a road sign pointed to Forest Hill. Indeed, Robin thought, that would be where they would go. With any luck, there might be a traveler's inn. This night, Robin did not want to sleep out in the open, with only the ghosts of his past to keep him company.

The sign for the inn was a rectangular wooden plank into which a border of branches and leaves and the shape of a tankard and a sleeping pallet had been burned. Robin drew nearer and detected the smell of roasting meat. As if he too knew that food and rest were nearby, Charger picked up the pace.

The two-storied half-timbered building had a sloped roof covered in thatch. A lad lounged at a small table in a tiny courtyard area and meat roasted on the spit in the outdoor kitchen.

As Robin neared the building, the lad sprang up from his bench and approached. "Good day, afternoon. Will you be taking hospitality with us?"

"Yes, I believe so," Robin said wearily. "Tend to my horse." Robin hadn't meant to speak so peremptorily but the time he had spent in the castle had reawakened all his kingly instincts and he had forgotten to censor himself. Charger wore the livery of Sea Gate Fortress which spoke to his pedigree better than Robin's rough traveling clothes spoke to his own. He hoped that the young man would assume his coarse appearance was due to the rigors of the road and would not doubt his rightful claim to such a fine mount. "If you would, young man, that would be very kind," he added to temper his sharpness. "He has been ridden long and hard. He needs food, water, and rest."

"It will be my pleasure to tend to such a fine animal, milord," the laid said, and made a short bow.

Robin smiled. Apparently Charger reflected well on him. He doubted that the opposite was true.

He entered the inn. Though the sun had not yet set, the windowless space was dark except for candle- and lantern-light. Due to the season, the hearth was cold but the room was nevertheless stifling with the collected heat of the day and the many bodies that filled the tables and crowded around the bar. Robin stood frozen in place, the shock of being around so many noisy, breathing, and laughing bodies after a day of preternatural silence was immobilizing.

"Come in, come in. Welcome, stranger."

Robin looked across his shoulder. By his white shirt, black waistcoat, and trousers tied at the ankles, Robin recognized the man as the innkeeper. He let himself be led by the elbow to the bar.

"Can I offer you ale, milord, or perhaps you would prefer wine? Tonight we have a tasty wine punch all the way from Spain, flavored with exotic fruits."

"Ale," Robin said, already feeling deadened as if he had spent the night before drinking. "And I haven't eaten."

"Ah, we do have a nice roast chicken," said the innkeeper.

"Yes, that would be fine," Robin said slowly. He was disoriented, as though he had awakened muddle-headed from a too-long sleep. He wasn't in fact even certain that he was awake. For all he knew, this was a dream, a nightmare, another bewitching.

The innkeeper handed him a tankard. "You look tired, stranger. Have you come a long way?"

From another world, Robin thought. "Yes. A long way," he replied.

The innkeeper held out his hand. "Danny," he said.

Robin shook it. "Please call me Robin."

"Well, relax, Robin. I will have my daughter Constance bring you some of that chicken." He called over a young woman whose stained apron and sweaty brow spoke to a long day of serving wayfarers. "We will have you feeling more like yourself in no time."

Like himself. Who would that be now, Robin wondered. "My horse —"

Danny waved off the concern. "Is being well taken care of. It's my son that will be seeing that your horse has water and hay."

"Much obliged." Robin tipped up the tankard and was surprised to taste only ale. No longer certain of anything, he would not have been surprised to find that tankard contained some potion, or even nothing but air. However the ale seemed ordinary enough and the plate of bread and roasted chicken that Danny's daughter placed before him was not only solid, it was flavorsome. He began to feel that if he had traveled to an unearthly realm from which he had managed to effect a return, and ate and drank with gusto.

Having drained the tankard, he called for another. "Have you had this tavern long?" he asked.

"Not long," said Danny. "I have not always been an innkeeper. Once, I plied a different trade, but that feels like a lifetime ago, although we have been in this location a year or so."

A year or so. Yes, to Robin too, that felt like a lifetime ago.

Danny folded his arms on the bar. "So, as the traveler, it is your job to bring us interesting tales from the road." He grinned. "Seen anything that makes a good story?"

Robin hesitated. He could tell his sad tale of betrayal again. So far, while no one disbelieved that he had been cuckolded, no one seemed to believe that he had once been a king. If he told what he had seen at Bell Castle, would the fine folk here at the Inn at Forest Hill think him mad? Did that matter? Would he be likely ever to be here again? "Indeed, I saw a strange sight. A deserted castle."

Danny waved his hand in dismissal. "Oh, deserted castles. They are commonplace these days."

Robin felt his eyebrows lift in surprise. "Are they?"

That sounded less like his personal tragedy and more like a spell. Had many queens absconded with an entire kingdom for parts unknown? What could cause that to happen? Could there truly be something like that, something so powerful and widespread that it could wipe out entire kingdoms? How? Why? What or who could wield such power? "So, do you know of the deserted castle a half-day's ride north of here?"

"You must mean the Bell Castle."

"Yes," said Robin. His head felt light and he didn't think that it was from the ale. "What can you tell me of it?"

CHAPTER TWENTY-TWO

"A most curious turn of events," said Danny. "I know them to be true because I heard about it from a trusted friend."

So Danny did not have a personal acquaintance with what had transpired at Bell Castle, just hearsay. Robin urged him to go on with his story nevertheless.

"The king there had gone off to fight a dragon. Word came back to the castle that he had been vanquished. No one knew for certain because his body was never found, but the word was that he had indeed lost the battle with the dragon. In any case, months passed, he did not return to the castle, no one had seen or heard of him so he was given up for dead."

Lies, Robin thought, all lies. He had not lost the battle, only his mind. "Surely the queen could have managed to continue in his absence. Marry herself to another ruler," he said, trying not to wince.

"Oh, she did, she had," Danny replied. He leaned closer. "I heard from a maid, who heard from a maid of the castle, that queen already had entered into, shall we say, an alliance with another king even before her husband left for battle. That had her husband not gone off to meet his death, she would have found another way to be rid of him."

Robin shuddered inwardly. Struggling to keep his voice even, he said, "That doesn't explain the deserted castle."

Danny nodded and poured himself some ale. "Ah, that. Now that's something that I know of personally. There is this lord by the name of Bernard —"

Robin frowned. "Him I have heard of." This did not bode well.

"Indeed. Many have, and wish they had long before he ruined their lives. Like mine. I was the royal baker, and still would be had the kingdom that I served not fallen victim to Lord Bernard."

"What happened?"

"My king desired to acquire a neighboring domain but his army was small. Lord Bernard provided him with many more troops. My king launched an invasion. However, the new knights that Bernard had provided did not receive the pay that they expected. Of course, they were not going to risk their lives for nothing, so they went rogue. My king lost and found himself at the mercy of the very man he sought to vanquish. Over concerns about our loyalty, many were imprisoned. Most of us who had served the king fled."

Danny's daughter Constance interrupted to inquire if Robin's food was to his liking.

"Yes, thank you," he said quickly. He turned to Danny. "That is tragic. And in the case of Bell Castle, what happened?" Robin asked, trying not to sound impatient.

"Excuse me one minute," Danny said, and stepped away to serve another customer.

"Done?" Constance asked.

Robin nodded and she reached for his platter. "My father has been telling you about how Lord Bernard got us banished from the castle?"

"Yes, he has. You are now another family I know that has met with misfortune at the hand of this man, including my own. He was about to tell me what happened to Bell Castle."

She chuckled. "Oh I don't think he really knows. But I know of someone who does. With the right 'encouragement' I could tell you who."

Robin fished in his pouch for a coin and observed that he had not many of those left. Since he knew not when or from where more of them were likely to come, he realized he should be conservative with them. But, since he no longer had a war chest to fill... Besides, he had all those ermine pelts which no longer had any meaning and for which he had no further use. They could perhaps be traded or sold. He handed over a coin.

"You want to talk to a woman named Centia," Danny's daughter said. "It is because of her that no one else will suffer at the lord Bernard's hands.

"Indeed? A woman? Is she a warrior? Did she smite him?"

Constance chuckled. "No, she is just someone very smart who figured out what he was doing and brought it to an end."

"And where might I find this Centia?" Robin asked, wondering if the answer was going to cost him his last coins.

CHAPTER TWENTY-THREE

Constance shrugged. "She likes to keep to herself. Her tale is very sad. The fewer people who know it, the better off she is."

Robin frowned. "Why would that be, if she stopped him from hurting others."

"It's how she did it that makes people uneasy. Still, she might talk to you, who has also suffered at the hands of Lord Bernard. " She pointed to a slim woman in simple, drab colored robe who sat alone, her forearms folded on the table. Her hands were wrapped around a tankard that she stared into but from which she did not drink. A thin gold fillet encircled her head and held in place a veil of long curling dark hair that hid her face.

"I would be happy to stand her to a drink," Robin said.

Danny's daughter shrugged. "A meal might earn you more favor," she said. "She doesn't drink much although goodness knows if anyone would have a right to lose herself in drink, it would be she."

"Would you ask her for me, then? Introduce me? I don't wish to disturb her peace."

"Peace? She's had little of that." Again, Constance shrugged. "Oh, all right. Wait here just a minute." She did not approach the woman but instead disappeared into the scullery. Robin stood in place as he had been told, trying to study the woman Centia without being obvious about it. He needn't have worried since the woman seemed not to notice the room but only stared into her tankard or off into the distance in an unfocused way.

Danny's daughter reappeared at Robin's side with a tray bearing a small wedge of cheese, some cut fruit, nuts, and a small cup of a dark brown liquid. "This will cost you," said Constance.

"The food?" As temptingly arrayed as it was, Robin didn't see anything especially spectacular about the repast.

"The drink. It's chocolate. Very rare, very expensive. But she really likes it."

Chocolate. Robin had heard of it, of course, and had even had it. In another life, when he had been a king, a merchant trying to curry his favor and secure a lucrative contract had brought him some as a gift. It was a curious and interesting hot beverage. Robin had found the experience to be something like drinking a pleasantly bitter liquefied dust that left him feeling energized.

He took the tray and approached the table. "Centia?" he asked.

She turned her head and looked up. Robin saw a youthful face made prematurely old by a visible weariness.

She sighed. "Yes, I'm afraid I am Centia. But I can't help you."

"I don't need help," he said, although he did, and desperately. "I just need to know what happened to my kingdom."

Centia winced. He placed the cup of chocolate before her. She looked at the cup, then at Robin.

"May I sit?" he asked.

She closed her eyes and sighed. A tiny smile pricked at the corners of her mouth. "I'm going to have to tell that girl not to make it so easy to bribe me." She held a hand out palm up and indicated the bench opposite.

Robin sat. "Please. I know how much I am asking of you."

"I don't think you do," she replied.

"Yes, I do," he said. "I was King Bewilliam, of Bell Castle. In the Chalklands."

The woman Centia sighed and buried her head in her folded arms. She hunched her shoulders and raised her head. "Milord," she said, tonelessly.

"You believe me? You do not find that surprising?" he asked.

"I find little surprising any more, milord."

"I am lord no more. Robin will do. Will you tell me, please, of Bernard?"

She sighed again. "I have told this story so many times."

"I know, believe me. I have spoken of my loss many times, but it doesn't make it any easier to bear."

"People want to hear about what I did, but they don't realize what it cost me. What it continues to cost me. I can no longer practice my trade."

"But I hear that you did a brave and clever thing. Stopped an evil man."

"No one refutes that. But they do fear it."

Robin nodded. It did not always serve to be too smart, as he had discovered for himself.

"Drink your chocolate. It's getting cold."

"And if I refuse to tell you what you want to know?"

"Drink it anyway. Something like that shouldn't be wasted."

She shrugged and sipped the drink, her lips puckering at its bitterness. She took a deep sigh and began.

"The world keeps getting bigger, more complex. Surely you've noticed." She lifted her cup. "We eat and drink foodstuffs we don't grow ourselves, from lands we've never seen, have only heard of. These could be magical creations, for all we know."

Robin shuddered at the suggestion.

"Once, you, people like you, were kings because you owned the land. You owned the land because you inherited it from your father, and your father before you, am I not right?"

"Right." And his sons, now, would inherit nothing. All he had to give them were a shabby cloak and dead animal skins. He closed his eyes against the tears that wanted to come.

"And your servants belonged to you because they belonged to the land. And as you prospered... I don't mean you personally, I mean rulers like you."

"All right."

"As you prospered, you wanted yet more. To do more, maybe even provide more for your dependents, yes?"

Robin nodded.

"And that takes more resources. The lands and the people that you owned, that might not have been enough to meet your ambitions. So you sought to expand your realm. Not so much by the sword, to conquer by force a neighboring kingdom. No, you are a modern ruler, you seek to do this by negotiation. You strike a deal with another domain that's struggling. They more or less lease themselves and the fruits of their labor to you in exchange for support. Am I right?"

Robin had done this, and so had Alexandra expanded her realm through what she called strategic partnerships. And as her ambassador and negotiator, he had struck such partnerships with Oliver John and Riverington.

"Is this bad?" he asked, truly perplexed because thus far he had seen nothing but benefits for both sides of the negotiation. Rulers such as he and Alexandra were able to expand their domains without, as Alexandra had said, stretching their resources too thin, and a needy community got new life.

"Not on the face of it, no," said Centia. "As a clerk, I myself assisted in the details and documentation of many of these alliances when I was in the employ of Lord Bernard."

Centia had been a clerk? Robin found that surprising. Women were not permitted to be clerks.

"Bernard was a very successful negotiator, a very persuasive man," she was saying. "One might say, a wizard, he was so persuasive. He would make dizzying promises to the subject community. They were astounding promises, they would so blind the listeners with visions of prosperity, nay even grandeur, that they would be as bewitched."

Robin winced. He did not like hearing of magic and spells as too much had happened already that he had been powerless to effect.

"Perhaps they were bewitched, as no one doubted him," Centia said. "Well, why should they? He would bury them in the trappings of success: fine textiles and generous stores of food, building supplies, oxen, horses even, and armaments. All the prospective subjects had to do was pledge their allegiance, sign away their holdings, assign to him the fruits of their labor which would come easier and be more plentiful. More than enough for all."

"Yes, I understand how this works. I have talked to people from several communities that had experience with him. What was the problem?"

"The problem was Lord Bernard really could not fulfill his end of the bargain to the extent that he had promised. Oh, he intended to make good his promises. But he oversold himself. He led the would-be new subjects to believe that they would all live like kings. And of course they believed him because he had the physical evidence of staggering wealth and prosperity. Wealth and prosperity that he didn't really have. And the loans would take years for the people to pay off. All the new subjects were already needy. Why else would they sign away their lands, their crops, their labor if they were not to at least some degree desperate? Even with Lord Bernard's help, their mines, their farms, their mills would not be at full production for many a season."

"So where did Bernard get all these enticements?"

"He borrowed them. He borrowed them, or borrowed money to acquire them, with promises to repay at a very high rate of interest, just as soon as the new alliances bore fruit."

"Rob Peter to pay Paul?"

Centia nodded. "And the new alliances were not as productive as he led his lenders to believe. They were good alliances, don't get me wrong. I would not have helped Bernard if they had not been." She clasped Robin's hands. "You believe me, don't you?"

Robin wondered how she might have refused to do what her lord bade her, but this seemed to be important to her, so he said, "Yes, I believe you. Do people doubt you? Do they blame you?"

"No," she said. "For that I am grateful. No, it wasn't the alliances that were Bernard's undoing. It was the loans that people made to him that enabled him to bedazzle so many. Those lenders are just as much to blame."

"So what happened?"

"The loans made to him came due and he could not repay them. He pressured the new allies for payment but as I said, it was too soon to expect those communities to be more productive. So Bernard borrowed yet more money at even higher rates of interest, to pay off his oldest loans. As word got out about how much in debt he was, many lenders insisted on immediate repayment. Others refused to extend him any more loans. Only the most vicious lenders would help him and they exacted a high price. Indeed, when he could not pay, they took everything that he had. Finally, he came to fear for his very life and went into hiding."

"So how did you get into trouble?"

"As I said, I was a clerk. I kept the accounts. After a while I came to realize just how much trouble Bernard was in. I saw the entire house of cards could come crashing down, and I saw how many people would come crashing with it." She hung her head. "I exposed him. I was the one who told the lenders how likely it was that Bernard would default on the loans. I betrayed him." She looked up with pleading eyes. "I couldn't let it go on. So many innocent people were being sucked into this quicksand.

"And yes, there are those who believe that it was righteous, what I did. It's the betrayal that they can't abide."

Yes, Robin understood that. If she came to doubt his ability to provide, Daya may have had good reasons for entrusting her future to another man. It was the betrayal that Robin could not excuse.

"Thus, I can no longer work. As a clerk, or really much of anything. Once they know who I am, people are leery of trusting me with their secrets. I mean, I ask you, would you hire me, knowing what you know?"

"I could say that I would, but that would be meaningless. I'm not in a position to hire anyone."

"Well, at least you're honest."

"So how do you live?"

She shrugged. "Like Danny, I no longer do what I did, so now I do what I can. I farm a little. I found that I'm good at a loom and I sell my weaving."

Robin said, "What I don't understand is how all this culminated in my losing my kingdom. Do you know?"

She nodded. "You vanished. Everyone thought you were dead."

"I am not, as you can see," Robin said.

"Well, that's what everyone believed. Lord Bernard had always been interested in the Chalklands. As you can imagine, the disappearance of the King of Bell Castle and the arrival of a new ruler led to some instability in the domain. Bernard sought to take advantage of that. He offered to loan men and arms who would reestablish control in exchange for ownership of some of the lands.

"The Queen and her new king relinquished the castle and the lands to Bernard as promised, planning to rule from afar. But Bernard did not command the men or finances that he had alleged. The kingdom of the Chalklands simply crumbled."

Robin clenched his fists. His kingdom, gone. His life, gone. His sons' future in ruins. "You said that this man, this sorcerer, this black magician is still alive, is in hiding. I want to see him."

Centia placed her empty cup on the table. "You realize that will not help you regain your kingdom. He can do nothing for you now. He is himself a ruined man."

Robin nodded. "I still want to see him. I have been thinking that I was under some magic spell, that I was the victim of an undefeatable witch or wizard. I think it would help me to know that he is just a man. You know of his whereabouts, don't you?"

Centia shrugged. "Do you think that will give you peace?"

"Yes!" Robin said, although he doubted he would ever have peace again.

"You must swear that if I give you the information you seek, you will tell no one where you heard it."

"I swear! Tell me, who knows where this man hides?"

"No one. No one besides me knows where he is. No one knows that I know where he is." Centia sighed. "I can take you to him."

"Is it far?"

"An hour's walk," she replied.

Robin was stunned to think that the agent of his personal downfall could be that close at hand. Still, Robin had had plenty enough of walking for one lifetime. "I have a horse," he said. A horse that would have to be returned. Much as he dreaded the journey to Sea Gate Fortress, he knew he would not be alone. For company he would have David, Dolores, Franklin, and their disappointments, even Daya and his sons.

Robin and Centia rode double in the dusky light, Centia pointing the way towards the farmlands on the outskirts of Forest Hill. Robin considered what he would do when finally he faced Bernard. He wanted to kill him. Which would be more satisfying, running the miscreant through with a sword or throttling him with bare hands? Perhaps, Robin thought, I'll shove my ermine skins down the man's throat until he chokes on them.

They stopped at a small hut on a tiny plot of land. The windows were dark.

"This is the home of Bernard?" Robin asked. Considering all the wealth that had passed through the man's hands, Robin would have expected at least a manor house.

"This is what he started with," she said. "And this is what's left."

"What do you mean, 'what he started with'? Where are his lands, his manor?"

Centia gave a bitter laugh. "You were thinking that he came from royalty?"

"People called him 'Lord.'"

"He called himself 'lord,' and thus, so did everyone else. No one ever asked for proof of his lineage." From a hook beside the door, she lifted down a lantern and lit it. She pushed open the door and ushered Robin into the dark room. Darker shapes suggested a table with a bench, a cupboard, sleeping pallets pushed up against the wall. She held the lantern high. The light shown on a man huddled in the corner, muttering.

"This is Bernard," said Centia.

Robin could not believe his eyes. This? This was the powerful and evil force that had ruined his life? Stolen his family, his title, his very life?

The man before him was but a shadow of the tall and regal visitor that had called on David that late night in Rose Bank. Now, he did have something of the look of a wizard and a mad one at that: wiry white hair fanned out around his head and a white beard straggled down his chest. Lines furrowed a high forehead and his eyes gleamed but whether with arcane powers or delirium Robin could not say. Robin could not make out what he was saying. Was he ranting or was he even now casting spells?

Robin's hand clenched his sword. "How is it that he is here? Is he not a wanted man? Are there not many who would see him imprisoned, if not dead?"

Centia nodded.

"So how is that you know where to find him?" Robin asked. "And why haven't you notified the authorities so that punishment can be meted out?"

"That won't restore kingdoms, livelihoods. He is an old, ruined man. He has lost everything, including his mind. Can't you see? He doesn't even know who he is anymore, much less what he's done. He will spend the rest of his days in this corner, cowering in fear. What more punishment is needed?"

"Nevertheless." Robin felt his own anger boiling. Why shouldn't Bernard be sentenced to spending the rest of his nights sleeping in a cow pasture or his days working in a foundry until he choked on the dust and went crippled and blind?

"Is that how you feel?" Centia asked. "That he should be punished?"

"Yes. Yes!" He glared at the man in the corner but Bernard seemed oblivious to their presence.

Centia gripped Robin's sword arm. "I'm sorry. I can't let that happen. And you gave me your word, you promised that if I let you see him, you would not reveal that you or even I know where he is." She fixed him with a steady gaze that dared him to go back on his word.

Robin felt his anger slowly dissipate like the steam from a pot taken off the boil. "I gave my solemn oath and I will keep it. But tell me, why are you protecting him when you know the destruction he has wrought?"

Her reply tore at his heart. "He's my father," she said.

CHAPTER TWENTY-FOUR

Atop the tower overlooking the sea, Robin stood next to Alexandra and stared straight ahead. He had felt wooden during the entire journey to Sea Gate, and awkward and out of step from the minute he had arrived back at the Fortress.

Alexandra had taken in stride his report of having failed to arrange alliances with Allenton and Rose Bank. What had upset her was how long he had been absent without even a message sent to the castle of his whereabouts. When she received word that he had returned she rushed to meet him, by turns angry and overjoyed.

"I worried so," she said. "I thought you had lost your way, were who knew where. I knew not what to think of what had become of you."

"No," said Robin, "I didn't lose my way. I found it, for all the good it did me." He told her about remembering what had transpired at the dragon-slaying, and at Bell Castle, about being betrayed by his knights and the Queen.

"The Queen?"

"Yes, the Queen. My wife, Daya."

Alexandra was silent, and Robin wondered if she regretted sharing her bed with him the night of the feast.

"I had told you that I remembered thinking that my knights seemed confused, hesitant. So too had been the Queen. For some months before I left for the dragon-slaying she had seemed distracted."

After a moment, Alexandra said, "Distracted? How?"

Robin fixed his gaze on the surf rolling gently and rhythmically to shore and wished that his future would present itself in such sure and steady waves. "As if some problem were perplexing her. As if...I don't know."

"Then, yes, she might have been in on it," she said softly. "Or even orchestrating it."

There was another moment when the roar of the ocean was the loudest sound. Then Alexandra said, "No man wants to hear that his beloved's heart has turned cold but you know it happens. You say you were gone for a long time. The plotters may have convinced her that you weren't coming back. She may have been convinced to cast her fate with he who planned to rule the kingdom in your stead. If her heart and her thoughts had been elsewhere for weeks, months, she may have already begun building a different future for herself."

Robin's own heart felt like a tightly-squeezed fist in his chest. In the last years of their marriage, little affection had passed between him and his wife. Though baffled and hurt by her estrangement, he had not been overly concerned. All married couples hit rough patches at some point in their relationship. He never would have considered putting her aside. They had a kingdom to run and two sons who were of a formative age when their parents' guidance would set their future course. If for those reasons alone, he would have done whatever was necessary to regain his wife's love.

"In any case, it is gone. All gone. I could go back but there is nothing to go back to."

"You could stay here," Alexandra said.

"And do what? Play the harmonica and tell you tales?" Robin asked.

Alexandra gripped his shoulders and turned him to face her. "Why not? No one else makes me laugh the way you do and goodness knows there's not much to smile about in my life."

Robin shook his head. "As true as that may be, Alexandra, I'm not a court jester."

"That's not what I meant and you know it. I had other roles in mind for you to play. You could do as you just did: visit other kingdoms and forge alliances." She embraced the landscape with a sweep of her arm. "It's difficult to journey to other domains and at the same time keep things running smoothly here.

"It wouldn't be if you didn't try to do it all yourself, if you had managers that you trusted." And yet she had managed, singlehandedly, to hold it all together for years.

"Trust. That's my point exactly. I trust you. You inspire confidence. You're good at establishing friendships, quickly."

"Apparently not that good," he murmured. He had failed, was a failure.

Alexandra pressed her lips together. "Not everything I've tried since the Emperor died has been an unqualified success."

"And yet here you are, Empress of all the eye can see, while I have nothing to offer."

She snorted in exasperation. "That's not true. So you didn't get the expected results at Allenton and Rose Bank. There were other factors in play of which neither of us had been aware. There will be other realms who need an ally. Who better to negotiate those alliances than someone who knows intimately the value of belonging to an empire?"

Robin turned to her. "And that would be your empire. Your empire, Alexandra, not mine."

"I don't understand why you can't see this. If you helped, it would be our empire, that we built together."

"No, it will always be your empire, the empire that you and your husband built. Your castle, your lands. Your life."

Alexandra frowned. "Running an empire is a job. It's not who I am. It's not my life."

"Still, I don't see you walking away from it."

"Well, not today."

"Or tomorrow either."

She folded her arms across her chest. "Be serious. I can't just walk away from it, just like that. To abandon all this prosperity would be such a waste, and there are people who depend on me for their livelihood."

"I understand. I don't think that you do."

"You're right, I don't," she said. "So, what will you do?"

He looked out across the bailey, past the viaduct and the city of Sea Gate, across the land that led back whence he had come. "I can't regain or recreate what I've lost," he said, trying to keep the tears from his eyes and his voice. "If I am not King Bewilliam, who am I?"

"Are you asking me? I have an answer, you know."

He shook his head. "It's an answer that I have to provide myself." Dreading the expression he would see when he looked at her, he nevertheless turned to face her. "It's not as if I've lost everything," he said.

Alexandra regarded him with raised eyebrows.

"Yes, I've lost lands, possessions, subjects. A life. A wife." He sucked in his bottom lip and sighed. "Somewhere, out there, are my sons. I need to find them."

He had nothing to bequeath them, no lands, no riches — nothing, save a lifetime of skills and experience. They were his legacy now. "I may no longer be a husband or a king but I am still a father. Can still, maybe, be a father." No, he could not teach his sons how to be kings. That would be pointless. He could teach them how to be dragon-slayers; could, perhaps, teach them to be men.

He took her hands in his. "You'll be all right?" he asked, knowing full well that on many levels, she would. Her hair was not fair, her gown not rose-covered, nor was she crowned with stars. Nevertheless, he had no doubt that she was indeed the Empress of David's Tarot cards: passionate, nurturing, and generous.

"Oh sure," she said with a rueful smile. "I'll just go on slaying my own dragons."

They were brave words, and he knew that she did believe them. Could and would, in fact, do just that. But he also saw the crushing disappointment in her eyes. It pained him to be the cause of it. Still, he could not form a mental picture of staying here playing the role that she had in mind for him.

"And you? What will you do?" she asked.

Indeed, what would he do? While peering into his past had terrified him into near paralysis, facing a questionable future did not fill him with fear.

Before him was the featureless ocean and a pale cloudless summer sky, blank as a parchment on which something had yet to be inscribed. If he turned his back to the water and looked back over the land, he saw an entire world stretched before him.

All that was left for him to do now was to find his place in it.

ABOUT THE AUTHOR

"What if?" Those two words all too easily send Devorah Fox spinning into flights of fancy. Best-selling author of The Bewildering Adventures of King Bewilliam epic historical fantasy series including *The Redoubt,* voted one of 50 Self-Published Books Worth Reading 2016, and *The Lost King,* awarded the All Authors Certificate of Excellence. She also wrote the historical thriller *Detour,* co-authored the contemporary thriller, *Naked Came the Sharks,* with Jed Donellie, contributed to *Masters of Time: a SciFi/Fantasy Time Travel Anthology,* and *Magic Unveiled: An Anthology,* and has several Mystery Mini Short Reads to her name. Born in Brooklyn, New York, she now lives in The Barefoot Palace on the Texas Gulf Coast with rescued tabby cats and a dragon named Inky, and writes the "Dee-Scoveries" blog at http://devorahfox.com
Connect online:
Email: devorahfox@aol.com
Facebook: https://facebook.com/DevorahFoxAuthor
Twitter: @devorah_fox
Smashwords: https://www.smashwords.com/profile/view/mbapub.